The Lindman Story
Freelance Fighter

B. B. Hartwich

The Lindman Story - Freelance Fighter

ISBN: 0615753949
ISBN-13: 978-0615753942

Cover art by Kaysie Donat
Edited by Kimberly Dunn

DEDICATION

First and foremost, this book is dedicated to my father, may he rest in peace. In 2002, he was diagnosed with cancer, and after a hard battle he slept in on May 18th, 2004. My dad told me when I was young that if I wanted to do something good with my very vivid imagination that I should write a book. It took me four years to the day after his death to realize I could do this. I began writing on May 18th, 2008, and now the book is finished, but my imagination continues. Here's to you, Dad: know that I will always think of you as I write.

Also I dedicate this to my loving wife Angela and wonderful kids Katie, Emmalee and Jackson. Without their support, I would not have had the energy to keep writing.

B. B. Hartwich

CONTENTS

| | Acknowledgments | i |

Prologue. — Pg 3

1   Chapter 1 – The Grimond Wolf.   Pg 9

2   Chapter 2 – The Aftermath.   Pg 19

3   Chapter 3 – Miranda.   Pg 27

4   Chapter 4 – The Helium.   Pg 35

5   Chapter 5 – Helena and Miranda.   Pg 43

6   Chapter 6 – The Academy.   Pg 49

7   Chapter 7 – The Recon Mission.   Pg 55

8   Chapter 8 – The Invasion.   Pg 65

9   Chapter 9 – No Hope.   Pg 73

10   Chapter 10 – The Rescue..   Pg 84

11   Chapter 11 – Miranda's Surprise.   Pg 93

12   Chapter 12 – The Peace Treaty.   Pg 99

13   Chapter 13 – 6 Years Later.   Pg 102

14   Chapter 14 – T-Minus Four Days.   Pg 111

15   Chapter 15 – Truth Be Told.   Pg 122

16   Chapter 16 – Let's Go Home.   Pg 129

17   Chapter 17 – The New Order.   Pg 138

18   Chapter 18 – Hostage.   Pg 145

19   Chapter 19 – Brilliant Idea.   Pg 153

20	Chapter 20 – The Thirty Usindes.	Pg 161
21	Chapter 21 – Jamie's Revenge.	Pg 167
22	Chapter 22 – A Fight for Justice.	Pg 176
23	Chapter 23 – Preston's Plan.	Pg 182
24	Chapter 24 – We Can Do It.	Pg 187
25	Chapter 25 – Never Leave A Man Behind.	Pg 198
26	Chapter 26 – The S.S.A.U Mission.	Pg 202
27	Chapter 27 – Thief Onboard.	Pg 209
28	Chapter 28 – Lucky Ladies.	Pg 216
29	Chapter 29 – The Book.	Pg 221
30	Chapter 30 – The Trikkyas Meeting.	Pg 226
31	Chapter 31 – Dreams Of Earth.	Pg 231
32	Chapter 32 – Home Sweet Home.	Pg 236
	Epilogue	Pg 239
	About the Author	Pg 243

ACKNOWLEDGMENTS

I want to thank my Editor, Kimberly Dunn, for outstanding work in editing the manuscript, and for all her patience with my many rants and questions.

Also, a big thank you to my Illustrator, Kaysie Donat, for the awesome work on the book cover and illustrations for my author page.

Again, a special thanks to my wife Angela and my kids Katie, Emmalee and Jackson for putting up with my many hours of living in a fantasy world while writing this book. Without their love and support, I would not have made it.

Andromeda-Galaxy

Prologue.

Jackson fell out of bed when the outer hull exploded. "What the hell was that?" he demanded.

"Damned if I know," Kingsly responded. He stood up from the floor in their shared quarters.

They paused in their movements, each one expecting another blast. Several seconds went by and all remained quiet until the alarm sounded. Overhead, the speakers announced, "Red Alert! Red Alert! Man your stations! We are under Attack!" Before the announcement was over, Jackson and Kingsly were running to their battle stations. They ran around the corner and tumbled into a young, red-headed girl. She dropped her laptop and gasped. Quickly, she pulled it back into her arms as if it were the only possession that mattered to her.

"Are you okay?" Kingsly asked, slightly smiling at her. The freckle-faced girl nodded and smiled back. "Go find your family. Make sure you stay hidden and safe," Jackson warned her. They turned around and ran off again.

Jackson and Kingsly considered themselves the best fighter pilots aboard the *Grimond Wolf*, a 3.5-mile long carrier of mostly small fighters and personnel but the best and fastest ship in the Presidential Fleet. With four Hangars holding 136 fighters, only the best of the 1800 crew members stationed on the *Grimond Wolf* flew the single-pilot sky beauties.

Jackson and Kingsley parted ways in the hallway before the Hangar door. "Come on, people! There's a fight goin' on, and you're still sleeping!" Jackson yelled. Adrenaline rushed through his limbs as his feet fought to keep up with the pumping of his heart and the million thoughts zinging through his mind. He ran around the corner near the sleeping quarters for the newly-enlisted men; he bumped into another buddy, his good man Michelson.

Michelson ran alongside him. "Sorry, sir, but it seems that *someone* decided to have this war in the middle of the fucking night!"

Jackson grinned. "Yes. Those damn Handlons aren't sticking to the 8 a.m. war schedule I ordered."

Michelson returned a smile before jumping into the cockpit of his 38-foot fighter jet, barely enough room for his large stature. "Hell, why can't they build these fighters to fit real men?" Michelson complained aloud. The outer hull exploded again, rocking him in his seat. He muttered a few swear words under his breath, snapped on his helmet, and gave the OKAY sign to Jackson in the plane on his left. Kingsley, a few jets to the right and behind, whispered a quick prayer as the air gate finally opened.

*   *   *

Captain Admiral Chugan Hanf of the Handlons drummed his fingers on the armrest of his chair. Patiently, he waited, barely suppressing the urge to give out commands in fear they'd be too early. He jabbed the intercom button. "They're coming. Be ready!"

Another moment later, Chugan sneered as he watched the *Grimond Wolf* fighters zip out from their Hangar: a perfect formation to destroy in a flash. He chuckled at his plan, and then gave the order. "Drop them now." This Handlons' own fleet of 250 Special Forces Fighters appeared from above at full speed.

They opened fire.

Seconds felt like minutes.

The only sounds on the Presidential Carrier's side were the fighter pilots' cries for help as the vicious surprise attack waged an awful battle of explosion and gore. Christian Henson, Captain of the *Grimond Wolf,* slammed on the inter-fleet distress button, and the signal broadcasted over the entire Presidential Space Signal Com (PSSC).

Hanf just smiled.

*   *   *

Millions of miles away, the mile-long freighter *Lindman* hovered near the Planet Driang. First to notice the distress call, First Pilot Tyler Nielson ordered a call out to his superior over the intercom.

"Captain Tallin, please report to the Control Center. Distress alert on the PSSC."

Kront Tallin sat up in his bed, rubbed his forehead, and

sighed, letting his head hang for a moment. "Damn. Can't get any peace around here either." He stood up, threw on his uniform top, and jogged down the corridors to the control unit, memories flooding his brooding mind

Kront had recently re-entered the service of the Presidential Fleet. Six years ago, he received a Dishonorable Discharge just because he "accidentally" knocked out his admiral, Silas Proked. Kront pleaded his case in court with his infamous phrase, "If you put my men in danger, I will kill you." Kront was very fond of his men, each and every one of them like a brother. When Proked had sent fourteen of Kront's men into the field, they understood it was a no-return mission, but no one told Kront before his boss executed the plan. By the time he found out, all fourteen were engaged in a heavy fight with the Handlons, and he heard the desperate cries over the com from the team's leading Sergeant: "Fall back! We need extraction! I repeat: we need extraction! Intel was wrong! Get our asses out of h—"

Kront's heart stopped in mid-beat. Silas didn't respond to the plea for help. Several men tried to stop him from what they knew he would do, yet others stood and watched, their own minds fuming at the indecency of their superior officer. Kront charged past the Admiral's secretary and into Proked's office. He took a swing and punched him in the nose. Within seconds of Kront wrestling the man the ground, two very large Presidential Security Officers (PSO's) grabbed the inferior officer and dragged the cursing man away, blood staining his knuckles from the Admiral's nose.

Kront arrived at the Deck. "Playback the distress," he ordered Nielson.

"It's a no-visual com, Cap." He pushed the button, and for the second time in minutes, everyone on the Deck stopped to listen: "This is the Presidential Carrier *Grimond Wolf.* We are under attack! Handlons are attacking our carrier. Position coordinates: 35-9-32 x 20-5-83 x 70-48-21, about 689.73 miles from the planet Loht 9." The message repeated after that.

"Damn it!" Kront cursed. "How fast can we get to them?"

Nielson checked the data on the computer. "About four hours, Cap."

"Set the course. Send the signal to the Presidential

Federation."

"Right away, sir!"

* * *

The PSSC Center on the planet Frigal erupted into total chaos when the distress signal came in from the *Grimond Wolf*. Com Operator Marshal Dess called PSSC Center Commander Groyt Hellond with the news.

"Sir, we received a distress call from the *Grimond Wolf* via a pass-through from the *Lindman*."

Groyt glanced at his visual com. "Pass it through to my screen.

Marshall pushed some buttons. "It's a non-visual call, sir." Groyt nodded. Tight-lipped he listened as Marshall quieted the others Soldiers in the large room. He lowered his head for a moment, and suddenly straightened his stance. "How far away is the nearest flagship to the *Grimond*?"

The Navigations Operator double-checked his screen. "About 120 million miles, sir."

Groyt frowned. He knew they would not get there in time. "Dispatch the *Vilantex* to assist the *Grimond Wolf*, and tell them to fly like hell!"

"Yes, sir."

Groyt turned to his second in command, a very nervous, puppy-like Senior Captain Drent Jenson. "Isn't the *Lindman* Captain Tallin's ship?"

Drent's hands shook as he pulled up the roster of the *Lindman*. "Yes, sir, He bought it five years ago, started his own freight company, Lindman OS – OS stands for "Over Space" – and from that—"

"I don't need the whole damn story! Call up the *Lindman*. I want to talk to Tallin."

Drent saluted. "Yes, sir. Right away, sir!"

* * *

"Signal from Frigal, Captain."

Kront joined Nielson at the deck Bridge. Kront gave the

"OK" for the call and smiled when he heard the familiar voice on the other side. "Groyt, my old friend! How can I help you?"

Commander Hellond laughed. "It's been three years, hasn't it?"

"Sure has. What do you need?"

"Well, as you might already know, I have a ship in distress."

Kront stopped smiling. "Yes. We've turned our ship about to assist, but I can't imagine we can do much by the time we get there. The Handlons have probably stripped the ship by now." Kront often found ships just drifting in space: no survivors, stripped to its skeleton, a literal ghost.

"You may be right, but I still want to give them a chance. Do it for old time's sake?"

"Anything for an old pal."

Groyt checked the radar. "One more thing, if you don't mind. On the ship, there's a safe with some papers concerning the King of Tilond from Planet Loht 9. If you happen to come across them, I'd be very grateful. It could prevent a war."

"You mean another one, right?" Kront lightly joked. "I'll do my best. *Lindman* out." Kront shut off the visual com. Without turning to Nielson, he ordered, "Wake the men. We're gonna go play some *war*."

PART 1

YEAR 2736

THE HANDLON WAR

Chapter 1 – The *Grimond Wolf*

The *Lindman* came up on the *Grimond Wolf*'s position. The second that Kront pulled the *Lindman* out of hyperspace, he could see that the Handlons had, indeed, stripped the ship apart for spare pieces and valuables. "Damn savages! They should all be hung and shot," Kront yelled. "Nielson! Scan for survivors."

Nielson scanned. "Nothing yet, sir, but let me increase the strength." Nielson gradually turned the signal button to the right, increasing it to maximum power. "Sir, there's a signal! It's faint, but definitely a life form."

Kront looked at the scanner and spoke over the intercom. "All Combat Fighters to the Hangar. This is now a Rescue Mission. We have detected a life form on the *Grimond Wolf*. Locate life form and report."

The forty-five Combat Soldiers Kront had onboard the *Lindman* were all retired Presidential Soldiers, all very loyal to Kront, and he knew it. He had been with almost every one of them in some form of life-and-death situation. When Kront was dishonorably discharged, they all resigned from the service to join their Captain on his new ship. Interrupting Kront's train of thought, five shuttles flew out of the Hangar. He mentally followed his soldiers through the visual that each group leader transferred via his or her helmet until each had landed aboard the ghostly *Grimond Wolf*. Now they would trek the ship on foot.

"Squad Alpha entering the lower deck now," Sergeant Sigu Flort radioed over.

Sergeant Helena Holley responded, "Roger that, Squad Alpha. Squad Bravo entering Bridge. All quiet, so far. Over."

Kront stared at the visual sent back from Squad Bravo, not willing to break concentration during the on-edge situation. All 5 squads had reported no activity.

"Squad Bravo, check the galley. The faint signal is coming from over there," Nielson directed over the com," Sergeant Holley replied. She shifted the heat sensor device to a closed door and listened. The sensor detected the life form on the other side, but it couldn't tell the Soldiers what *kind* of life form. Each Soldier had a slight sense of fear, nerves, or bold determination to figure out the mystery, whether human, alien, or motion-activated bomb.

Sergeant Holley swung her head around to face her crew when she heard slight whispers in the halls. "Everyone shut up!" She put her ear to the door and called in, "I hear something, Cap. It's faint, but something *is* in there"

"Roger that, Sergeant Holley. Proceed with extreme caution," Kront replied, knowing he didn't need to remind her.

"Koffman, cover me. The rest of you standby to engage." Sergeant Holley's 1st gunner, Chuck Koffman, kneeled down and took aim at the door. He nodded, looking ready to handle a surprise attack from the room. Slowly, Sergeant Helena turned the door handle; the heavy steel door squeaked, showing signs of blast fire. She knew that whatever was on the other side had put up one hell of a fight. "*It's incredible someone survived this,*" she thought to herself. Taking a quick breath, she jumped through the door and rolled to the right, Koffman tightened his grip around the rifle and took aim while Sergeant Holley's 2nd gunner, Janic Mosnhet, jumped to the left and cocked. Instantly, an awful, high-pitched scream erupted. Helena dropped her weapon. "Don't shoot! Don't shoot! She's just a kid!" She turned her attention to the child. "Hey! It's okay! We're here to rescue you!" The voice softened to a whimper, but she made no move to escape. Grabbing her com, Sergeant Holley radioed, "Everyone stand down. Bravo Squad, Stand down. It's just a young girl." Replacing the com, she slowly walked over to the child.

Not looking much over 11 years old, the small thing had short red hair and plenty of freckles. Sergeant Holley always loved freckles; they looked so cute! Coming back to the present moment, she side-stepped three bodies lying on the floor, two men and one woman. The girl hovered in the corner in the fetal position. It was all too clear to the military leader that this poor girl had seen more than she should have.

Sergeant Holley bent down to the crying figure's level. "Hi," she softly stated. "My name is Helena. What's your name?

The girl looked up, tears spilling from her eyes, and in a split second, she jumped up and attacked Helena, screaming at the top of her lungs without mercy!

Sergeant Holley defended her face from the adrenaline-forced punches and firmly grabbed the girl's forearms. "Calm down, sweetie. We're here to help you!"

The girl's green eyes burned with uncontrollable fire, an inconsumable hate that could quickly cause psychological instability, but Helena would not blame her if it happened. The Bravo Squad Sergeant slowly released her grip on the child as the freckles faded and normal breathing returned. "Let's take you away from here, okay? We'll get you some blankets and new clothes, and maybe you can help us out. Sound good?" Helena hoped for a nod, in the least, but the frail frame only blinked.

*   *   *

Helena and the rest of the Bravo Squad received a warm welcome of applause and cheers as they entered the *Lindman*. "Cap!" Helena called out to Kront. He turned her direction and smiled, the nervous trickles of sweat long diminished after watching the little girl try to take on Helena back on the *Grimond Wolf*. Helena, all smiles and beautiful, white teeth, gently tugged from behind her back the little red-headed fighter. "Captain Tallin, I'd like you to meet our guest."

Tallin eyed the girl, her head hanging down, and nodded at Nielson. The First Pilot called over the com, "Doctor Frank Trad, please report to the hanger hall. Patient arrival on the *Lindman*. Medic crew, standby."

Tallin turned back to Helena. "Sergeant Holley, I need to report back to the command center. As you know, our other squads are still on that skeleton ship."

She nodded. They saluted, and he left, nearly colliding with Doc as the older, yet spry, gentleman burst through the hangar hall door to join the ever-growing crowd of curious soldiers. He pushed his way to the center of the circle. "Quiet down! Where is the emergency?" He stopped short in front of Helena, his hands on his hips, a stern frown lining his face. "Well, Sergeant Holley?" All other noise seemed to dissipate.

"Doctor Trad, I would like you to meet my friend." Helena gently tugged the girl's hand and directed Doc's eyes down to the small figure. "We found her onboard the *Grimond Wolf*. No visual injuries, but she won't talk and is very frightened from the events of the past few hours."

The frown quickly dismissed into a caring, concerned demeanor.Doc kneeled in front of the girl. "Hello. I'm Doctor Trad, but everyone calls me Doc. What's your name?"

She didn't answer.

"Do you know why we brought you here?"

A slow head nod confirmed his question.

He glanced up at Sergeant Holley and then back to the guest. "Would you like Sergeant Holley and me to help you find your own room so you can rest?"

The young girl raised her eyes to meet those of the doctor's, and his heart melted at the sight of the pain in her face. Doc stood up, unable to bear another moment of personal connection. "Sergeant Holley, please accompany us to my office. We need to make our guest comfortable for as long as she would like to stay with us." He turned on his heels, quickly venturing out of the hall and toward his office. Sergeant Holley nudged the red-headed figure and gently pulled her alongside, following Doc's trail of loud, verbal orders to his medic team.

*   *   *

"Alpha Squad, check the cargo level. We need to find that safe."

Sergeant Flort responded to Captain Tallin, "Yes, sir."

Kront called Charlie Squad next. "Sergeant Pladu, report. What's your position?"

Drenge Pladu whispered, "Cap, we are just outside the Captain's Quarters, preparing to enter."

"Roger. Proceed with caution. Over. Delta, what's your position?"

No response. "Delta, come in. Over."

Still no response. "Sergeant Lodre, report, damn it!" Kront impatiently tapped his foot and slammed his hands down on the table. Meanwhile, Nielson stared at John Lodre's camera visual that transmitted back to their screen an eerie, black static.

"What's on the scanner, Nielson?"

"The scanner is clear, sir. We are picking up our own

thirty-six soldiers on the *Grimond Wolf*. No signs of any other activity over there."

Kront radioed out again. "Delta Squad, Sergeant Lodre, come in!"

Kront didn't waste much time waiting before he chose to find them another way. "Echo Squad, report!"

"Echo here, sir. Sergeant Jinko."

"Sergeant Jinko, what's your position?"

Michael Jinko responded, "We are at the personnel quarters. Last saw Delta at the fighter Hangar."

Kront whipped toward Nielson, a fearful tingle running down his spine. "Nielson, Check the Hangars. Scan the hell out of them! Those Handlons might be concealing their life signatures with some new technology!"

Nielson's fingers flew across his keyboards while his eyes monitored the screens in front of him. "Boosting the scan to Power Level 5X, sir."

Tallin paced the room for the few seconds it took Nielson to complete a new scan. "Sir! We have company! I read twenty new life forms on the *Grimond Wolf*: eight in the Hangar, six in the engine room, and six on the outer hull near the Bridge. All life forms are Classified Handlons!"

Kront yelled over the intercom, "All Squads: Red Alert! I repeat, Red Alert! Handlons are onboard!" Immediately, all the Squads emergently went in to defense mode, each squad changing radio frequency and tracking back to their fighters in the Hangar. "All Squads report now!"

"Alpha Squad, Sergeant Flort reporting.

"Charlie Squad, Sergeant Pladu reporting."

"Echo Squad, Sergeant Jinko reporting."

"All Squads proceed to the Hangar, immediately!" Kront yelled. "Delta has been compromised! Leave no one behind!"

The familiar phrase from his days in the service of the Presidential Security Force burned inside his chest. For over 900 years, its existence kept people safe. In the old days, they were called Marines, but while the name evolved over time, its defenders remained true to each other and their core beliefs: 1775 – 2235 the U.S. Marines, 2236 – 2428 the Royal Planet Admirals (RPAs), 2429 – 2684 the Green Planet Defenders (GPDs), and

2685 – now Presidential Security Force (PCF). The halls of the *Lindman* echoed the famous phrase, and Kront required that each man's quarters held a plaque frame on the wall with the words, "A Marine Leaves No Man Behind" in bold, black-outlined, crystal-clear white letters. Suddenly, the voices of his squadrons interrupted his reminiscences.

"Captain Tallin!" Sergeant Flort radioed in. "Squads Alpha, Charlie, and Echo at the Hangar door. Waiting for your command, sir."

Kront joined Nielson at the scanner screen. "All squadrons listen up: Delta Squad has been compromised. This is a combat search and rescue mission. Handlons are around the corner to your left, 10 o'clock." He paused a moment. He could not let his anger against the Handlons control his decision-making skills, but for all he knew Delta Squad was lined up to the wall in preparation for the firing squad. "Take no prisoners…unless they surrender on sight."

"Roger, Cap. Entering Hangar now," Sergeant Pladu reported. Sergeant Flort and Alpha Squad stormed through the Hangar door, followed closely by Sergeant Jinko and Echo Squad while Sergeant Pladu and Charlie Squad covered the rear. Upon entrance, Sigu quickly scanned the area for the position and number of Handlons in the Hangar and took out the first one with a headshot; bullets sprayed through the air as the Handlons grabbed their weapons and charged back. They dropped left and right with guns as Alpha and Charlie covered the front while Sergeant Jinko and his men engaged in battle with the 2 or 3 Handlons that tried to escape from a secondary Hangar entrance a few feet away. For a few moments, all was quiet. No one moved or even took a breath.

A sudden shot sounded out as a dying Handlon aimed his weapon at Jessica Helpha of Alpha Squad. The bullet broke a slit in her armor just above the right clavicle at her neck. Two of her companions immediately shot back, shredding the Handlon with another 120 bullets in a furious rage. Jessica's blood gushed out too quickly for them to stop. Fortunately, she only suffered for a few moments before her eyes rolled back. Quietly, Alpha Squad shut her eyelids and laid her down on the floor, surrounding her body with their armor and tears.

In less than a minute, the eight Handlons in the Hangar had

painted the concrete floor with their blood and bodies. In less than a minute, a team mate had died trying to free a squad of friends. The 2nd Gunner of Delta Squad, Regan Drogly, was injured as well.

Impatiently, Kront waited for reports. He refused to watch the fight on the screens, not so for the others in the command center.

As he heard the shot that got Jessica in the neck, he twinged. A stabbing pain grabbed his heart as he heard the gasps and muttered curses of his crew.

"Cap?"

Slowly, he heaved a sigh and grabbed the radio, still facing away from the cameras.

"Captain Tallin here. Report."

"This is Sergeant Pladu, Charlie Squad. Delta Squad secure, sir. Only one injured: a Regan Drogly. Took a blast to the lower back. Um…"

Kront knew what was coming next. "Go on, Drenge."

"Sir…um, one…dead…from Alpha Squad…Jessica Helpha…they got her…in her neck, sir…in a slit between her armor."

Kront bowed his head. He hated to lose any of his crew or squadrons, but war had taught him that you can't make an omelet without breaking a few eggs. He had known Jessica since the Academy. Back then, he was just a Sergeant. She had been one of his best students: never questioned orders unless she had a better idea – and when she questioned the orders, she *always* had the better idea.

"Delta Squad, return to the station. I'll have Doc on standby." With a slightly stronger voice and straighter stance, he tightened his grip on the radio. "Alpha and Echo, Engine room, six Handlons. Charlie, Outer Hull, six Handlons. Take them all out."

Alpha and Echo took out the Handlons in the Engine room without any injuries. In the Outer Hull, Charles Hamkoc from Charlie Squad got a bullet in his back, also damaging his pressure suit. He stumbled to the rear of his squad. His suit was venting air as he slid to the floor, and if it didn't stop soon, he would suffocate. He called out to his twin brother, "Jindso! They got me! I need a Pressure patch on my suit back!"

Jindso and Charles joined the Academy together seven years ago when the Handlons attacked a civilian freighter and killed all onboard, their parents included. The boys had sworn that they would fight the Handlons until the day the twins died or peace was declared.

Jindso took another shot and pulled to the rear to find his brother, his face pale and sweating from the pain of the bullet and loss of oxygen. Jindso ripped out a pressure patch and stabilized Charles' suit. "There you go, bro. All fixed. Still looking after you, just like mom always said I'd have to!"

Charles smirked, "Smart ass, mom never said that." Jindso stayed near his brother, ready to take his kin's defense, but as they prepared to rejoin the fight, the Handlon mission was already finished.

*   *   *

On the Bridge of the *Lindman*, Kront stood, impatiently waiting to welcome home his squadrons, their successes, and their losses.

Sigu was the first to salute. "Captain Tallin, sir."

Kront returned salute. "Welcome back, Alpha Squad. Report."

Sergeant Flort's voice quivered for a moment. Not a man to show emotion in front of his squad, he could not help but know the Captain's ties to their loss of Jessica. "All members returned. One down: Jessica Helpha. No other injuries reported, but morale is low over Helpha, sir."

Kront's eyes began to water. "Thank you, Sergeant Flort. I know she will be missed. Please arrange a memorial service for her."

Sigu nodded and turned back to his squad, leading them inside for emotional and physical relief from the day's work.

"Charlie Squad, report."

Drenge saluted Kront. "Captain Tallin, sir. All members returned. One wounded: Charles Drogly. Shot in the back. Suit was punctured but Jindso fixed him up. Also, we did find these documents in the Captain's Quarters at your request, sir."

Finally, something to smile about! Kront nodded, making a

mental note to send a full report to Groyt about the accomplished and tragically successful mission. He sighed aloud and gratefully accepted the folder from Drenge. "Thank you, Sergeant Pladu. Hope Drogly's pulling through. Should be with Doc by now. Job well done finding those papers."

Drenge saluted. Sergeant John Lodre held a severe and disappointed look on his face. "Delta Squad reporting, sir. We entered the Hangar as ordered but saw no activity. Suddenly, a Stun grenade went off nearby, and the next thing I remember, I saw Alpha, Charlie, and Echo Squads bustin' in and savin' our asses. All members returned. One wounded: Regan Drogly, also shot in the back."

Another mishap that shouldn't have happened. Kront saluted John and released his squad for relief.

"Echo Squad reporting, sir!" Michael was not smiling: Regan was his best friend. They had been roommates all through the Academy, and Regan had saved Michael's life during the First Handlon War. "All members returned. No injuries reported. Permission to check on a friend, sir?"

Kront nodded. "Of course. Thank you, Sergeant Jinko." Kront turned to address the remained of the squads, "I need two volunteers to deliver these papers to the King of Tilond on Planet Loht 9."

Sigu stood up to respond. "Sir, I think Fonty Dlags and Reggi Grout from Alpha Squad would like to have a few days off. They can deliver the papers."

Kront nodded, "Thanks, Sigu. I'll discuss the trip with them later."

*   *   *

Groyt paced in circles in his office, waiting for results from a mission to a recent ghost ship was the worst he knew. Someone knocked on his office door.

"Commander!"

He rushed to the door and pulled it open. "Yes?"

Com Operator Marshal Dess stood at attention. "We have an incoming Visual from the *Lindman*, sir."

Groyt sighed in relief and quickly led the way for both of

them back to the command center on the PSSC. Groyt slammed on the receiver button. "Kront! What's your report?" Commander Hellond noted the lack of a smile on his friend's face, even though Kront wasn't usually a smiling person.

"Sir, we entered the *Grimond Wolf* and found no signs of life. A deeper scan of the ship found one life form onboard: Bravo Squad found a young girl about 12 years old in the Galley."

"Job well done, indeed!" the Commander smiled, waiting somewhat patiently to hear about the important documents. "Continue."

"Yes, sir. Thank you, sir. During the mission we lost contact with Delta Squad." Kront took a deep breath. "Nielson boosted the signal on the scanner and another twenty life forms appeared on the scanner, all Handlons."

Groyt's shock didn't leave his face as he questioned the possibility. "Twenty Handlons? How the hell did they get past your damn scanners?!" In the visual, he saw Kront pick up and display an item for him to see.

"This is a piece of the armor we pulled of one of Handlons we killed. Its high-duty platinum and titanium alloy, sir. Very expensive, but blocks the scanner signatures. We had to boost the scanners to near-maximum capacity. I'm sending you the laboratory results of the compounds now."

As the test readings printed off next to him, Groyt continued to hear Kront's report. "We were able to locate and rescue Delta Squad in the Hangar. In the fight with the Handlons, Regan Drogly and Charles Hamkoc were injured, and…Jessica Helpha…was shot in the neck. She…she didn't suffer for long."

The men around Commander Hellond seemed to parallel his grief of the tragedy. "I'm sorry for your loss my friend. I will personally report to the Senate and inform her family."

Kront gave Groyt a short nod. "Thank you my friend. However, I believe we found the documents you needed."

Commander Hellond grinned. "Amidst the tragedy, it's nice to have a bit of good news. When can I expect to receive them?"

"I'm sending out two men tomorrow. *Lindman* out."

Chapter 2. – The Aftermath.

Thon Jukle dashed through the hallways of the Senate on Planet Troklon, nearly knocking over two officers. "Watch out boy!" the lieutenant yelled out at him.

Normally, Thon would reply, but this was a not a normal situation. He burst through office doors. Papers flew out of a woman's hands; suit-clad men raised voices over spending and fraud. Others gathered around desks, hovered over books, or stood casually chatting as though Thon had entered the wrong room.

"Senator Milons?"

The senator did not hear the young lad's squeaky voice.

He cleared his throat and tried again. "Senator Milons."

The senator looked Thon's direction and smirked, but turned back toward the letter consuming his present attention.

Finally, Thon had had enough. He gathered the courage of a Senate courier and raised his voice: "Senator Milons! Special com from Frigal: the *Grimond Wolf* has been destroyed, only one survivor, sir."

The senator's coffee cup shattered on the floor. All voices silenced. Typing stopped. Even the air within the building seemed to hallow the words he had said.

The senator stood up. "The *Grimond Wolf*? Are you sure?"

Thon handed Senator Flopre Milons the Com Disc. "Sir, it's a visual com. The *Lindman* crew sent pictures of the…ghost ship…and their fight against the Handlons."

Flopre slowly sank into his seat. "Handlons. How could they? The *Grimond Wolf* was one of our strongest carriers." He straightened his back and addressed the young man, "Call the Admirals. *All* of them." Thon nodded and ran out of the room to accomplish his next task.

*   *   *

"How is she, Doc?"

Frank didn't have to look up. He knew which young woman had crept in to his Medic Center and to whom she referred.

He made another stitch in the wound on Charles' back before replying. "She's doing better, Helena. I gave the little girl some broth and water; however, I'm sure her mind will not allow her body to stomach anything for a while, if you forgive my pun."

Helena smiled.

"She's in the next room, dear." He barely heard her reply, "Thanks, doc!" before she was out the door and into the next room.

Helena was happy to hear the girl was doing fine, but she wasn't sure how to proceed from this point onward. Quietly, in case the little girl slept, she cracked the door open. To her surprise, the little girl locked eyes with Helena, fascinated by the older woman's streaks of pink, blue, and purple running through midnight-black hair. Finally, Helena broke eye contact to shut the door behind her.

"I'm sorry I attacked you," the girl whispered.

The Marine descendant's heart softened even more toward the girl. "You didn't know if we came to help or hurt you. I can't blame you for defending yourself."

"How are my mom and dad?"

Forget a softened heart. It melted into a puddle of "how-am-I-going-to-explain-this-one?" as she remembered the bodies they found in the galley aboard the *Grimond Wolf*: two men and one woman. *Damn*, she thought to herself, *that must have been her family*. "Well, I'm not sure. I have to check with the manifest first. What's your full name?"

"Miranda Holliday."

"And your parents' names?" Helena grabbed a pen and paper from one of the drawers and began writing down the information.

"My dad is Warren, and my mom is Britny, spelled B-R-I-T-N-Y."

Helena called in over her com unit. "Nielson, our extra special passenger's name is Miranda Holliday."

"Roger that. Nielson out."

The older woman replaced her unit and snuck her hand into a different pocket. "I have a feeling that you and I will be good friends."

"Really?" Miranda's green eyes of fear and hate turned to a more pure emerald.

"Yes, and you know why?"

Miranda's opened widely as she shook her head.

Helena lowered her voice and pulled a small bar from her pocket. "Because I brought you some chocolate."

Miranda's giggle was the most innocent sound to Helena's ears. A tear formed at the corner of her eye from the thought of the loss of Miranda's parents. The little girl's voice jilted Helena back to reality. "What was that, sweetie?"

"Why did the Handlons attack us?"

"I honestly don't know, but we'll find out. Don't worry." She wiped a smudge of chocolate from the girl's chin and smiled.

"Inbound com from the *Lindman*, sir," Com Operator Marshall Dess informed his superior, Commander Groyt Hellond.

"Patch it through, please." The commander's visual screen came to life. "Kront! Good to see you again. Did you get any information out of our little survivor?"

Kront nodded. This is the visual from the Medic Center. Her name is Miranda Holliday. She lost both parents on the *Grimond Wolf*. We've sent out an inquiry to search the registries for any known relatives."

Groyt's first-hand man, Senior Captain Drent Jenson, approached. "Here's a printout regarding the little girl, sir."

"Thank you, Jenson." Groyt knew that finding the family of this innocent was important, but bringing the Handlons to justice for their havoc to the *Grimond Wolf* must come first. "Anything else, Kront?"

"No, that was all, but please inform the Senate that the *Lindman* is for hire if they need us."

Groyt laughed. "Will do, my friend. Frigal out."

*   *   *

The Senate was in absolute chaos. Admirals yelled at each other, Couriers ran all over the place with coms aplenty, Senators trying to discern between truth and rumor in the recent news of the *Grimond Wolf*, and Officers listening and volunteering for various duties of station.

"QUIET!" Senator Milons managed to yell over the rest.

"We have a direct com from Planet Frigal."

The noise skidded to a halt with random whispers piercing the silence until the large visual com appeared before them on the Senate screen. Commander Hellond's face came in view.

"Admirals, Senators, Officers, and all others of this particular Senate com: I have an update from the *Lindman*." Groyt took a moment to pause before continuing, noting that whispers among the media persons began as their pens and pencils flew across their notepads and electronic mediums. Inwardly, he rolled his eyes. "Personnel have identified the sole survivor of the atrocious attack on the *Grimond Wolf*. Her name is Miranda Holliday; she is the 12-year old daughter of First-Lieutenant Warren Holliday and Nurse Britny Holliday."

Conversations hummed in the Senate room as Groyt continued. "The *Lindman* has offered their services to find those responsible for the attack."

"The *Lindman*, you say?" Senator Milons asked. "Isn't that Kront Tallin's ship?"

"Yes, sir. It is."

Admiral Silas Proked's voice rose from the sea of nameless shadowed faces in the room. "You can tell that low-lying, dirt-faced, bastard Tallin to go back to—"

"Enough!" Senator Milons exclaimed. "Admiral Proked, you will not - I repeat, *not* - interrupt my com! I will make decisions on whether or not we need the *Lindman*. Is that understood?" The Senator knew that Kront and Silas had a history. He had been on the jury that had discharged Kront; the vote had been 20-4 in favor of a discharge. He was one of the four.

Admiral Proked's glare never left the Senator's face as he grumbled an apology.

Commander Hellond restrained himself so as to not laugh at Admiral Proked's counseling. Groyt turned back to Flopre. "Sir, what word should I give to Captain Tallin?"

"Tell the *Lindman* to report to the Spaceport on Planet Frigal. Equip them and send them on a recon mission." Flopre paced the floor as several of his scribes took notes and couriers ran from the room to deliver instructions. "We need to know who ordered the call. The Handlons have been fighting amongst themselves for many years, dividing into hundreds of clans, and not *all* of them have decided to continue under the Handlons' creeds. We need to know which clan is responsible."

Groyt nodded, "Yes, sir. But there is one more thing, Senator. The *Lindman* discovered that the Handlons have a new armor type. It hides their life signatures from our scanners until we raise the scan to near-maximum capacity."

Flopre shook his head. "The things they think of...if that's true, we could have Handlon spies on all our ships and not even know it!"

The Senate floor burst into noise. Admirals and Officers yelled orders over their com systems. Media persons and couriers raced around to gather information and spread the word of Handlons hiding in the halls of every ship and planet.

Groyt spoke above the Senate floor garble, "Yes, sir, that's very true. I saw the readings the *Lindman* sent us. The compound is platinum and titanium alloy. Very expensive, but also very good."

Flopre turned to the Admirals in the room. "Call all of our ships. Boost scanners to maximum capacity for a full search. Capture any enemy spies. I want a report from each of them by the end of the day!" He slammed on the visual com button to turn off Commander Hellond's message. "We've got work to do."

*   *   *

Back in the Medic Center, Helena continued to build a relationship of trust with the little girl. Miranda reminded the sergeant of her own little sister living with their parents on Planet Troklon. Their parents were both teachers, so they didn't have to travel away from home. "Miranda, I have some more questions I need to ask you."

"I'm tired, Helena. Can I rest?"

"Just a few more questions, and then you can, okay?" Miranda shook her head in agreement. She liked being around Helena, no matter what. "When the Handlons attacked the ship you were on, they killed everyone except you. Do you know why?"

"My dad told me to hide under the sink. He said it was steel and would hide my signature."

Helena smiled and tousled the girl's red locks. "Your dad

was very smart to tell you that."

Miranda's face quivered. She looked down, and Helena's heart sunk as she knew the words Miranda was about to ask. "My mom and dad…they're dead, aren't they?"

Helena took Miranda into her arms in a warm hug. "I'm so sorry, honey. They were trying to protect you, and it worked."

Miranda held Helena tight and cried, "What do I do now? Where am I going to live?"

"Well, we've sent out a search to find some of your relatives. How about that?"

"But there isn't anyone else."

The female soldier looked down at the little girl. "What do you mean, Miranda?"

Before little green eyes could answer, a message came over the com system: "Attention all Squad Leaders: report to the Situation Room." Nielson's voice sounded harder than usual.

Helena kissed the top of Miranda's red head. "Sorry, sweetie, but I have to go. I'll be back later, and I'll bring some chocolate." Her last ditch attempt to get a smile out of the teary-eyed child worked as Helena left the room, closed the door behind her, and straightened her posture as she headed out to meet the other squad leaders.

*   *   *

"Where the hell are the reports from the Admirals?" Senator Milons yelled over the com to his com officer. Flopre was furious. More than twenty-four hours had passed, and he still didn't know if he had spies on any of his ships.

"Sir, I have been informed that the reports will be arriving within the next few minutes."

Flopre gave a tight-lipped smile to the man on the visual. "Thank you, Tony. Sorry about the outburst."

Com Officer Flakes smiled back. After five years of working together, Tony had become accustomed to Flopre's personality. Very little surprised him now. "Sir, the Admirals are here. I'll let them into your office."

"Thank you." A few moments later, several gentlemen walked into the room in cleaned and pressed uniforms. "Please, take a seat. We'll begin with you, Admiral Miskl."

Admiral Holger Miskl nodded. "Sir, all ten of our ships in the Gamma Sector reported no foreign life forms aboard their vessels."

"Good to hear. Next?" Flopre stood up from behind his desk and walked to the window behind him, looking out at the families playing on the Senate lawn.

"Sector Charlie reports one of our fifteen ships - the *Independence* - found two Handlons hiding out in a storage room. One sergeant was wounded in combat, but both Handlons have been captured." Admiral Wrent Haqmil sat down to give the floor to Silas.

"Sir, seven of our ten ships in the Delta Sector reported no extra Life forms. The *Flying Rope* engaged two Handlons, killed in combat. The *Strider* detected five Handlons. Unfortunately, we lost two of our people: Sergeant Phillip Nilhk and Under-Officer Doris Groms. We have been unable to get in contact with the *Helium*."

Flopre whipped around. "What do you mean 'unable to get in contact?'?"

"Sir, they're not answering our radio calls. We still have them on radar, and their transponder is sending out their position."

The Senator slammed on the com button. "Tony, call Frigal and pass the commander through a direct line to my com."

"Yes, sir. Right away."

*   *   *

Helena stepped in to the Situation Room. Sigu, John, and Michael were already there. Only Drenge was missing.

Kront gestured to her seat. "Please, take a seat."

Must be something big, she thought to herself.

Drenge came running through the door a few moments later. Kront nodded to him and began, "Now that we're all here, let's get started." Kront pushed a button to bring up a 3D model from a table projector. "As you can see, this is a model of Planet Loht 9. We cleared the *Grimond Wolf* about 690,000 miles away. We've been ordered by the Senate to investigate if this planet may have been used as an ambush point." They all nodded. "Good. Gear up. We leave in two hours."

As the squad leaders left, he turned to Helena, "Helena, if you could stay a minute." She walked over to him. "Helena, I'm going to ask you to sit this one out. I need you here to take care of Miranda and be acting commander while I'm on the mission. I will take command of Bravo Squad."

Helena snickered. "No offense, sir, but do you even remember how to fight?"

They both laughed. "Maybe it has been two years since our fight on Planet Dabni, but I do remember."

Helena raised her hands in concession. "Bravo squad is yours, sir. I will take good care of Miranda and the *Lindman*."

*　　*　　*

Commander Hellond picked up the call from the Senate in his office after pushing everyone else out. "Senator Milons, how can I help you?"

Flopre rubbed his forehead. "Groyt, we've lost all contact to the *Helium*. She still sends her position, but no one's answering the com."

"Tell me what you need done, Senator."

The Senator took a deep breath. "We need the best. We need the *Lindman*."

Groyt nodded, "On it, sir. Frigal out." He turned off the com. "Marshal, get me the *Lindman*."

Com Officer Dess patched through the *Lindman*. "Captain Tallin, sir."

Groyt could only smile as he thought of how Admiral Proked's frustrated face would turn flush red when he found out about the Senator's mission for the *Lindman*.

"Kront here. What's up, Groyt?"
Tallin's voice was like music to the commander's ears. "I've got a mission for you, Tallin. From the Senate."

Chapter 3. – Miranda.

"Helena, what's going to happen to me?"

The squad leader stroked the girl's red hair. "Well, sweetie, either the Senate will get you in a school program, or you'll be assigned to a foster family."

"I don't want another family. I want to stay here with you." Miranda pushed away slightly.

"Miranda, I—" Helena didn't finish before Nielson called her over the com unit.

"Sergeant Holley, emergency com from Frigal. Please report to the Bridge."

Helena stood up to leave, but a hand locked on to her arm. "Can I come?"

Helena smiled. "Okay, but you have to keep quiet when I am on the com."

Hand in hand, Miranda and Helena walked up to the Bridge.

"Lock and load, men. We have a direct order to shoot-to-kill any and all Handlons." Kront stood at the front of the shuttle so he could see both his soldiers and the pilot, Chuck Koffman, who took over assignments in place of Helena.

"Sir, our scanner indicates over 140 Handlon life signatures, approximately twenty human signatures…and one dog…"

"Signal the other squads; we're going in hot." Koffman started the back thrusters to slow their descent.

"Ready to drop in t-minus five….four…three…"

Kront opened the hatch. "Go, go, go!"

Thirty-seven soldiers on the ground with rifles stood ready for combat. Moniqé Nastas from Bravo Squad was first to engage the enemy. Quickly, she identified and took out three targets before the second soldier hit the ground.

"Move out! Clear the area," Kront whispered over the com.

Buck Cypher ran point for Charlie Squad; he entered the first building, rifle at the ready. "Hold!" he called over the com.

"Twelve targets: four left, four right, and four center. Three humans center on the ground, tied down. Looks like one needs medical attention." Buck went left and fired eight fast shots. Four Handlons collapsed to the ground. Cradan Trippen jumped to the right and shot seven times; three of the Handlons dropped dead, but the last on the right fell to a prone position and started to fire, hitting Cradan in his right shoulder. He grabbed his arm in pain, lifted his rifle, and fired another five shots. Drenge Pladu came in to cover Cradan and fired eight shots. The four center Handlons buckled. One of their rifles went off after a Drenge-shot: the Handlon bullet killed one of the captives.

Drenge radioed in to Echo Squad. "All clear. Twelve targets down. Cradan wounded. We need extraction to the shuttle."

"Roger, Charlie Squad. A three-man team is entering the target building."

Luis Lashus, Tena Grissham, and King Davis from Echo Squad were with Cradan before the com transmission was over. "Grissham and Davis, get the Hostages out of here!" The two soldiers that accompanied Lashus followed his directive.

Kront radioed in after watching Lashus' team escort the hostages. "All clear. Delta Squad, check in."

Sergeant Lodre replied to the com call. "Delta squad has cleared the target building." He paused a moment before continuing. "We lost Steven Blisy when we entered. A Handlon caught us off guard."

Forty soldiers returned to the shuttle unharmed. Cradan Trippen was wounded, Steven Blisy was dead, sixteen human hostages survived, and all of the Handlons were shot down.

"Bravo Squad, collect their weapons and armor pieces," Kront called in. He boarded the shuttle.

"Commander Hellond. Sergeant Holley, sir. How may the *Lindman* be of service?" Helena smiled at the visual com from Frigal. She knew Groyt very well; over the years, her father had trained many of the commander's men at the Academy.

"Helena it's good to see you, but I'm afraid I need to talk to your captain."

"The Captain is on the ground on Loht 9, sir. He left me in command." Although she tried to play it smooth, she knew Groyt meant serious business when he didn't smile.

Well, I have a mission - Priority Alpha - for the *Lindman*. Captain Tallin and the *Lindman* are needed now. The *Helium* is dead in space; we're not receiving any coms from them. I'm sending you their coordinates."

Helena's smile faded, as well. "Yes, sir. I'll contact Captain Tallin immediately. *Lindman* out." Helena ended the visual com and turned to Nielson. "Get the cap on the com, Nielson." A sudden sigh from behind her broke her concentration. She had completely forgotten that Miranda had accompanied her up to the Bridge.

"Oh, sweetie! I'm so sorry!" She hugged Miranda and then pulled her back to talk to her. "I need you to go back to the Medic Center, okay? I'll come down there as soon as I'm finished up here."

Miranda jumped down from her chair and saluted Helena with a slight smile, running back to Doc's office. Miranda had a feeling this was serious. *I wish I could help out somehow*, she thought.

"Captain, we have an emergency call from Frigal: mission briefing."

Kront stopped in his tracks as he walked onto the Bridge of the Lindman. "Thank you for that introduction back to the *Lindman*, Sergeant Holley."

Helena shrugged. "Sorry, cap. Frigal reports no contact with the *Helium* for three days."

Kront frowned. "I have a feeling that's not all."

"The Admirals from the Senate reported Handlon invasions on three ships."

Kront slammed his fist down on the table, causing Helena to wince. "How the hell could the Handlons get on any of the Presidential ships without getting detected? Don't they patrol their ships anymore?" Kront turned to Nielson, "Get Frigal on the com."

Tyler nodded. "Yes, sir."

"This stinks of a traitor in our ranks." Tallin put his hands on his hips. "Someone somewhere is helping the Handlons."

Helena coughed to clear her throat. "Sir, we can't prove that...at least not yet."

"But we will. Somehow."

"Where are we going?"

Helena held a frightened Miranda in her arms. The little girl didn't understand everything that happened on the Bridge, and a few hours had passed since she had returned to Doc's office. "Sweetie, we have to fly to Delta Sector to look for the *Helium*. It's a four-day flight, so we'll have lots of time together."

"I'd like that." Helena could feel Miranda's smile even though she didn't look down to see it.

Now let's talk about your future. How do you—"

"I want to be a soldier like you."

Miranda's statement shook Helena a bit to the bone. She suddenly felt protective of this fragile child. Even at twelve years old, the freckle-faced girl seemed too young to be thinking of being in the military.

"What made you decide that?"

"Because you're so brave and strong."

"How do you know that I'm not a chicken that hides behind my friends?"

Miranda grinned, "I saw the recordings from The *Grimond Wolf*."

Helena's smile faded. "Those files are classified. How did you open them?"

Embarrassed, Miranda admitted to Helena of her technological gift, especially in computers. "Three years ago, my dad gave me a computer. A few days later, the Presidential Security Force knocked on our door and asked to see our computer records. I had hacked in to the Senate Security Network."

Helena took a deep breath in, and just as she was about to scold Miranda, the little girl jumped the gun. "Please don't be mad."

"What else have you seen on that computer?"

"Your Presidential Military Record."

Helena cocked an eyebrow. "Let's keep this a secret. Just between you and me, okay?"

* * *

The last three days aboard the *Lindman* were full of fun times for Helena and Miranda; for the sergeant, it was like being back home with her little sister again. She thought of their most recent conversation as she waited in the Conference Room for the other members of the meeting to arrive.

"Helena, do you think I can live with you when we get to Troklon?" Miranda looked so hopeful.

"I don't know sweetie," Helena lied, knowing it was highly doubtful their situation would be approved. "It depends on what the Senate says. If you want to be a soldier like me, you have to start at the Academy on Planet Troklon very soon, but you will be in good hands there. My parents are both teachers at the Academy."

"That's great, but where do I live when I'm not in school?" Miranda seemed to have a million questions, but who could blame her? She lost all security in life with the disaster aboard the Grimond Wolf.

"We'll figure something out." Helena smiled, and Miranda bought it.

"Hey, Helena." Sigu, Drenge, and Michael walked through the door, interrupting her flashback.

"Hi, guys," Helena smiled at them.

"So, how's our little mascot down in the Med Center?" Michael started.

"She's doing very well, considering what happened."

Sigu nodded. "The poor girl…imagine, witnessing the murder of your parents."

"Yes, but she's getting better every day. Just yesterday she asked me to write a letter to the Senate: she wants to apply to join the Academy on Planet Troklon. She thinks of us as heroes and wants to be one of us."

Drenge crossed his arms. "Gotta be careful with that one. No offense, but we don't want a possible revenge-bent killer joining our ranks."

Helena braced the table. "What do you mean by that?"

"Easy, Helena," Michael warned. "I'm sure Drenge just means what we all think of when anyone who has lost family or friends suddenly desires to soldier-up."

Drenge narrowed his eyes. "Yeah, that's all I meant. But I am concerned about your increased feelings for her. You don't want to cross the line, Helena. We are still soldiers, and she's a victim."

Helena jumped to her feet. "Don't tell me about crossing lines, Drenge. I'm doing my job. Yes, I care for her, and yes I worry that she may be joining for the wrong reasons, but I'm also a woman and have a better connection to this little girl than you could get."

Sigu's strained laugh tried to break the tight air, "We don't argue you there, Helena."

Kront and Nielson walked through the door, the former immediately noting a high level of intense feelings in the air. He subtly placed his hand on Helena's shoulder and gently pushed her down into her seat. "Easy, tiger," he whispered into her ear. He made sure none of the others could hear what he had said.

"Okay, now that we're all here, let's get started." Kront gestured to all of the individuals in the room as he spoke, "As you all know, the *Helium* has now been D.I.S. – "Dead in Space" – for seven days, absolutely no contact whatsoever."

They all nodded. Helena's arms were still crossed. Drenge had a half-smile cocked on his face. Kront knew Drenge liked to tick people off, but he probably wanted a little more out of Helena. And it wasn't going to get him on Kront's good side.

"The *Helium* has 1350 crew members. Our mission is to shuttle onboard and conduct a section-to-section search for survivors." A 3-D model of the *Helium* appeared over the conference table. "As you can see on this model, the Hangar is located in the bow. Entering it will be tricky. Last time we did this, we were met with great resistance by only eight or so Handlons on the *Grimond Wolf*. We must be more prepared for this trip." He looked at each person intently. "We won't be able to scan for Handlons until we are less than thirty minutes away, so I want all five Squads to search the ship together. No squads go off on their own. One squad will transport the wounded back through the secured areas. Is that understood?"

They sounded off with a, "Sir, yes, sir!" They began to file out, but Kront couldn't help but notice the slight snicker Drenge sent Helena's way. Michael took Drenge's arm and dragged him out of the room opposite of Sigu who headed toward Helena to offer her a few words out of Kront's earshot. When Sigu left, Kront caught himself gazing at Helena; he shook his gaze before she noticed.

"Captain, can I have a word?" Helena addressed Kront.

Shit, he thought, *she caught me. Maybe I can change the subject.*

"Sure, but may I ask what happened in here before Nielson and I arrived?"

She shifted in her shoes. "That's part of what I need to talk to you about. It's Miranda."

Kront's eyes widened. "What's wrong? Is she okay?"

"She's fine. She's all right. But, she wants to apply to the Academy on Planet Troklon. I might have encouraged her a little, but she's a bright kid, and she just wants to belong somewhere." She crossed her arms and sank back into her chair. "Drenge got me worked up about it, but he might be right: what if she's joining for the wrong reasons? What if she's hell-bent on revenge, and her actions cause more damage than help, like damaging the reputation of this institution?"

Kront breathed a sigh of relief as he realized only part of Drenge's nonverbal communication was about Helena herself. "You're getting very attached to Miranda, aren't you?"

Helena nodded. "Yes, Captain. She reminds me of my little sister. I may have jumped the gun a little, but I've already made arrangement with my parents to give her my old room while she's not attending the Academy."

Kront took her hand and looked her in the eyes. "Be careful, Sergeant Holley. I don't want you losing your heart to this little girl, only for it to be broken when she grows up on you."

Helena's eyes nearly filled up and burst with tears as she realized just how motherly and attached she had become. She pulled her hand back out of embarrassment. "Thank you, Captain Tallin, but I'm sure I can handle it." She saluted her superior officer and left without saying another word.

*   *   *

"Incoming com from the *Lindman*, sir," Marshal told

Commander Hellond.

"Thank you Officer Dess. Patch it through." Groyt sat down in front of his com unit with his mug of piping-hot black coffee, just the way he liked it. "Captain Tallin, always a pleasure. My long range scanner tells me you're only one day away from the *Helium*, so I hope you're not calling to back out of the mission."

Kront laughed, "No, sir, but I do have a little bit of business to discuss. Miranda Holliday, our little survivor from the *Grimond Wolf*, has sent in an application to join the Academy on Planet Troklon."

"Well," Groyt stated. "Isn't that interesting?"

"Indeed, it is. Sergeant Holley has been talking to Miranda about it, but she's not sure if the little girl is joining out of revenge or true interest and loyalty. Maybe as a personal favor, we could let the little thing have a go at it and see how she does."

"I don't think it would hurt." Groyt took a sip of his blackened drink. "Either she'll enjoy it and prove a worthwhile soldier, or we'll find out her ulterior motives and she'll fail the psychological portion of the examinations. But who is going to pay for it?"

Kront smiled. "I have a feeling that once the crew finds out, she'll have enough donations from the *Lindman* to send her to the Academy several times over, failed psychological test or not."

Even Groyt laughed at that. "Well, then, why not? I tell you I had a feeling that Helena would get attached to the stowaway. But, if it's good for the girl, and it's not hurting anyone, then I just happen to know that there's an opening at the Academy, and I'll make sure it has Ms. Holliday's name all over it."

"Thank you, sir," Kront remarked. "I think I'll go inform Sergeant Holley and Miranda right now, if you don't mind."

Groyt held a fatherly countenance on his face for a few moments as he told Kront, "You go do that, son. Groyt out."

Chapter 4. – The *Helium*.

After Kront delivered the news, Sergeant Holley and Miranda nearly threw a party in the latter's recovery room. It was practically her own living quarters until the mission with the *Helium* was over. It had been one mission after another with very little time to figure out what to do with Miranda, but at least one thing had been determined: she was going to get a shot at the Academy.

"Now, you have to work hard," Helena started. Both girls sat down on the cot in the room, hearts racing and smiles from ear to ear. "It's not an easy job being a soldier. You'll get to the fighting and shooting parts soon enough, but there is a lot of reading and learning, like foreign languages, for instance."

"Well, what do you do in the military?" Miranda asked.

"That's another thing you'll have to figure out at the Academy. I mean, not what I do, but what you want to do: you have to choose a profession in your first two weeks. There are eight professions from which to choose: Pilot, Com Officer, Explosions, Medic, Gunner, Special, Intelligence, and S.S.A.U."

"How do I know which one I want to be?" Miranda's puzzled face brought a laugh to Helena's lips that she found quite hard to stifle. "Oh, I know! Hold on!" Miranda dashed over to a counter, rummaged through the drawers, and returned with a small notepad and a stubby pencil. "Okay, I'm ready."

Helena smiled. "Obviously, a pilot flies the ships and shuttles, but they must have the ability to think fast. For example, if the Landing Zone is under fire, they need to report it and quickly relocate without being compromised."

"Okay, that one's easy to understand."

"A com officer carries the com unit and rifle on his or her back, and acts as a gunner when necessary, but the primary responsibility is to keep communications clear and open. Aboard the ship, they are responsible for visual coms as well, not just audio coms. Com officers are very handy with technology." Helena nudged Miranda and smiled.

Miranda took the nudge and nodded. "It sounds okay, but I'm not sure."

"Well, the explosions officer is a gunner with an explosions pack. They open up blocked doors or remove barricades that prevent us from continuing onward. The medic—"

"Let me guess," Miranda interrupted. "The medic is like Doc. They know first-aid and stuff, and save lives…and stuff."

"…And stuff…" Helena joked. "Medics never carry a weapon, but they save more lives than any of the fighting soldiers. If we have medics in our squad at a particular battle zone, we make sure we keep them alive, or we're doomed."

"The gunner—well, you know, why don't we go talk to a gunner."

"Really?" Miranda's eyes widened and lit up so brightly.

"Sure! Let's go talk to Charles."

Miranda and Helena walked over a few doors to another recovery room. Helena knocked, and then opened the door when she heard Charles invite them in.

"Well, well, well. What do we have here?" he joked. He crossed his arms and tried to sound serious, but they both knew it was hard for either of the Jindso brothers to have a serious bone in their body.

Helena pushed Miranda to stand in front of her. "Miranda wants to attend the Academy, and I was explaining a gunner's responsibilities when I suddenly thought that it may sound better coming from a gunner personally."

Charles uncrossed his arms and put them behind his head on his pillow. "Gunners are the only ones that the other squad members can count on to cover their backs. You have to be a perfect shot, no exceptions. Your rifle is always at the ready. Your job is to carry out orders and shoot whatever enemy you see."

Miranda looked down at her toes for a moment, then back up at Charles. "What happens if you miss? Or if you're too slow? Or if your gun gets jammed? Or if you get shot?"

"Why do you think I'm in this bed?" Charles tried to smile. "It's a dangerous job. I'm not trying to downplay it, Miss Miranda. It's a serious responsibility. You can either do it or not, but not everyone can. I'm in this bed today because a Handlon beat me to it. I'm very lucky, though, because this is only my second time getting shot."

Miranda looked at Helena. "Aren't there other soldiers with

guns in case the gunners get shot?"

Helena looked at Charles who looked slightly shocked at the young girl's intelligence. "I told you, Charles."

"Yes, you did."

"Miranda, let's go back to our room and finish this discussion, okay? Mr. Charles needs his rest." Helena took Miranda's hand and began to pull her toward the door.

Miranda waved goodbye, and Charles closed his eyes, a slight smile on his lips. The two ladies continued their discussion as they walked down the hallway back to Miranda's room. "What was the next one, Helena?"

"The next one is called the special. The special is like Sigu and Drenge. Technically, they're gunners with extra training. They master almost every weapon, so they can literally pick up any kind of weapon and know how to use it correctly. Also, they have sniper training. Sniper training really helps when taking out targets from long-distance ranges. Got it?"

Miranda nodded, so Helena continued. "The intelligence or the spies are only for the smartest students at the Academy, like those who are able to hack computer files."

Helena knew that Miranda's cheeks blushed. What she didn't know was that Miranda herself wasn't sure if she was smart enough for intelligence work.

"The last one is S.S.A.U. or Special Space Attack Unit. These soldiers are the best of the best. They can do all of the other jobs, and much better, but they have secret assignments that only some people get to know about. It's a very hard, but very rewarding, position."

Miranda's pencil slowed in her note-taking. "So…which profession are you, Helena?"

Helena smiled. "The Academy will teach you that position is nothing if you can't do your job well and if you don't have a good attitude. We don't go around telling people which position we have to get gain or glory or fame or anything. I won't tell you my position, but I'll give you one guess."

Miranda smiled. "Fair enough. I think your S.S.A.U."

Helena winked.

Nielson's voice sounded over the com system, "All squads gear up. We'll arrive at the *Helium* in less than one hour. Repeat:

all squads gear up."

"Okay, Nielson, start the scan." Kront crossed his arms, ready to hear the worst possible news.

A few moments passed by before Tyler reported. "Sir, I read five human life forms and over 100 Handlons. With the way they are scattered all over the ship, it looks like they are trying to steal it, not destroy it. The Bridge alone has fifteen Handlons, and the Hangar has forty-five of them. Good thing the Presidential Fleet began securing the ships with the L.S.V.R. Chips."

Kront agreed, "Yes. Without them, the ship won't fly. The Life Signature and Voice Recognition Chip. Man, whoever came up with that idea was one smart cookie." He looked to Sergeant Holley. "Sergeant, this is going to be a tough mission. I need a five-soldier squad to infiltrate from the outer hull. Entry is through the hatch at the Bridge."

"Sir, with your permission, I choose Buck Cypher from Charlie Squad, Robin Sammy from Delta Squad, and Mason Jung and Moniqé Nastas from Bravo Squad."

Kront didn't even finish writing down the names of her companions before he realized just what she had done. "I see, Sergeant Holley. Good choice: an S.S.A.U. Squad." He brought up a 3-D visual of the *Helium* for her to study. "Your objective is to take back the Bridge."

Helena looked over the schematics of the *Helium*. "Captain, with your additional permission, I have an idea."

"Go on."

"I can send Chuck Koffman out in a space suit. He can fire an acid grenade into the Hangar. If the timing is right, we can take out 80% of the Handlons in the Hangar before the other squads get on board."

Kront mused over the idea. "An acid grenade may permanently damage parts of the *Helium*, but I'd rather hurt a ship than lose a soldier. You have my approval. Let's get this show on the road." Kront began to walk away, but Helena interrupted him. "Captain? Just one more thing."

Kront, slightly surprised by what was about to come out of his own mouth, stated, "My, Sergeant Holley, you certainly aren't afraid to ask for what you want this evening."

A blush equal to that of her pink hair fell across her cheeks, but she quickly recovered. "Cap, I know it's out of regulation, but do you think Miranda can follow the mission on the visual screens? If a student wants to learn, what better way is there?"

Helena and her S.S.A.U. Squad arrived at the hatch to the Bridge. While waiting for the grenade to explode in the Hangar, the team snuck into the airlock, took off their helmets, and waited, watched, listened. Helena gazed up at the stars and the vastness of space through the tiny window of nine-inch-thick glass. When the Presidential Service invented the P.S.A. (Protection against Space Air) Suit, soldiers could travel back and forth from shuttle to ship without wearing heavy spacesuits. The first time she put one on and floated out in space, she had been amazed at how much empty sky had been blocked by a space suit. Now, with a clear helmet, she had a 360° view of true nightlife.

"Koffman ready."

Koffman's voice interrupted her thoughts. Helena got herself together and replied, "S.S.A.U. ready. Fire at will."

Chuck was floating in his space suit thirty miles from the Hangar doors. "Standby, S.S.A.U. Firing in t-minus five seconds." Chuck took aim, zoomed in at the Hangar doors with the scope, and slowly squeezed the trigger. An enormous blast of light and flames propelled the grenade towards the Hangar doors, soaring off in a perfectly straight line of dangerous color toward the *Helium*.

"Thirty seconds to impact…twenty seconds…ten seconds—Helena, be ready!" As Koffman counted down the last few moments, Helena and her squad watched from their position above. "Five, four, three, two, one, impact!" He didn't have to say it; Helena and her crew felt the impact in the hull.

"Go, go, go!" Helena commanded her squad members. She opened the door leading from the airlock to the Bridge; Mason jumped through first, followed closely by Buck. Helena was third to enter, and by the time she landed, Buck and Mason had already shot down six of the fifteen Handlons in the way.

Helena opened fire, knocking out her own Handlon with four bullets, but as the excitement of being on another mission began to kick up her adrenaline, she barely heard Buck call out "Helena, behind you!" before everything turned black.

"Helena. Helena, wake up. Man, she's gonna hate her head when she gets up from this! Helena, how are you feeling?"

Helena opened her eyes. Buck was shaking her; it hurt her head, so she punched him in the arm. "Stop shaking me. You're killing my head." She tried to sit up, but between a pain-searing back, a bleeding neck, and dizziness enough to make her vomit, she lied back down for a few more moments. "What the hell happened?"

Buck smiled at her and told the others, "Told you she wouldn't like it." Turning back to Helena, he said, "You got knocked down by a Handlon. He was hiding in the corner of the Bridge, and when he saw you, he jumped forward and knocked you out with an iron rod. He tried to hit you again after you went down, but we took him out before he could do it."

Helena glanced at the dead Handlon beside her. "Thanks. What's our status?"

"The Hangar was clear when the squads landed. Grenade took out all the Handlons except a few, but they were too injured to fight. While Delta Squad held the Hangar, Bravo and Echo Squads cleared the top two levels, and Charlie and Alpha Squads cleared the lower two levels."

Helena tried to stand. Buck helped her up. "Okay, good. Any human survivors?"

Buck shook his head as he offered Helena his forearm her support. "Four survived; one died when a Handlon started shooting them off as Echo Squad approached."

Helena didn't answer, but Buck could understand. Her balance was severely off as she teetered back and forth, leaning on Buck yet trying to hold her own.

"Damn. Now I have to see Doc, huh?" she smiled.

Chuck walked up and joined the conversation. "That's right. Frank will be balls of joy to see you as a patient."

"Shut up and report." Helena's scowl was only half-true. Although she was a woman, Helena gave her all in trying to be the best in her gender and class at the Academy, all without getting hurt. Now it seemed as though Doctor Frank Trad aboard the *Lindman* would be her first doctor ever.

"All one-hundred Handlons are dead. Echo and Bravo

Squads are collecting what little weapons and armor weren't completely destroyed in the acid grenade."

Helena winced as her headache began developing into a monster migraine. "Fine, just fine. How are the men? Any injuries or deaths?"

Chuck laughed, "Only you Helena. Mission was a success."

Helena half-smiled through the pain and turned on her com. "Patch me into the Situation Room."

"Captain Tallin here. Report."

"Cap. Come in. This is Sergeant Holley."

He smiled and allowed Miranda to climb up on the seat next to him. "Helena, how are you doing? Miranda and I saw what happened. She was a little freaked out, but I showed her the Life Monitor System. Your vitals were fine, so she calmed down."

"No worries on this end, Cap. I'm fine, just a little headache."

Kront quickly covered Miranda's ears before yelling out, "Oh, bullshit, Helena! I watched what happened! You will report directly to Doctor Trad the moment you board the *Lindman*, am I clear, Sergeant Holley?"

Shit, Helena thought. *The last thing I need right now is for him to be upset with me.* "Sir, yes, sir."

"Good." Kront uncovered Miranda's ears, but her widened eyes and curious smile gave away that she still heard his outburst and probably thought it was cute that he was reprimanding Helena. "Continue with your report."

"Yes, sir. The *Helium* is clear: one-hundred Handlons dead and four human survivors. One died."

"Thank you, Sergeant Holley. Charlie and Delta Squads will remain on the *Helium*, and the rest of you will report back to the *Lindman* immediately. *Lindman* out." He slammed the com button to turn it off, getting a jumpy reaction from Miranda. He turned to speak to the girl. "Ms. Helena is tough, and I'm sure you will be just as tough, my dear. But don't ever downplay an injury, especially one that knocks you out unconscious so you miss the rest of the battle."

Miranda smiled, "Thanks, Mr. Kront, but I don't think I'll choose S.S.A.U."

"You've made your decision, then?"

Miranda shook her head of red hair. "I think I'll enjoy Intelligence more."

Her answer got an outburst of laughter from the Captain. "Yes, I must agree. You have great computer skills, and you're very observant."

Miranda's face blanked. She thought she was in trouble for sure. She gulped, "How do you know about my computer skills?"

"Oh, don't worry. I have some of those skills, too. I can tell when someone hacks my system. You're good for your age, and I can show you some tricks that will come in handy, but I'll deny I ever showed you anything if you tell anyone I taught you. Understand?

Miranda gave him a big hug. "Thank you, Captain Tallin!"

He gently pulled her off. "Run down to Doc's office to greet Helena when she boards, and make sure she listens to him. You report to me in one hour."

Miranda saluted her "superior" and ran off down the hall.

Kront turned back to his work and pushed the com button. "Frigal, come in. This is the *Lindman*."

A few seconds passed by before the visual came up. "Kront," Groyt said, "I hear you loud and clear. What's your status?"

"The *Helium* is clear, sir. All one-hundred Handlons are dead. We have four living and one dead survivor from the *Helium* crew. One small injury of our own: Helena got knocked out by a Handlon from the back."

Groyt stopped smiling. "Is she okay?"

"She'll recover in a day or two just fine. As for the *Helium*, please inform the Senate that we are on our way to deliver it to Frigal."

Groyt smiled. "I will. Thanks again. Frigal out."

Kront turned off the com and glanced toward the hallway leading to Doc's office, dreading how Helena would take being a patient instead of caring for her own little red-headed patient.

Chapter 5. – Helena and Miranda.

Tony Flakes pushed the button on his com. "Sir, there's a visual com from Frigal. They've secured the *Helium*."

Flopre smiled. "Good job, Kront," he said to himself. He pushed the com button to reply. "Tony, please patch it through."

"Roger that."

Within milliseconds, Commander Hellond appeared on the Senator's screen. "Groyt, I hear the *Helium* is safe. What's the status?"

"As you can see, sir," Groyt began as he pushed a few buttons. A list appeared before the both of them in their separate and distant offices. "This is the list of the dead. Over 1300 crew members from the *Helium* are confirmed dead. The *Lindman* crew found only four survivors, but they killed all Handlons onboard trying to steal the ship. The *Lindman* is currently escorting the *Helium* to Frigal."

Flopre hung his head. "Only four survivors? What could have driven the Handlons to do this? How are they getting on board our ships? We've lost over 3000 crew members between the *Helium* and the *Grimond Wolf*, and we still don't know what's going on?"

Groyt cleared his throat, obviously uncomfortable with the situation as well, but not sure how to respond to the Senator.

"I'm sorry, Commander. Please tell Captain Tallin that I appreciate his help in this endeavor, and please make sure he gets paid for his service."

Groyt nodded, "Yes, sir. I'll take care of that, but there is one more matter, slightly unrelated and less important."

"Yes, Groyt? What is it?"

"I'm sending you some files right now." Groyt looked to his right and nodded to his com officer, then turned back to Flopre. "Our extra passenger from the *Grimond Wolf*, Miranda Holliday, has applied to the Academy on Planet Troklon. I've put in my letter of recommendation, but since she is such a special case, I was hoping to have your signature on file, too."

"Done deal. It's the least I can do for the lone survivor of the *Grimond Wolf.* She may be an orphan in life, but I have a feeling she's going to affect us all one day. I'll notify the Academy and have the papers ready. Captain Tallin may escort Ms. Holliday to her new home at the Academy."

Groyt smiled and sighed. "Thank you, sir. She'll be ecstatic to know that she has your support. Frigal out."

*   *   *

Helena was furious.

I don't need medical attention. It's just a bump on my head and a small cut on the back of my neck. I have a little...somewhat big...headache. So, what? It's nothing, she argued with herself.

"Sorry, Helena. Captain Tallin requests that you stay here for a minimum of two days. You've lost a lot of blood, and already you're so angry you're going to bust through those twenty stitches, so please lay down and relax." Doc Trad had no problem telling Helena what to do so long as he had Kront's backing.

"Helena! Helena!" Helena heard the voice of the green-eyed angel as she flew into the room and past Doc.

"Shh!" Doc scolded, winking at Helena. "You're going to give her another headache if you're not careful, young lady."

Miranda smiled. "Sorry, Doc. Sorry, Helena. I just came to tell you that the Academy approved my application!"

"That's great news!" The sergeant hugged her little friend tightly. "When do you report?"

Miranda jumped up on the bed next to her mentor. "Next week as soon as Captain Tallin can get us to Troklon."

"Good. Now remember, it's going to be a lot of hard work. If you want to succeed, you'll need to study hard and be the best in your class. This is the only way to nearly-guarantee that you'll get the best choices in assignments when you graduate."

Miranda nodded. "That's what Mr. Kront said, too. I was hoping you could train with me to get me ready for some of it, since I'll be six months behind when I start."

"I have a feeling you'll catch up quite quickly." Helena pushed some strands of Miranda's hair behind her right ear. "Go up to Nielson and ask to borrow these three books: *The Study of*

Weapons: 3rd Presidential Edition, *Handlons History*, and *Space - Sector by Sector*. We'll start with those."

*   *   *

Jamie Holley ran in to the house from the door to the backyard. She dropped her backpack in the entryway and ran in to the kitchen to see her mom. "Mom, is it true? Is Helena coming home to visit?"

"Yes, dear. I received the com this morning. She'll arrive tomorrow and stay for four days," Ida Holley excitedly informed Helena's younger sister. "Your father doesn't know, yet, so I'm planning on surprising him tonight during dinner."

Jamie kicked off her shoes and slumped back in a chair. "It's been eight months since the last time she visited. It's about time!"

"My, my, you really do keep track on that calendar she bought you, don't you?"

Jamie laughed. "What do you think she'll bring me this time?"

"I don't know, dear, but I do know that she's bringing a friend."

Helena's little sister jumped up in her seat. "Did she get a boyfriend?"

Ida laughed, "Maybe. Why would that be so terrible? She does need love, you know. Space can be a cold, empty place for a single woman." The woman laughed as she watched her youngest child roll her eyes and shake her body.

"Yuck! Boys are gross!"

"I bet you'll change your tune in four or five years, and want one for yourself!"

"No way, mom. Not me!"

*   *   *

The *Lindman* slowly descended toward a spaceport at Planet Troklon's Academy. First item of business: drop off the new student. "Academy Troklon, this is the *Lindman*. Request permission to land." Nielson waited for an answer on his end of the com.

"*Lindman*, this is Academy Troklon. You are authorized to land on platform 14 Foxtrot. Welcome home."

"Roger that, Academy Troklon, and thank you. We're glad to be back." Slowly, Nielson sat the big freighter down on the platform. "Academy Troklon, this is the *Lindman*. We have landed."

Kront shut down the engines and sighed. "It's good to be home. Come on, Nielson." The two made their way to the large Hangar where the crew of the *Lindman* awaited instructions from their superior commander. Kront stood at a higher balcony and address the soldiers at attention below. "We have four days here at home. I suggest you spend them wisely. The Senate is planning a recon mission for us, so get your affairs in order and be back here by Tuesday." After a proper salute, Kront bellowed, "Dismissed!" and turned from the cheers toward the hallway that led to Helena's recovery room. He knocked on her door and entered. "Sergeant Holley?"

"Captain Tallin, come on in."

"How are you feeling?" He shut the door behind him and gave a big hug to Miranda as she pounced on him from behind.

"I'm not sure if this headache is from the blow to my head or all the studying I did with that one over there," she suggested, hinting at Miranda. "But, damn, it hurts"

Kront winked at the red-headed girl. "She must really miss the Academy if she helped you study."

Helena shook her head. "Pardon me for saying so, but hell no, sir."

Kront laughed again. "Well, take good care of Miranda. She has three days before she starts at the school. I presume she'll be staying with your family, yes?"

"Yes, sir. We're going there right now."

Kront bent down to Miranda's level. "I guess this is goodbye, for now. I'll be following your progress while you're at the Academy, and I hope that we get to hear from you on the com from time to time."

Miranda hugged Tallin again. "Captain, sir, this crew has been really nice to me. Thank you all for helping me. I know you're worried about my intentions for becoming a soldier, but I know that this is what I want."

Kront stood up. "Attention on deck: Honorary Crew Member Miranda Holliday resigning from duty aboard the *Lindman*." Although the crew had been dismissed prior to this moment, Doc, Helena, and Kront saluted Miranda as she walked partway down the hallway before turning back to grab Helena's hand and pull her along.

Miranda turned around to say, "I'll be back. Don't worry about that! Your computer just better be ready for me in eight years!" With that, the two ladies left on the *Lindman* left the ship, leaving Doc to clean up and Kront to stare after them.

*   *   *

Nikolej Holley was so happy! Finally, after eight long months, his military daughter would come home and stay for four days. "They're on the way right now! I just heard the com! Quick, Jamie, go get a Slonga Water. I'm sure Helena has missed her favorite drink."

Jamie ran down to the basement to get the Slonga, but then the doorbell rang. Forgetting Helena's drink, she ran up the stairs and yelled, "I got it!" She wanted to be the first to see Helena. She threw open the door and jumped into her older sister's arms. "Helena!"

"Who are you?"

Jamie jumped down, confirming it was definitely Helena, and asked, "Are you okay?"

Helena smiled. "Yup, just kidding." She grabbed her little sister in a second embrace.

"Helena, I missed you so much!"

They parted, and Helena pulled Miranda out from behind her. "Sis, let me introduce you to a friend of mine. This is Miranda Holliday. She starts at the Academy in three days."

Jamie smiled at Miranda and extended her hand for a proper introduction. "Hi, I'm Jamie. Come on in and meet my parents."

Miranda looked at Helena, the latter ushering the former inside. "It's okay. Go ahead." Miranda shook Jamie's hand and followed Helena's younger sister inside. Before Jamie could introduce Miranda, her parents hugged, cried, and gushed over Helena's return.

"Mom! Dad!"

The parents quieted. "Oh, goodness!" Ida began, "I'm so sorry! I forgot: Nikolej, we have a visitor, remember?"

"Yes, yes, I do," Nikolej agreed.

Jamie stood up a little higher. "Miranda, this is my mom, Ida Holley, and my dad, Nikolej Holley. They both teach at the Academy, so you'll get to see them a lot. Probably more than me."

Helena tousled Jamie's hair. *She's getting so big,* Helena thought. *I need to come back and visit home more often. I'm so glad to be home.*

Chapter 6. – The Academy.

"Wake up, Miranda! Today's the day," Jamie exclaimed as she shook Miranda awake.

"What? Who? When? I'm up! I'm up." Miranda was having such a good dream, imagining she was sitting on the Bridge of the *Lindman* with Helena and Kront. They flew across the galaxy and fought the evil Handlons—

"When do classes start?" Jamie, again, interrupted Miranda's thoughts.

The red-head looked at Helena's younger sister with tired eyes. "In three hours, but I need to eat breakfast and get ready, first." Jamie smiled, and then dashed off with a bounce in her step.

Miranda smiled. Just as nice as Helena, but more her age, Jamie was a great best friend. Although they both attended the Academy, they had different classes: Jamie wanted to be a Com Officer, and Miranda still opted for Intelligence. It didn't take much to get Captain Tallin and Commander Hellond to pull some strings for them to room together. Normally classmates of the same profession would stick together, but they understood Miranda's special situation. She didn't mind being known as the lone survivor of the *Grimond Wolf*, but she wanted to prove that she was good enough on her own, as well. Thinking of her rescue made her think of Helena and their conversation the night before.

"Miranda, this is important," Helena warned. "You'll learn stuff you can't share with anyone, including Jamie. Being in Intelligence means you learn things that you have to keep to yourself."

Miranda understood what that meant, no matter how hard it may one day be for others – including Jamie – to understand.

"One more thing: you'll get an implant in your wrist. It's a chip that can eventually give you access to all computers and the ability to control all ships

*commanded by the Presidential. But there are
levels you must pass in order to gain more
access. The pain from the procedure itself
will hurt for a day or two, but as your pass
your classes with highest marks, even greater
responsibilities will be given to you over
other classmates.*

*Miranda nodded, slightly worried.
"When will I get the implant?"*

*"Before your first class tomorrow. I'll
be with you."*

A voice startled Miranda's thoughts. "Students, I want you to meet the newest member of the Academy, Ms. Miranda Holliday." The Grand Master of the Academy stood at the center of the stage with Miranda and Helena. Miranda wasn't sure what to do; Helena nudged her, so she smiled and gave a little wave to the 800 or so students before her. "Miranda hails from the Planet Dringls."

Miranda was quick to pick up on the whispers. She knew why, too. The Grand Master continued speaking. "As you all know, very few humans survived after the massive Handlon attack on that planet. She was relocated to a life aboard the *Grimond Wolf* with her parents until recently…when, again, Handlons attacked, and she alone survived."

Miranda's eyes began to water as the Grand Master's words hit home. She turned to Helena and asked, "Why is he telling them? That's very personal."

Helena whispered back, "We have no secrets at the Academy except when working on classified projects." She gave the girl a smile in hopes to alleviate some of the misunderstanding.

"Miranda has chosen the Intelligence profession, and I hope her classmates will take good care of her. Now, let's stand and welcome her with our Academy Troklon manners." The Grand Master signaled the students to stand; with their voices raised as one sound, they shouted, "Miranda, Miranda, Miranda, HUR!"

Helena translated, "That's the Academy Welcome. Now, bow and say thank you."

Miranda did as she was told. The whole room started to

clap, and suddenly Miranda felt very welcome.

Miranda slowly slid her hand into the machine's hole. Helena watched and acted as a guide since she had the procedure done in the past. "It will sting a bit, but it'll be over very quickly. Try to act tough."

The machine buzzed and whirred, and like a scorpion stinging its prey, she felt the needle jam into her wrist and the accompanying burn where the chip was implanted under her skin.

Sting a bit? Miranda reflected. *Hurts like hell!* "That wasn't so bad." A few other Intelligence students gathered in the room to watch the new student; others waited in line to get their chip.

"Let's go get something to eat," Helena offered the new student. Miranda smiled. *Food sounds great! I felt like I haven't eaten in ages!*

With plates loaded full of food, they sat down in the cafeteria. Helena spoke first. "Your chip is set to Level 1. As you pass various tests or levels, your chip will be upgraded. In time, you can opt for a more advanced chip if yours is incapable of storing enough data, malfunctions, or anything else. Chips are used in everything we do; even some weapons won't fire if you don't have the chip that matches the weapon." Helena smiled, an impish look in her eyes. Miranda liked that look. It meant a lot of fun in the future. "I've talked to Captain Tallin and Mr. Holley—"

"Your dad?"

"Yes, my dad," Helena confirmed. "It's just so weird to call him 'dad' when I'm talking to an Academy student. Anyway, we've agreed that you should take your first test today. You're going to start with Advanced Computer Security Level 4."

Miranda nearly choked on the food in her mouth. "What about Levels 1 through 3?"

Helena laughed, "Well, with your skills in hacking computers, you probably don't want to waste everyone's time with those trivialities."

"Okay, I trust you three. When is my test?"

Helena looked at her watch. "In a few more minutes. The tests happen in the Great Hall. Your class will be there, but only you will take the test." She took another bite of food and swallowed. "There is one more thing you should know before you take the test."

Miranda cocked an eyebrow.

"Captain Tallin designed most of the Academy's Computer Security courses."

Miranda smiled. *This will be a piece of cake.*

Kront was sitting in the front row. He received special permission to attend Miranda's first test, especially since he designed the course. She looked up and saw him, waving wildly. He smiled and winked, hoping his presence would boost her confidence a little more.

"You have thirty minutes to find and close as many back doors as possible in the system. You may begin." Grand Master of the Academy, Professor Hugsly Thandson, started the clock. Miranda started up the computer; the other students in the room watched her progress on the big screen above and before them. A 1st year student had never passed the test before; the youngest had been Kront, and many years ago. He felt a little old as he realized he had held the record for 38 years now. He shifted in his seat. Helena noticed out of the corner of her eye and gave him a cocky grin, seeming to perceive his sudden discomfort. He brought his thoughts back to the test, going over the schematics and wondering if he made it too hard or too easy. There were two ways that Miranda could break the record: she would have to close more than sixteen back doors in the program – Kront's record was sixteen – but by doing so she'd be the youngest ever to pass the test.

She can do it, he assured himself. *If she broke into my system on the* Lindman *and found Helena's files, she can break into this system just fine.*

Miranda worked fast. After an initial eight minutes of frustration, she found a cluster of back doors. Quickly, she identified them by name and creators, logged them in the system, and closed them. By seventeen minutes into the test, the whole crew of the *Lindman* had entered the Great Hall, unnoticed by Miranda. Another five minutes had passed, and a challenge appeared: she found what seemed to be a back door, but it did not want to open for her. Three more minutes passed. Miranda's fingers began to hurt, and finally the door opened. She identified it, logged it, and put a new security measure on it. Mumbling words under her breath too quiet for anyone to hear, Helena could tell it was a good thing no one could hear them; her words probably weren't meant to be spoken over a microphone.

Twenty-eight minutes into the test, she found two more back doors that were locked. With fingers cramping and wrists tingling, she wrote a new sub-routine and pried them open, logging and securing them right before the clock buzzed her out.

Grand Master Professor Thandson stepped forward and turned off her screen. "Sorry, Ms. Holliday, but your time is up. Let's look at your log." He pulled out a printout from her test and held it up to read. "In order to break the record, you must have located and closed at least sixteen back doors." After a few moments, he put the paper down at his side and announced, "Ms. Holliday successfully located and closed eighteen back doors. She has secured a new Academy record."

Helena was the first to hug her tightly. "Congratulations, champ!" Miranda smiled, feeling radiant. It was then, when she looked to Kront and his bright-white smile, that she heard the extra-loud shouts coming from the crew from the *Lindman*. She nearly ran to them, but Helena stopped her. She knew the protocol that came next before any additional celebration.

"Ms. Holliday," the Grand Master began. "Please place you wrist under this scanner to update your chip." Miranda did as she was told, turning up her wrist and watching the red laser beam connect her implanted chip wirelessly to the computer she had used to beat Kront's old record. A beeping noise confirmed the update. "Welcome to Computer Security Level 5. You are dismissed."

Kront walked up to her on stage. "Miranda, the crew and I went in together and had this made for you." He gave her the package he held in his hands. She ripped it open. A stunned expression fell upon her face. She didn't say anything. "Well, don't you like it?"

Miranda sniffled. "It's a *Lindman* Uniform. How could I not like it?" She looked up to Kront, tears in her eyes.

"Why are you crying?"

"I feel like I have a real home, a place where I finally belong."

Tears fell from Helena's face. She wiped them away when

Kront noticed, but she smiled when she saw tears gather in his eyes as well. He cleared his throat and directed his attention back to the red-headed smarty pants. "Please note the insignia."

Miranda held up the uniform up and read out loud, "Miranda Holliday: Junior Security Officer, The *Lindman*." Miranda smiled through her continuous tears. "Thank you, Captain Tallin. Thank you, all of you!"

Kront kneeled down in front of her. "I know we've pulled a lot of strings to help you out, but it's not because we don't think you will do great on your own. Since we rescued you from the *Grimond Wolf* and scared the daylights out of Sergeant Holley—"

"Hey!" Helena interrupted, slapping Kront on the shoulder. Everyone laughed, and he could only remark, "Well, it's true, and it's hard to scare you, too! I know!" She shook her head, and he continued, "Since then, the *Lindman* crew feels that you belong with us. So, we spoke to the Academy, and the Board has approved my request to allow you to wear this as your school uniform."

Miranda threw her arms around him in a bear hug, but he pulled her back. "Wait, I'm not done, yet. In addition, I have recruited you on board the *Lindman*. You're an official a member of the *Lindman* crew."

At the sound of this news, Miranda felt like fainting from an overload of joy. However, she didn't want to disappoint her new superior commander and fellow soldiers with that kind of dramatic presentation. Instead, she allowed the butterflies to settle, closed her eyes to relax and focus, and then saluted Kront and Helena at attention. "Thank you, sir!"

Kront smiled. "Junior Officer Holliday, until you board the Lindman, I expect nothing but the best work from you. Is that understood?"

"Sir, yes, sir!"

He laughed and saluted her back.

Chapter 7. – The Recon Mission.

Miranda turned on the visual com. "Hi Helena."

Helena smiled at Miranda, "Hi, sweetie. We take off in a few minutes, but I just wanted to say goodbye and wish you good luck at the Academy."

Miranda pushed a few buttons, and an extra, smaller screen popped up on Helena's visual. "Before you go, two things: first, I've sent you an attachment that includes a security sub-routine I wrote last night. Can you make sure that Captain Tallin at least takes a look at it?"

"No problem. He'll be so honored to take a look at your first piece of handiwork, especially if he deems it good enough to implement on board A.S.A.P."

The red-headed student laughed. "It's not perfect, and I'm certainly not that good, yet. Someday I will be."

"I'm sure it's just fine, but what does it do?"

"It closes the back doors I found when I located your files on board."

Helena threw back her head and laughed. "Yep, he'll like this one just fine. What's the other one?"

"It's a surprise, and also for Captain Tallin."

The sergeant arched an eyebrow, but didn't push the subject. "Okay, I'll make sure he gets both of them. Miranda, I've got to go now. Study hard, and I'll see you soon!"

Miranda nodded, "I will, Helena. Miranda out."

"Academy Troklon, this is the *Lindman*. We are preparing for takeoff." Nielson smiled. He loved to be home and visit his parents, but nothing was better than deep space. The *Lindman* started her engines. The Academy's platform shook.

"*Lindman*, we have confirmed your takeoff. Have a safe journey, and we'll see you soon."

Nielson smiled to the young woman on the visual. *Damn, she's pretty,* Nielson thought to himself. *She has to be at least 18 years old to be a Com Officer, although she barely looks 17. I'm only 22, so maybe I'll check her out next time we visit.* Focusing back on the mission when Kront nudged him in the back, Nielson cleared his throat. "Thank you, Academy Troklon. *Lindman* out." Nielson smiled and winked at the pretty officer, and saw her smile and wink back just before the screen blanked.

"Listen up, everyone." Kront paced the Control Center as his com officers and squad leaders surrounded him, waiting for instruction. "We have a six-day flight ahead of us. The Senate has given us a recon mission. Our target is Planet Helgin. Intelligence has unconfirmed reports that the Handlons have built a base there made of spare parts and looted items from The *Grimond Wolf*." The captain brought up a 3D model of the planet. "I want everyone to study the planet. All Com Officers: scan the planet for humans; I want to know where they live. Helena and Sigu, I want to know every possible site for a Handlon base and every possible entry to get to the base. Any questions?" No one spoke up, so he turned off the model. "Get to work. You have four days to get me the information I want."

As the squad leaders filed out of the room, Helena stayed behind—as usual. "Sir, I have a disc for you from Miranda."

Kront smiled. "I haven't even been gone for one whole day, and she already misses me. What is it?"

"It's a present."

"Okay, Helena. Play the disc."

Helena put the disc in the player and started it. "Captain Tallin, this is Junior Officer Holliday. Sergeant Holley informed me prior to your departure that the *Lindman* must be within thirty minutes of a destination in order to scan for Handlons, thanks to their new and upgraded armor. Well, let's battle their new and improved with our own new and improved. I've rewritten some coding for the scanners aboard the *Lindman* that should improve the scans to much more desirable circumstances."

Kront looked at the screen and saw the program on the visual. "Damn! She just gave us the option to detect and pinpoint targets two days out!" Kront blurted out.

Helena laughed. "She sure earned her uniform, sir."

Kront smiled and placed his hands on his hips, resting at his belt. "I'll say! Nielson, install this as fast as you can, and get me Frigal on the com."

"Sir, the *Lindman* is on the com."

Groyt looked up from his report. "Thank you, Marshal. Patch it through." He smiled instantly as green- and purple-dyed hair filled his screen. "Hi, Helena. How can I help you?"

"Well, sir, I think it is we who can help you, but we have a small demand that comes with it."

Groyt seemed beyond confused.

"Maybe Captain Tallin should explain." Kront came on to the visual. "Sir? Our friend, Ms. Holliday, has just made our lives a whole lot easier."

"You don't say?" Groyt sat forward in his chair, extremely interested in what Kront had to say. "Yes, sir. She's rewritten the coding of the scanners aboard our ship and made it possible to detect Handlons in their new armor, and two days out, to boot!"

"This could turn the war," Commander Hellond mumbled, though the com picked it up."

"Yes, sir, it just could," Kront agreed. "Look at the pre-formatted program coding and compare it to the post-formatted coding." He gave Groyt a few moments to flip through a few pages of notes. "Now look at these test results from the *Lindman*."

His superior commander sat stunned in his chair. "All right, you've got me. What's your demand?"

Kront smiled. "We want the Presidential to pay Miranda according to talent and ability, age and background aside."

Groyt laughed and slammed his fist on the table. "Done! She damn well deserves it, too! I'll make sure this little spitfire gets the all-out treatment."

"Thank you, sir. *Lindman* out."

*   *   *

"Captain," Neilson called over the com. "Please report to the Control Center."

Kront looked up from his book. "Finally," he said aloud. He pushed the com button and replied, "I'll be right there. Call the Squad Leaders to the Bridge." Kront got up from his chair. "Okay, Miranda, let's see that program of yours in action." He had no doubt it would work wonders.

"All Squad Leaders to the Bridge," Nielson's voice

sounded over the com.

When Kront arrived, Neilson was first to grab his attention. "Sir, I assume you know why I called you up here?"

"Our destination target?"

"Yes, sir. It just appeared on the radar."

Helena and Sigu arrived as Neilson and Kront continued their conversation, closely followed by Drenge and Michael.

"Please, take a seat," Kront designated with his hands. "Let me update you on the situation." He explained Miranda's contribution to the Academy and then turned toward his squad leaders. "The only dilemma now is that I don't know what it's called. She didn't give it a title in the DVD presentation."

Helena interrupted with a smile. "Sir, Miranda told me she wants to call it the L.D.S.S., or *Lindman* Deep Space Scanner."

"I'm so touched. I think I might be blushing," he joked. "The next chance that any of us get to speak with Junior Officer Holliday, tell her it is an honor, and we accept." Clearing his throat, he turned his attention toward Nielson. "Upload the new coding sequences and start the scan."

"Uploading the new coding sequences, sir." Nielson held his breath. "Upload complete. Switching to scan. Sergeant Holley, will you do the honors?" Sigu, Drenge, and Michael left their seats to join the front-seat view with the other three in front of the various computers monitors and flashing buttons.

Helena switched the screen to Planetary View. "Scanner at minimum power for first run, sir."

"Thank you Helena." Kront crossed his fingers. "Nielson, have Frigal on standby."

"Contacting Frigal for standby."

A few minutes passed by. Toes tapped, arms crossed, and machines whirred. No Handlons appeared on the radar. Kront couldn't handle it. "Sergeant Holley, up the power to twenty-percent."

"Yes, sir." She slowly pushed a large-handled lever up and stopped. "Power at twenty—"

"Sir!" Sigu interjected, pointing to a screen on the right with numerous lime-green specs popping up all over. "Over there! Handlons."

Michael chimed in, "There's so many of them."

Drenge snorted. "They light up the screen like Christmastime, damn bastards."

Miranda did it! Her new scanner coding works! Helena sighed. She looked at Kront who seemed to have the same thoughts in mind.

"I had a feeling you would contact me soon," Groyt smiled.

"Commander Hellond, we just conducted a full scan of Planet Helgin at forty-two hours away." Kront was so excited to share the news that his hands shook as though he were on a caffeine high. "Our report indicates an underground base with over 900 Handlons, and they chose to build the base out of the same material as their armor, which makes us wonder what they're using the pieces of the *Grimond Wolf* for."

Groyt shook his head. "Unfortunately, we'll never know the answer to many questions we have concerning their race and why certain of them choose to cause so much evil in the galaxy. On a better note, I sent Ms. Holliday's coding program updates to the Senate, and they've already approved the acquisition of her work at the Standard Programmers Fee of 150,000 Credits for every unit they install."

Kront nearly stopped breathing. "Sir, if you don't mind my asking, how many are they planning to buy?"

"Well, I imagine they are going to outfit the entire Presidential Fleet with her coding sequences. It's an absolute miracle, I tell you! And just in time!"

Kront did some calculations in his head to make sure his initial gut reaction was right. *Let's just say, for the sake of math, that there are only 200 ships in the fleet.* Kront snorted. There were well over 200 ships, and he knew it, but his mind was going nuts right now. *If she gets paid that fee per ship, she's getting at least…oh my—*

"Kront?" Groyt interrupted. "Did you hear me?"

Kront shook his head. "Sorry, sir. I was making some mental calculations on her…*income.*"

Groyt chuckled. "Yes, I know. Junior Officer Holliday, a millionaire at her age. The Senate is sending her a contract to install her coding in 37 ships starting tomorrow. They'll send her a later contract for another 100 ships, and a third contract for the remainder of the fleet as they come in for repairs or recoup time. I've sent Drent Jenson to personally deliver the news to Ms. Holliday along with her Credit Chip of 5.5 million credits." The commander leaned back in his chair. "Makes me really proud to know that little girl."

Kront smiled. "Yes, sir. I must agree with you on that."

"Makes you wish you had one of your own, huh?" Groyt raised an eyebrow, expecting a half-snide remark to come from the lifelong-single man on the other side of the visual com.

The captain just smiled. "*Lindman* out."

* * *

Kront was startled by a sudden face on his visual com. "Miranda?"

"Hi, Captain!"

"Are you okay? Is everything all right?"

"Things are great!" her voiced bubbled over in happiness. "I just passed my second test, so now I'm a Level 6. Oh, and I broke another one of your records. Sorry, but you're no longer the fastest hacker in Academy history."

Kront laughed and shook his head. "I should have known what I was getting into when I okayed you for studies at the school." He sat forward in his seat, a more serious atmosphere settling upon their conversation. "Do the other students know about your recent financial accomplishments? Are they treating you any differently?"

Miranda blushed, "Captain, they don't know, but I don't want the money to change me, either. I feel awkward having all this money and still only twelve years old. I was only trying to help your crew and you."

Her superior commander smiled. "A few days ago, I was talking to Senator Milons about your code and its great success. If you think you've got a lot of money now, just wait until they've paid you for the entire Presidential Fleet."

The student's jaw dropped. "Captain? That's a lot of money."

"You're telling me." He gave her a few moments to soak it all in before he continued. "Miranda, it's important for you to continue in school, doing the best you can, no matter how rich and famous you may become. Do you understand?"

"Yes, sir, Captain Tallin."

"I received a visual message from your Professor. We here at the *Lindman* are very proud of you."

A second hint of red fell across her young features, competing against her fiery-red locks. "That means the world to me, Captain. Thank you, sir. I want to be the best so I can earn a spot on your ship."

Kront laughed, "Junior Officer Holliday, when you graduate from the Academy, your first assignment will be on this ship, so have no worries there. I'll make sure of it myself."

Miranda sighed. "Thanks, Captain. Miranda out."

*   *   *

Nielson was one of the best at his job. Very keen with an ability to sense things right before they happened, he looked up at his screen. *Blip.* He smiled and pushed the com button. "Captain, the *Vilantex* just appeared on the radar."

Kront pulled up the radar image on the monitor in his office. There it was: a 13,200-foot long carrier with a 1600-member crew and over 100 fighter jets. "Roger that. Get me their Captain." Kront adjusted his uniform and sat up straight in front of his visual com.

A few seconds passed by before an elderly man appeared on his visual com. "Captain Tallin, it's good to see you again. What are you up to, boy?"

Good ol' Captain Johan Grillo, Kront recollected. "Good to see you. Not doing much since we fought against the Drikly Clan of Handlons some eight years ago. Remember that?"

"Sure do. My age don't make me dumb, boy. Word is that you need my help killing some Handlons."

"Word is right as usual, sir," Kront laughed.

"What are your plans?"

"Coming to you now." Captain Tallin pressed a few buttons and sent the files through the digital version of space over to the *Vilantex* and its commander. "Two of my best squad leaders – Sergeants Holley and Flort – came up with a two-front attack.

Your men attack from the south, and we come at them from the north. We can have our ships and the remainders of your men guarding any escape holes and side entrances in case Handlons decide to surface instead of stay and die for their cause." Kront's voice dripped with sarcasm.

Johan threw back his head and cackled. It always made Kront smile the way the old man laughed. "Good one, Tallin. Very well, the mission starts in exactly four hours. I'll give you one hundred of my men to help out with the northern attack. I'll send out four hundred of the others for the southern attack."

Kront nodded, "Roger that. At least forty members of my crew will be out there fighting. *Lindman* out." Kront turned off the visual com just as Helena knocked on his office door.

"Enter."

"Sir, Charlie and Regan have requested to join the landing. Doc has cleared them for duty as of this morning."

Kront tapped his desk. "Great to hear. Request granted. I was hoping to have them with us. Any news on Cradan?"

"The wound in his neck is still infected; Doc says that he's looking at another two weeks in the very least."

"Well, Doc knows best. Looks like forty-five troops and I are going to battle." Kront pulled a visual screen from his desk drawer and gave it to his soldier. "By the way, this com came for you earlier today." A sneaky smile stole across his facial features.

Helena peered his direction, waiting for him to throw something at her or cause a ruckus. Although the age difference between them kept them from dating, they had a special place in each other's heart. They were known for causing hell to each other—both good and bad. As Kront got farther down the hallway, she sat down in a chair in his office and looked down at the screen. The smiling and happy faces of Jamie and Miranda popped up on the screen. "Hi, Helena! HAPPY BIRTHDAY!"

Helena laughed. "Silly girls!" she spoke aloud.

Miranda started, "We know you're far from home, but we wanted to call and wish you a happy birthday.

"Yeah! And Miranda just bought mom and dad a new SHX 2000 Personnel Transporter! It's super smart! She said it's a thank-you present for letting her join our family."

"I know what you're thinking, Helena." She mocked

Helena, in a motherly voice, "'Miranda, that's too much money.'" Miranda shrugged her shoulders. "But if I don't use my money, then why have it?"

Jamie filled the screen with her face up-close and personal. "We've got to go, so happy birthday, and we'll talk to you soon!"

Miranda took the screen back and said the same. The visual closed out. Helena wiped a tear from her eyes, placed the personal monitor back on Kront's desk, and closed the door behind her on her way to the Bridge. *Thank you, girls,* she mused in her mind. *That was the best birthday gift ever.*

When Helena made it to the Bridge, all of the squad leaders were already sitting in their seats, big smiles on their faces. She glanced around the room and then looked behind her. "What? Is my hair out of place? Is a clown popping out from behind me?"

The men laughed, and Kront motioned them to all shout together. "Happy Birthday!"

Sergeant Holley smiled. "Thanks, guys. You're all sweet."

Sigu asked, "So how old are you now?" He flirtatiously winked at her.

"Not answering that, Sigu." The others laughed at her reply. Sigu made a duck-face at her.

Kront pulled her along to the door that led to the Hangar. "I promised Miranda I would give you her present to you, so if you would follow me to the *Vilantex*, please."

"Wait," she said, stopping their walk. "What do you mean? I'm confused. I thought the com was my present from Jamie and her."

"Nope. You'll see."

Helena and Kront took a short shuttle hopper over to the *Vilantex*. Johan met them on their landing. "Welcome aboard the *Vilantex*."

Kront shook Johan's hand. "Good to see you in person, Johan. Sergeant Holley, this is Captain Grillo of the *Vilantex*."

Helena shook Johan's hand. "Nice to meet you, sir."

"You, too, Sergeant, and happy birthday." Before she could ask how he knew it was her birthday, he motioned for Kront and her to join him. "Please follow me to Hangar 7." As they arrived, one of the bodyguards accompanying Captain Grillo flipped on the lights to Hangar 7.

Helena gawked at the most beautiful and advanced piece of advanced spacecraft ever built for personal use. "No, it can't be."

"Yup," Captain Grillo confirmed.

Helena looked at Kront. He threw up his hands in his defense. "Hey, don't look at me! All I did was answer a question. I didn't know why the red-headed child asked."

"But it's…it's…"

Captain Grillo harrumphed. "It's a Frigate Deluxe, Model XT 9000, soldier. Spit it out."

"Is that for me? That's impossible."

Kront shook his head. "There are only eighteen of these out there, and now you are the proud owner of a space cruiser that hits Hyperspace 4+. That's 0.2 faster than the *Lindman* herself! It can have up to twenty-five people, but the greatest part is that Miranda had the L.D.S.S. built in for you."

Captain Grillo butted in, "Well, don't just stand there! Take the thing for a ride. I'll be in my quarters when you return so we can discuss the invasion of the Handlon base." Just as quickly as he appeared, he disappeared behind his group of bodyguards into the black surroundings of the other Hangar dividers.

"Captain?" Helena smiled. "Would you do me the honor of accompanying me on my first tour?"

"I'd be delighted!" Not even ten minutes into flight, Kront wanted to take back his words as he held back the contents of his lunch meal.

"Easy now, Helena." He burped to try to relieve the upset feeling in his abdomen. "What will you name her?"

"Sir, there's only one name that fits her: the *Holliday*."

Kront managed to get out a chuckle. "Not only does it honor Miranda, but I have a feeling this cruiser will be like that child when she hits adolescence, a fast and wild, unstoppable force."

Helena looped around, finally steering it back to the Hangar with ease. Kront jumped out and kissed the Hangar floor.

"Sorry, sir, but I needed to test some of its capabilities at first run."

Kront's smile wavered. "I understand. Loops are just not my cup of tea."

Chapter 8. – The Invasion.

Helena called Kront over the com. "Captain, we're ready to be briefed."

"Thank you," he replied without looking up at the visual com. "I'll be right there." He stood up from his chair, stretched a bit, and began what seemed to be a long walk from his office to the Hangar of the *Lindman*. How he hated briefing his troops. Briefings meant battles, and battles meant blood. He knew he would be sending one or more of his crew to their death; the worst part was that he knew the crew knew, as well. He entered the Hangar and heard Sigu call the troops to attention.

"Listen up," Kront began. "We are about to launch a major attack – an invasion – against the Handlons on Planet Helgin. There are nearly one thousand of them. They know we are here, and they expect us to attack. Their defenses are strong, and they are armed. They may be willing to die for what they believe in, but we all know that what we fight for is better and stronger. It's more pure and good. Being a soldier is a privilege with heavy burdens, but you are more than capable of carrying them to success. Captain Grillo of the *Vilantex* is giving us one hundred of his own men for our northern attack, but before we join up with them, I have some important business to attend. Sergeant Holley, please step forward."

Helena was only two feet to his right, but she stepped forward as commanded. Everyone's eyes fell on her. And her flaming pink hair. "Sergeant Helena Holley, you are being promoted to the rank of Lieutenant based on your service aboard the *Lindman* and numerous battles against the Handlons enemy." Kront pinned a Lieutenant badge on to her uniform. "Congratulations, Lieutenant Holley."

Helena shook Kront's hand. "Thank you, Captain Tallin." She stepped back in line.

"Chief Engineer and Gunner Buck Cypher, please step forward and come up to the platform." A very surprised Buck stepped forward and marched up to the platform. He saluted Kront and turned to face his comrades. "Chief Engineer and Gunner

Buck Cypher, you are being given the Medal of Courage for your heroism in saving the life of Lieutenant Helena Holley. Without your fast action and quick thinking, Lieutenant Holley may not be with us today to distract our attention with her daily changes in hair color." His remarks received a few laughs from the soldiers, as he had hoped would happen in order to break the serious feeling in the air. Kront pinned a medal on to Buck's uniform. "Furthermore, by recommendation from Lieutenant Holley and Sergeant Drenge Pladu, Chief Engineer and Gunner Buck Cypher will be promoted to Sergeant and given leadership over Bravo Squad." Kront pinned the Sergeant badge on Buck's uniform and shook his hand. "Congratulations, Sergeant Cypher."

Buck's face was full of smiles. "Thank you, sir!" Buck returned to his position, receiving pats on the back and handshakes from a few soldiers around him.

"Everyone to the shuttles. We land in half an hour. Dismissed!" The soldiers scurried off to their positions. Helena stayed put. Kront smiled at her. "Helena, as second-in-command, it's your responsibility to ensure that everyone does their job. If mistakes make bodies, I prefer fewer than more."

Helena nodded, "Understood, Captain." She saluted Kront and ran over to Bravo Squad's shuttle. "Sergeant Cypher?"

Buck grinned, a toothy smile from ear to ear. "Yes, Lieutenant Holley?"

Helena's smile was just as wide in hearing her new title. "Lock and load."

"Roger that, Lieutenant."

Kront sat down in the Command Shuttle. "Ready signal. All squads report."

Sigu was first to reply. "Alpha Squad ready."

Newly-promoted Buck answered next. "Bravo Squad ready." The others squads checked in, as did Grillo's men in their own shuttles. Kront tightened his seat harness. "All squads, we have a green light: mission is a go. Bravo Squad is running point, touchdown in one minute." Kront flipped between the various screens showing the vitals of his forty-five soldiers on their way to Planet Helgin. *Let's not lose anyone today. Please, not today. And definitely not Helena.*

One of the pilots of a *Vilantex* shuttle called over the com within moments of takeoff. "Lieutenant Holley, I'm spotting some...'traffic' ahead, copy?"

"Joy," Buck told Helena in the pilot seat of their own shuttle. "My favorite toy: Planetary Defense Blasters." The rain of blaster rounds fell upon the shuttles.

"All shuttles use extreme caution. Handlons are using PDBs. Squad leaders, take control of the guns." Helena turned off her com and flipped on the anti-blaster gun. She could hear Michael, Sigu, Drenge, and Jinko do the same. Within seconds of blasting some of the PDBs to smithereens, she watched three of the *Vilantex* shuttles explode into millions of pieces. *Damn*, she thought. *It's like someone had their number on speed-dial or something.* "Buck," she called up to her copilot. "We lost some of the *Vilantex* crews. Hurry up and land this bucket of metal!"

Buck swore under his breath. "Roger that, Lieutenant! All squads, standby for landing."

Helena took over the com as she blasted the last PDB into bits. "Secure the landing zone. I want a perimeter around the shuttle immediately." She jumped out of her seat and joined the others in Bravo Squad at the rear door. The moment Buck had the shuttle touch the planet's surface, the hatch opened, and the troops ran out to do as they were told. Helena called over the com. "Captain, Bravo is on the ground. The others squads are following plans according to their orders. We lost some of the *Vilantex* crews to PDBs, but the rest are disseminating as ordered. Bravo Squad proceeding to Checkpoint Hector."

"Roger that," Kront replied.

Checkpoint Hector was the designated name for the hill that overlooked the Handlon base. Bravo Squad, led by Lieutenant Holley and Sergeant Cypher, jogged several hundred feet over to the checkpoint and then burrowed down below the top when they spied enemies ahead. The nearest star that served as the planet's source of light wouldn't set for a while, but it still hung low in the horizon. *A dusk battle*, Helena noted. She motioned to the others in order to avoid conversation. *Chuck, James, and Mason: three targets, 2 o'clock. Go left. Signal when ready.*" They nodded in response. Chuck, James, and Mason moved to the left and took position. They signaled back that they were ready. She double-checked the targets and their positions before giving the gunners the OK.

Three quiet shots barely louder than the sound of pins hitting a concrete floor sounded off. The three targets went down. She motioned for the team to move forward. At the top of the hill, she looked down the other side. She wiped her brow with her forearm and motioned in silence. *Forty targets. Position around me. Signal when ready.* Helena set up her own weapon, scanned her crew for readiness, and gave the OK.

Shots fired out from Bravo Squad startled the Handlons. Several died instantly while many more dropped to the ground, grasping for their weapons in a chance to shoot back, but Bravo Squad denied the enemies their chance. Nearly twelve of the Handlons were lucky enough to find cover instead of being fatally shot. It was a bullet from one of those twelve that suddenly found itself lodged in the skull of James Montas, a member of Bravo Squad positioned next to Moniqé Nastas. The accuracy and skill of Bravo Squad eventually beat out the Handlons that came out from hiding to both shoot at Buck's team and Helena and run from them. It was only after the last Handlon fell and Buck ordered a perimeter check that Moniqé noticed James wasn't moving.

"James?" She pushed him over. Blood filled his head gear. She wanted to scream, go into a rage, and shoot every last Handlon. But she didn't want to compromise their position or cost them any more time. This was a full-scale invasion of a Handlon base. This was no place for broken hearts and tears.

Helena walked over to Moniqé. "I'm sorry, Moniqé. We have to keep moving." Moniqé didn't answer. She just stared at James' body. Helena grabbed her com, leaving the female soldier behind with the casualty. She followed at the rear of Bravo Squad led by Buck. "Captain, this is Bravo Squad. Checkpoint Hector clear, but we lost James Montas. Moniqé Nastas is staying behind. Request for her to accompany him back to the ship. Personal matter, sir."

Kront bowed his head. "Damn, why didn't I see that?" He had a strict rule in his ranks that romantically-involved soldiers should never be in same squad. "Request granted. Continue with the mission. I'll send someone to pick up Moniqé and James."

Helena caught up to Buck, a pissed-off look on his face.

She hit his arm, "You ready?"

He glared straight ahead. "Oh, yeah. Time to finish this." Just as they jogged around the corner of another hill, a com call came over the radio.

"Lieutenant, we need assistance!" It was Sergeant Pladu. "Charlie Squad is pinned down. We are 800 feet from Checkpoint Kilo. Over!"

Helena peered around the corner, careful to avoid contact with Handlon eyes. She grabbed her com and radioed, "Drenge, this is Helena. Thirty more Handlons headed your way. We're around the hill to your 9 o'clock. Hold on!" She turned off the com and turned to Buck. "Your call, Sergeant."

He yelled out, "Bravo, go!"

Helena ducked behind various objects to block her from enemy fire as she prepared to send fire back their way. Bravo Squad had separated into various lines as planned in the event of a squad-rescue. She dropped to one knee, peeked out from behind her temporary shield, and shot several Handlons unaware of her position. She hid behind her shield as Buck took a turn several feet away behind his own cover. She heard the cries of pain as several more Handlons screamed in pain, fatally falling to the ground thanks to Bravo Squad. Then, she heard a noise she didn't like to hear.

"I'm hit! I'm hit!" Heidi Kalt from Bravo fell to the ground, grasping her right knee cap. Mason Jung shot off a few more rounds and then stopped to assist her. He dragged her to a safe cover and grabbed his com. "Lieutenant Holley, this is Jung. Kalt's been hit in the kneecap. She's out."

Helena nodded to Buck to take over and then join her while she answered the com. "Get her to safety. Holley out." Buck shot off a few rounds, running across an open line until he joined cover with Helena. Firing with deadly precision, another five Handlons dropped dead. Helena covered for Buck's last two seconds; she took aim and fired. The last Handlon dropped, hit in the head by her shot. Bravo Squad remained silent as they waited for movement and sound. They popped out from behind their covers and checked the area.

"Captain, this is Lieutenant Holley. Checkpoint Kilo secure. Charlie Squad secure." Helena ran over to see Heidi.

Drenge was down on one knee inspecting Kalt for other injuries. "How bad is it, Drenge?"

Heidi removed her bloodied hand. She sucked in air through her clenched teeth. "It's not that bad."

Drenge smirked and stood up, crossing his arms. "It's bad enough that Doc will still need to see it."

The lieutenant nodded. Buck grabbed his com. "Captain Tallin, this is Sergeant Cypher. Kalt took a blast to the knee. Need medic extraction."

Kront tapped his pilot on the shoulder and nodded. The pilot nodded in response, and they took off. "Sergeant Cypher, this is Captain Tallin. Roger that. ETA one minute."

"*Vilantex* Ground Crew, this is *Lindman* ground crew, please come in." Helena waited for the answer, hoping all was going as planned. One lost life and another lost to injury was enough already.

"*Lindman* crew, we hear you loud and clear. Over."

"What's your status on the south side?"

"*Vilantex* south side has fourteen casualties and nine wounded. Approximately 150 Handlon casualties. Over."

Buck shook his head. "Damn, the Captain won't like those numbers."

Helena closed her eyes for a moment. "*Lindman* north side has one dead and one wounded, approximately 190 Handlon casualties." She looked back over her shoulder at a noise to see squads Alpha, Delta, and Echo walking up to join them. "No contact from *Vilantex* north side. Have you heard anything?"

"Roger that, Lieutenant. Fifteen casualties. The other seventy troops are on their way to join you. Standby to enter base."

Helena welcomed Sigu, John, and Michael back. Facing the five squad leaders, she said, "Give 'em the orders, Sergeants."

Buck and Drenge half-saluted and faced their troops while Michael kissed John on the cheek who nearly shot him for doing it. Sigu got a good laugh of it and clapped Buck on the shoulder. "Bravo Squad, lock and load," Buck called out.

"Charlie Squad," Drenge said. "Let's go kick some Handlon ass." John nodded his approval, still glaring at Michael's antics.

*　　*　　*

Sigu and John shot open the Handlon base's north door. Helena called over the com to Kront, "*Lindman* entering base." She signaled Buck; he jumped through the door and rolled to the left. Janic and Mason followed him closely. Buck opened fire and dropped three Handlons. He jumped over to the next door and secured it. Janic and Mason pulled out one knife apiece and slit the throats of two unsuspecting Handlons with their backs to the *Lindman* crews. The two then crept along and called back, "All clear!"

The lieutenant stepped through the door. "Squads, do your thing, and do it quick!"

In seconds, the squads split down various hallways and disappeared, but before Bravo Squad could take another step, she heard what sounded like a door handle jiggling to her left. She waited and then shot four times at the wall. She heard a cry of pain and a subsequent thump. "Camo door! Secure it, now!!" she yelled.

Janic jumped over to the door and nodded. Helena kicked it open and pointed her rifle through it, firing several more rounds as Handlons came into her view. Buck, Mason, and Janic jumped through the door and shot four more Handlons as they tried to escape through an exit on the other side of the room.

"Lieutenant, this is Sergeant Flort." Sigu called Helena over the com, "We found the items from the *Grimond Wolf*." Level 4, south side."

Helena smiled. "Great job. Give me your report."

"Level 4 clear. Eighty-five Handlons dead. No casualties or injuries."

Helena smiled. *Thank you, Lord.* "Charlie Squad, report."

"Level 3 clear," Drenge began. "Forty Handlons dead. Jindso Hamkoc shot in the hand. He can still fight, but he needs to see Doc."

Seriously? How did he get shot in his hand? she questioned. She shook her head. "Delta, report."

John's voice was loud and clear. "Level 5 clear. Over one-hundred Handlons dead. No injuries…but…two casualties…Robin

Sammy and Linda Milas. Bastard Handlons had the door booby-trapped."

Helena lowered her head as she waited for Echo's report. *Two more casualties. That makes a total of five bodies since the* Grimond Wolf, she scolded herself. "Echo, report."

"Level 4 clear. Over one-hundred Handlons dead. No casualties or injuries."

The lieutenant sighed. "*Vilantex* Ground Crew, check in. What's your report?"

A few seconds of static passed by. Then, a voice came over the com. "*Lindman*, this is *Vilantex* Ground Crew. Mission complete. All Handlons dead. Another thirty-two casualties and twelve injuries, but we are heading back to our ship to go home. Congratulations, *Lindman*."

Helena gulped at the number of casualties and injuries between the troops of both ships. In a voice near a whisper, she uttered, "All squads, report to the south entrance. Mission complete. Bring the casualties, and let's take them home."

Chapter 9. – No Hope.

Helena boarded the *Lindman* with her squads and troops. She winced as the battle casualties were brought out of the shuttles.

Kront entered the Hangar, glanced at Helena, and yelled, "Attention!" At his command, the troops stood at attention and saluted. Even the injured stayed to salute before Doc wheeled or led them away to his area of the *Lindman.* The moment the casualties were removed to Doc's casualty rooms, Kront and Helena returned to the Control Center.

Nielson's grim face met his superior officer. "Sir, we have a...situation." He flitted a glance at Helena. "It's Miranda."

The lieutenant felt her heart bottom-out. "What's wrong, Nielson?"

Nielson looked to Kront who nodded at him, unaware of how the impending news would affect him, as well. "While you two were out on the Helgin mission, I received a com from Professor Holley. The Handlons waited to exact revenge for you taking out their base until you had landed on Helgin."

"Well," Helena prompted Nielson. "What do my parents have to do with...?" All of a sudden, Helena's face whitened. "No..." she whispered, shaking her head in denial.

"They've kidnapped Miranda and Jamie."

Kront grabbed the nearest com. "All squad leaders, report to the Situation Room immediately!" He turned to Nielson. "Get me all the info you have on it and meet me in the Situation Room in five minutes." He grabbed Helena by the shoulders. "Focus, Lieutenant. They need you to focus right now, and so do I."

Helena seemed stuck in a gaze, but she gathered enough breath to convince him she was fine and jogged behind him to the Situation Room. The others had just arrived.

"What's up, Captain?" Sigu asked.

Just as Kront was about to inform his squad leaders, Nielson appeared. "Nielson will explain, and then I'll take over." He nodded to his com officer who took a position at the front of the room.

"Here's what we know so far," he began, taking fair notice

of Helena sitting in a chair in a far corner, a distant look in her eyes. "While the *Lindman* and *Vilantex* crews were deployed on Planet Helgin, an unknown number of Handlons infiltrated the Academy on Planet Troklon and kidnapped Miranda Holliday and Jamie Holley. The only—"

"They what?!" Drenge interrupted. He got Sigu's attention to discuss the matter.

"I second that!" exclaimed Michael. "John, did you hear that?"

He crossed his arms. "Sure did. What are we gonna do about it?"

As the other four leaders talked amongst themselves, Buck glanced over at Helena. She still looked to be in total shock. *Probably thinks it's all her fault,* he thought to himself. Before he could get a word out of her, Kront demanded their full attention.

"Hey! Hold on a minute." He firmly planted his fists at his belt line. The room quieted. "Nielson, please continue."

"It comes down to this," he summarized. "I think we have a traitor on the inside, possibly at the Academy and maybe another in the Senate."

This time, John was first to speak up. A usually quiet man, the leader of Echo Squad had been especially touched during the rescue of an emotionally-executed, freckle-faced child that reminded him of his nieces and nephews back home. "If I'm thinking what you're thinking, Captain, you might want to ask the troops before you go any further with this issue. I'm not saying they'll back out, but it's still a personal choice in this matter. A whole lot more than just a rescue mission is on the line here."

Kront sighed. "Lodre, you're right. I completely agree. Squad leaders, get your troops together. Form ranks in the Hangar in ten minutes. Dismissed.

"So, as you see," Kront informed the troops in the Hangar. "The choices is yours. No one will hold it against you if you choose a temporary station aboard the *Vilantex* while we carry out this rescue mission to save Miranda and Jaime." He had already described what had happened to Miranda and Jaime. After several outbursts of "Let's go get them!" and "Those Handlons will pay if they've hurt the girls!" that nearly brought tears to Helena's still-blanched face, Kront knew his troops could be counted on to join forces with him in finding and bringing to justice the girls' captors.

Kront turned to Helena. "It's your turn. I'll call Frigal to inform them of our mission. I'm not asking their permission."

Helena, head lowered, stated in a near-whisper, "Captain, we are breaking so many rules. I can't have you or any of the troops get in trouble for what I do about this. I feel like it's my fault."

Kront gritted his teeth. "If you weren't a woman, I would punch you in the face, Lieutenant. Those words are the most lie-filled I've ever heard. Their kidnap is *not* your fault, and these troops and our squad leaders have made their decision: they're coming with. Now, it's up to you to put together your own team for your own shuttle while I prepare this ship for battle." He straightened his stance and saluted her. "Lieutenant Holley, command those whom you need. I'm dismissing myself to the Control Center. I'll be there if you need me. Kront out." He left the Hangar – and her – with the hint of a smile on his lips, just enough to boost her into action mode.

She faced the troops in the hanger and announced, "I need five troops to help me equip the *Holliday* for battle." Reggi Grout, Thomas Masters, Jonas Dron, Adam Pander, and Tena Grissham stepped forward. Helena couldn't be more pleased with the outcome. "All right, then, follow me. The rest of you are dismissed to your stations. Prepare for a rescue mission."

Reggi Grout was the weapons expert aboard the *Lindman*. He quickly drew up a blueprint for the *Holliday*'s new load of weapons: sizes, kinds, and numbers. Thomas Masters was the electronics expert. His special skill was in engine boosting and automotive design. He was extremely adept in adding extra equipment to overstuffed ships. Jonas Dron earned the title of Best Interplanetary Pilot three years in a row. He acted as copilot to Kront during the invasion of the Handlon base on Planet Helgin. His job was to relieve the pilot of duties and make the cockpit easier to use and more accessible. Adam Pander was the equipment master. He knew what Helena needed and where to get the stuff from. Tena Grissham was an electronics expert like Thomas, but her specialty lay in the prevention of overheating engines. It was a common malfunction for Hyperspace 4+ shuttles, including Helena's new ship, so Helena had a great need for Tena to be on board.

*   *   *

Miranda opened her eyes. It took a while for her eyes to adjust to the darkness. "Where am—Jamie! Jamie? Are you here?" She crawled around on the cold, bumpy floor, searching for her friend by feeling out for Jamie's body.

"I'm here," Jamie called out.

"Where are you?" Miranda tried to tune her ears to the direction of Jamie's voice.

"I don't think I'm too far. I think I'm getting closer," she sniffled. Miranda's heart panged. She knew this kidnap was her fault.

"Ouch!" they both cried out as their heads collided. Miranda pulled Jaime into her arms. "How long was I out?"

"I don't know," Jaime whimpered, wiping tears from her face. "I called out your name every so often, but you put up such a fight that I didn't think you'd ever wake up after that Handlon knocked you out."

"Well, how long have we been here?"

"I don't know. Maybe a day, I think. They let me use the bathroom once, but they won't give us any food. Just water. I'm so hungry, and I want to go home!"

Miranda tried to focus on the walls, the floor—anything that could give her a hint of where they were. "I doubt they kept us anywhere on Planet Troklon. What happened after the fight?"

Jamie shivered, so Miranda tried to warm up her friend's arms by quickly rubbing her hands over them. "They took us on a shuttle. We flew for several hours. I heard them talk of a small base. I didn't hear the whole word, but it sounded really weird."

"That actually narrows it down quite a bit. Most of the Handlons live in peace with the humans or our kind, or live very, very far away. Eight hours doesn't fit either category, and there are only two planets that have really weird names that may be the answer we're looking for: Planets Voplin and Wrisjok. The only problem is Wrisjok is a desert planet, and it's way too cold here, so we must be on Voplin."

Miranda and Jaime stayed quiet for a few more minutes, the former focusing on how to bust out and the latter thinking of how to stay warm and get food. Miranda broke the silence. "When they let you out to use the bathroom, how did they open the door?"

"It was a key. I noticed because it made so much noise. It seemed like they had no idea how to use a lock-and-key themselves, as if they had never used one before. Also, the base on the door was really old, so the key squeaked and hurt my ears."

Miranda sighed. "Most doors use codes or voice prints these days. Old-fashioned is not good news."

Jaime began to cry again. "Do you think Helena knows we've been taken?" Miranda nodded, "Yes, I'm sure of it, and I know Captain Tallin and the crew will come rescue us."

Suddenly, the door opened and a very large Handlon came in. "Follow me. The Prime Commander wants to talk to you."

*   *   *

Two days after finding out the news of Miranda and Jaime's disappearance, Helena wiped the sweat from her brow and overlooked the work done on her *Holliday* ship. "She looks ready!" She gave a hint of a smile, more than what she had offered anyone who had tried to cheer her up in the last forty-eight hours.

Kront entered the scene and stood next to Helena. "Looks nice. What have you added?"

"Four blasters in the front and two in the rear, an ion cannon on top, and a missile launcher underneath. She's covered with armor, a bit like a flying tank. We gave her another paint job so she looks the same as before." Out of the blue, Helena hugged Kront. She needed it, and she knew it, and Kront knew it, too. He hugged her back. "Please tell me we'll find those girls. Tell me we won't be too late."

"With you acting as Miranda's mother, those damn Handlons won't have a chance to hurt those girls." He pulled back to look in Helena's eyes. "I talked to Commander Hellond. According to him, the Handlons flew a small freighter in and out of Troklon the day the girls disappeared. Their shuttle was last seen heading in the direction of Planet Wrisjok. However, we're

77

not stupid. We've had that planet covered in troops since the last major Handlon war. It's nothing but desert now. We think they diverted to Planet Voplin. It's got a small base of less than fifty Handlons. They won't think we'll suspect it because it has so few Handlons, but we won't fall for that trick."

"But what did Groyt say?"

Kront shook his head. "The Senate has not okayed us for battle. If we go, then when we return, we will be arrested and charged with treason."

Helena's eyes lit up as red as her flaming red hair, dyed in honor of Miranda's red-headed locks. "That's not—"

"That's not something we need to worry about right now, is it? We focus on getting the girls back. I have a feeling we'll find something that will change the Senate's mind about all of this soon enough."

Helena's temper was calmed for the moment. She closed her eyes and tried to imagine the girls' current situation. "Poor Miranda and Jaime. I hope they're okay."

*   *   *

For the fourth time, the girls followed the large Handlon into what seemed to be a throne room. "Kneel before the Prime Commander," he demanded. He pushed the girls to the ground; they fell to their knees, and Jaime began to cry.

Miranda's blood boiled over in rage. "What right do you think you have to kidnap us?" she yelled at the Prime Commander.

She tried to stand up, but the big Handlon pushed her down again. "You will stay down until the Prime Commander says you can stand." Miranda chose to listen only because he was so much bigger than she.

The Prime Commander rose from his chair. In a deep-throated, sick voice, he declared, "You are Miranda Holliday and Jaime Holley, friend and sister of Helena Holley, enemy and murderer of many Handlons on Planet Helgin." He paused a moment before continuing. "I have every right to exact revenge. Unless she chooses to pay for her deeds or take your place, you two must pay for the actions of Helena Holley." He sat back down in his chair. "Admiral Silas Proked has not failed me, yet. He's been right so far, and I'm sure he's right about Lieutenant Holley: she'll gladly take your place. I'd prefer executing a hero anyway." He turned to the Handlon that had brought the girls. "Take them back to the dungeon."

Dragged down the hallway and thrown back into the cell, the large Handlon left the door open long enough to light a single candle and leave it in the cell with the girls before slamming it shut and locking it behind him. "You'll get some food later today."

Jaime screamed for joy. "Miranda, did you—"

Miranda silenced Jaime until she heard him use the key. "You were right; it's a lock-and-key door. Definitely not good."

Jaime pushed Miranda's hand away from her mouth. "He said food, Miranda! Food!"

But the red-headed student wasn't listening. She picked up the candle and began to notice the entire interior of the cell. Bits and pieces of metal plates and other objects laid scattered across the floor. She snapped her fingers. "Help me move these, Jaime. I've got a plan."

*　　*　　*

"Academy Troklon, this is the *Lindman*. Request permission to land." Nielson waited for the visual to appear.

"*Lindman*, you are clear to land. Welcome home." It was the same young girl he winked at when the *Lindman* left for the Helgin mission.

He wanted to smile back, but he just couldn't muster it. "Thank you, Academy Troklon. I'd say it's good to be home, but the circumstances aren't the usual. *Lindman* out." Nielson turned off the visual com before she could ask why, and he landed the *Lindman*.

"Nielson, make sure we get supplies and upgrades for the *Lindman*," Kront ordered. "Helena and I are going to talk to Grand Master Thandson to find out what happened."

"Roger that."

Helena and Kront ran down the ramp and toward the Academy. "First, we talk to the Thandson," Kront stated. "Then we seek out any possible witnesses or accomplices."

"But, students, Kront? Do you really think some of the

students were involved?" Helena's worries were a true concern to Kront. He stopped her partway down a road.

"Can you do your job or not, Lieutenant Holley?"

She straightened her posture. "Yes, sir, I can."

"Then you know that anyone and everyone is a suspect until disqualified."

Helena nodded, "You're right, sir." They continued down the road. "I believe they have cameras set up in the hallways. That may be to our benefit."

They made plans up to the moment they faced the Grand Master's office door. Helena knocked but walked right in, not waiting for an invitation. Grand Master Thandson stood up. "My dear Lieutenant Holley, I'm so sorry to hear about this ordeal. We here at the Academy are here to help you in anything you need."

"I need to see the recordings from each hallway camera."

Thandson fidgeted. "I have strict orders from the Senate to offer emotional support and related kinds of aid, but I'm afraid I cannot turn those over."

"Fine," Kront said, crossing his arms. "Replay them because you wanted to see them, and no one will ever know we saw them while peering over your shoulder from behind you when you weren't looking."

Thandson smiled. "I like the way you think, Captain Tallin. Follow me to the com room." A few doors down from the Grand Master's office, the com room looked like a simple, white-walled door from the outside, but the inside looked like a com officer's dream with multiple monitors and visual boards lining the walls of the very large office.

"This is Academy Troklon's Junior Com Officer Jamina Sonklod. She speaks to your com officer at every landing and departure."

"Ah, yes," Kront said, squinting his eyes. "I believe I know who you are."

Jamina's cheeks blushed, and Helena nudged him in the ribs quite hard. "Focus, sir."

Thandson, oblivious to what was said and done, pressed a few buttons and then stood back. "Jamina, please play the recording from Saturday last week at around 8 am."

Jamina's fingers froze. "The time of the kidnapping, sir?"

"Yes, Jamina."

She gulped. "Yes, sir." Her fingers flew across numerous keyboards and within seconds, a recording popped up on a computer monitor on the left and began playing. "There's Miranda and Jamie. Looks like they're being detained – harassed even – as they walk toward the cafeteria."

Kront nodded, and then froze. "Stop the tape!" Jamina paused it. "What's that?" Kront pointed to a particular figure on the screen that was not Miranda or Helena. "Jamina, please zoom in."

"Yes, sir," she replied. "It looks like Greely McMichaels, sir. One of the 7th year students."

Kront crossed his arms again. "Play the tape, but slowly this time, and keep going until I stop you." Jamina did as she was told, and within moments Kront had her stop the tape again. This time, the focus was on Greely alone. "Zoom in on his arms."

Jamina zoomed. "He has a watch on his left arm. It looks hella nice, too! Probably custom made."

Helena finally piped in, "Can't be many of those at the Academy."

Kront agreed. "And if you've got one, you probably never take it off." He turned to Thandson. "Grand Master, please call an assembly in the great hall. Post security guards at each entrance and exit so no one can leave while we interrogate."

The Head Master questioned, "Don't you want to question just Greely?"

"No," Helena answered. "We don't want him to think we're on to him. Otherwise he'll run before he gets anywhere close to us."

Thandson nodded and left the room. Kront and Helena thanked Jamina and left shortly thereafter. Helena rubbed her arms. "I've got a bad feeling about this one, Captain."

"What do you mean?"

She shook her head. "I don't know. I'm just not sure things are about to go as planned."

Kront half-chuckled, "Do they ever?"

As the sixth year students were being escorted back to their classes from the cafeteria, the seventh year students – including

Greely – were being led into the cafeteria. Greely looked very uncomfortable. The seventh year students had all day to hear the rumors of what was going on: from the administration of booster shots to required chip testing for forgeries to testimonies on the disappearance of Miranda Holliday and Jaime Holley. Sweat drops formed on his forehead.

Kront and Helena didn't conduct the investigation. They left the questioning to Thandson to make the interrogation more proper and aligned with Senate rules. Unfortunately for Greely, this gave them a better chance to keep an eye out for him.

Helena spotted him first. "There. On the left. Thirteenth from the back in the green-striped polo and long khaki pants."

Kront narrowed his eyes. "Good eye, Helena. He's nervous. Sweating already, and he hasn't even been questioned."

"Where's the watch?" Helena and Kront waited. Without the watch, they had no case. Even with the watch, they had to prove it was Greely wearing it on the video, and not some other kid, but after discussing Greely's juvenile record with his parole officer and talking to his counselor about family issues, they were sure they had the right boy. Suddenly, a glint of gold flashed their way.

"There it is," Kront smiled.

"Bingo."

But it was too late. Greely noticed them watching him, and just before he entered the cafeteria, he pushed some kids out of his way and ran for the front entrance.

"Stop him!" Kront yelled. Three security officers turned to run after Greely, but he pushed down trash cans and knocked over several other students as he barreled toward the doors. "Don't let him leave!" Kront barely finished his statement when he saw Helena charge past him, light as ever on her feet, and jump, landing right on top of Greely. They both plunged to the floor. She twisted his arm behind his back.

"What did you do to them?" she yelled. She twisted it further. Greely yelled out in pain. "Where did the Handlons take them? Where are they? How could you?"

"Helena!" Kront bellowed. He yanked Helena off Greely as two security guards pulled Greely off the floor and put him in laser cuffs. Helena fell into Kront's arms as he chose to grab her up instead of letting her fall to the floor. "Helena, are you mad? I know you're upset, as am I, but we can't lose it like that!"

Greely nervously looked around. Professors and students stared at him, and the whisper began. Greely had always been the butt of the joke. Not this time. "I didn't do it. You have the wrong person."

Kront shoved a copy of a still photograph from the security footage showing Greely's arm with the watch. "Son, is this your watch or not? Simple question."

"Yeah, so what? Maybe another kid stole it and wore it while he hurt those two bitches."

Helena tried to free herself from Kront's tight grasp. Even Kront restrained himself from knocking the daylights out of the foul-mouthed child. "Easy, McMichaels. You don't want to get on my bad side."

"Oh, yeah? And why's that? The Handlons offered me 100,000 credits to delay those girls so they could grab them. Do you know how much money that is?" Tears began to well up in his eyes. "I don't care who they are or who you two are. That money is enough to bust my mom out of jail so I can have her at home again."

Helena turned away from Greely, unsure of what to think but still angry at his words and the hurt he had caused for his selfish actions, mom or no mom to boot.

Captain Tallin shook his head. "Take him away."

As the guards took Greely away, the student called out, "Lieutenant Holley, the Handlons have a message for you." The guards stopped in their tracks. Kront and Helena looked Greely's way but made no effort to go his direction.

"If you don't give them the ransom money or give up yourself in place of the girls by the end of the fourth day, they're gonna kill those two girls. And then they're going to kill you." He smiled. "By the way, today's day three."

Chapter 10. – The Rescue.

"The Senate has chosen not to negotiate, Kront," Groyt argued. "I'm sorry, but they don't feel that the lives of two little girls are worth 1.5 billion Credits."

"And how do you feel about it?" Kront argued back.

Groyt's face turned red, the color matching the rise of anger in his voice. "Don't make me tell you how I feel. You know how I voted. I want those little girls home just as much as you, but we don't negotiate with terrorists, Captain Tallin!"

Kront slammed his fist on his desk and lowered his head. "I know. I know."

Each man took a few seconds to recoup their senses.

"Commander Hellond, sir? Permission to conduct an investigation."

"Granted!" Groyt nodded. "It's about time someone outside the Senate wanted to do something about this abduction. I tell you, I'm so sick of Silas shutting down every operation to find out about the girls' disappearance..." Groyt continued mumbling on about Silas as though Kront hadn't been listening, but he had.

"Sir, what did you say? Something about our favorite person in common?"

Commander Hellond snorted. "Who, Silas? Yes, it seems as though every organization, group, team, or person that wants to investigate is shot down. Silas claims he's leading his own team to find out the location of the girls, although I've seen enough bullshit from him to make him choke on his own words."

Kront shook off a feeling that he couldn't allow himself to feel right now. "Sir, when we first found out about the missing girls, Com Officer Nielson informed me that he believes we have a traitor or two in our ranks. We found a student at the Academy who assisted the Handlons in the abduction process, but if there were someone in the Senate, it would explain a whole lot more."

Groyt seemed to catch on. "Such as why we have only partial tapes showing a Handlon ship landing and takeoff near the Academy without any Handlons actually appearing anywhere, and how the girls were taken from the Academy without their chips alerting school security."

"Exactly."

The older gentleman pushed back in his chair, palms pressed together at his lips as though he were praying. "This is a serious accusation, Kront."

"I understand, sir, but we must seriously consider the possibility, especially since Miranda Holliday has been such a success lately with her ability to rewrite coding to detect the new Handlon armor. Imagine what her skills could do for the other side, sir. No wonder they took her. I'm sure Jaime was used as bait to get Miranda to cooperate."

Groyt tapped his desk. "You're starting to make more sense than most of the Senators here, Kront. Have you ever considered running for the Senate, son?"

Kront smiled, "No, sir, but I'm honored that you think I could. What do you think?"

"I think you'd make a great senator."

"Thank you, sir, but I wanted your opinion about my theory of a traitor in the Senate."

"Oh, yes." Groyt cleared his throat. "Well, like I said, it's a serious accusation, but I think your words make sense and all precautions should be taken. Innocent people have nothing to hide. They shouldn't have a problem with being investigated."

Kront smiled. "Oh, yes. I'm sure I will, sir. *Lindman* out."

*　　*　　*

Helena stood in front of the completed *Holliday*. "Captain, I only have a few more hours until it's day four and the Handlons—"

"And the Handlons what?" Kront interrupted. "Do you really think they'll kill Miranda and Jaime? We both know they want revenge, yes, but they want you to come after them. They want to kill you, and we know that won't happen." He paused for a beat. "Right?"

"Of course, Captain," she smiled. Still, she felt uneasy about taking so long before leaving to rescue the girls. She tried another subject to ease her mind. "I know I can have up to twenty-five crew members aboard my ship, but I only need a fourteen-man team for the mission."

"Are you sure?"

"Yes, sir," she sighed, trying to believe her own words.

Kront clapped his hand on her shoulder. "We'll be on Planet Troklon for a full-scale investigation into the disappearance of the girls, starting with Silas Proked in the Senate." Kront snapped his fingers. "Don't forget to take out the transponder from your ship. We don't want the *Holliday* appearing on the Presidential's radar."

"Thank you, sir." They walked over to the troops standing in formation in the Hangar.

"Do you know exactly who you want on your team?" Before Helena could respond, he interrupted her. "Why am I even asking? You're Lieutenant Holley. You always know what you want, and you're never afraid to ask for it or go get it." They smiled at each other. *She and her ocean-blue hair,* Kront pondered. *If only we were closer in age.* Kront's staring at Helena earned him an "Ahem" from Sergeant Pladu. Michael and Sigu ribbed each other, and even John gave a hint of a smile. They all knew Kront's little secret, and they knew Kront would kill them all if they even hinted at it. So they immediately put on serious faces when Kront turned their direction.

Helena looked over the troops. "I have chosen fourteen crew members to accompany me on this mission. If you want to find a replacement, do not hesitate to inform me. I won't hold it against you. When I say your name, please walk over to the *Holliday*: Melissa Heart, Chuck Koffman, Moniqé Nastas, Mason Jung, Buck Cypher, Jack Holland, Jindso Hamkoc, Mort Klav, Adam Pander, Tena Grissham, King Davis, Melvin Phillips, Janic Mosnhet, and Jens Nessau." Each person walked over to the *Holliday*, saluting the lieutenant as he or she passed Helena. She stifled tears of honor in having a perfect crew and turned back to the others. "The rest of you will assist Captain Tallin in an investigation into the Senate to find any possible traitors who may have helped in the kidnapping of Miranda Holliday and Jaime Holley. Dismissed."

A mere two hours later, Helena sat in the cockpit of the *Holliday*. "*Lindman*, this is the *Holliday*. Request permission to takeoff."

Nielson looked warily at his superior officer who didn't return a glance his direction. "*Holliday*, this is the *Lindman*. Permission granted. Bring those girls home. Safe travels."

Kront turned on the visual, "Be careful, Helena."

Helena winked at him through her visual. "Aw, Captain. If I didn't know any better, I'd say you cared about me." Although she couldn't see it, his face flushed, and Nielson stifled a laugh with a cough. Kront watched Helena navigate her ship into deep space and then hyperspace. *If only you knew, Helena*, he told himself.

The *Holliday* entered hyperspace mode and took off, leaving the *Lindman* far behind. "Hang on," Helena warned her crew. "We'll enter the planet's atmosphere within minutes."

Sure enough, as Buck turned off hyperspace mode, the ship immediately began gravitating toward Planet Voplin, a not-too-distant planet of gray and yellow hues. "Switching on scrambler mode," he announced. Helena turned the nose of the ship straight down. She knew the best way to disappear from a Handlon radar was to fake a crash. She pulled back on the steering rod as hard as she could. Her shuttle leveled just thirty feet above the ground. She fired a rocket at a pile of metal trash lying on the ground nearby, making it look like they had crashed. In addition, the weapons were concealed under the camouflaged paint colors. If anyone found the shuttle, they couldn't tell it had weapons unless they shot at it or took the ship apart.

"Three minutes to target," Helena yelled over her shoulder to the other thirteen crew members behind her. "Helmet coms on." Everyone immediately reached up to turn on their ear and voice pieces. "Remember: all non-humans are targets." They loaded their weapons, checked their extra magazines, and adjusted their fitted armor pieces. They gave a thumbs-up to Buck.

"They're ready, Lieutenant."

She nodded, speaking to her crew through her microphone to their ear pieces. "When you exit the shuttle, the Handlon base will be at your 8 o'clock. I'm scanning for Handlons now." She maxed out the scanner, just to be sure. "Twenty-one Handlons: four at the gate on the right as you exit, at your 3 o'clock." She noted two small figures huddling together on a higher level in the

Handlon fortress. She touched the screen ever so lightly. "The girls are on Level 2. Nearest Handlon is fifty feet away. Make it quick." Buck moved to the back door. "Touchdown in ten seconds. Buck, you're on point," Buck moved over to the door, rifle at the ready. "Three, two, one. Go, go, go!"

As the ship hit the ground, Buck was first to jump out, fire, and fall to the ground to recover. His bullets hit their first target; the Handlon fell backwards and dropped his weapon. Handlons were all too glad to return fire. Second to jump out, Janic landed beside Buck and fired his gun; two more Handlons dropped. A third Handlon avoided the twosome's shots and pulled out a rocket blaster, pointing it at the cockpit of the *Holliday*. From the back door of the shuttle, Mort aimed and fired his rifle. The Handlon pulled the trigger just as he was hit; the impact of the bullets was enough for the Handlon to lose his target, and the rocket flew up and over the ship. The rest of the troops jumped out and scanned the area.

Helena exited the shuttle last after securing it. "The last scan indicated the Handlons can't get into the girls' cell. My guess is Miranda found some metal and had a bright idea in barricading themselves inside."

Mason smiled, "Smart girls. Bet they learned a lot from you, huh, Lieutenant?" Helena only blushed. "Let's keep moving, troops."

Janic opened the base door and threw in a stun grenade. A body cried out in pain and hit the floor. "Well, what do you know? Someone was waiting up for us."

Tena and King jumped through the door and started shooting. "All clear," Tena reported. "Six Handlons out."

Helena walked in, "Melvin and Jens, take the next room. The rest of you, act as a 360° shield."

Jens opened the door, and Melvin started to shoot. Another cry of pain; another much louder thump against the hard floor. Jens laughed, "I think you got someone." They turned toward the inside and continued firing for several seconds. Melvin reported, "All clear. Nine Handlons out."

King and Adam moved ahead to the stairwell leading to the second floor. "Helena, over there," Jindso called to his superior commander. "I think King and Adam found the way up."

"Find another way up in case we meet trouble at the top," Helena ordered. "Moniqé, Melissa, and Chuck, take the rear. Mason, go with Jindso." Helena pulled out her portable scanner as her team began to dwindle in splitting up.

"What's it say?" Buck asked.

"Two Handlons are a few doors down from the girls. Looks like they found some equipment to force their way into the room."

"We'd better hurry!"

"Jamie?" Miranda called out in the darkness. The single candle had long since died. They huddled in a corner. Jaime's tears had stopped when the Handlons gave up trying to force their way into the room. She didn't know what Miranda had done. All she did was help push large metal pieces to her at the doorway. She was too hungry to think. She was too cold to think about hunger. She was too sad to feel anything, really.

"Jaime, did you hear that? I heard it again!" Miranda excitedly announced. "It sounded like a spread blaster! I think Helena's here!"

Jaime suddenly found life in her eyes again. "What else can you hear?"

Miranda put her finger to her lips. She listened for a moment. Suddenly, she grabbed Jaime and pulled her to the side as a large blast hit their door.

Jaime's voice shrilled through the air. "They're taking us away, Miranda!"

Another large blast hit the door. It would only take one more hit before the door would fall into pieces and the Handlons would take them away forever.

Please let it be Helena, Miranda hoped in her heart. *For Jaime's sake, and mine, please let it be them!*

A female voice sounded on the other side. "Girls, are you there?"

Miranda squeezed Jaime's hand. "Jaime, it's Helena! She came!"

"She came! She came!" the younger Holley sister screamed. "Helena, we're here!"

"Oh, girls! Hold on, we're going to blast you out. Move as far away from the door as you can! We'll wait three seconds."

Miranda and Jaime ran farther from the door and hunkered down to the floor, covering their ears. The last blast blew the door off its hinges and metal pieces flew all around. Helena stepped through, and the girls ran up to her. The three hugged each other desperately, tears flowing down their faces.

"Helena, you came for us!" Jaime cried.

"Of course, I did," the lieutenant assured her. "Why wouldn't I? You're my little sister."

Miranda had no words to say. She was content to know her heroine had come again.

Buck stepped into the room. "Lieutenant, we've got to go. The scanner indicates several Handlon ships have landed. We don't want to deal with this amount of trouble."

Helena pulled back and held a hand from each girl in one of her own hands. "Let's go home, ladies. And fast!"

While Buck, Helena, Miranda, and Jaime took one path out of the fortress shielded by Jack, Mason, and King, the others of the team fought off some of the Handlons that dared to catch up to them. In separated groups, they boarded the *Holliday*, and Helena started up the engines as quickly as she could. "Buck, let's do this quick!"

"You got it, Helena." He flipped on controls just as fast as he could shoot off a rifle. "Girls, sit down and hold on tight."

Jens, Melissa, and Chuck were last to enter the shuttle. The back hatch closed up, the ship took off, and the Handlons raged as their chance for revenge took off toward Troklon.

An hour later, the ship was safely headed toward Troklon with no Handlon shuttles following or intersecting them from any direction. Helena unattached her seat harness and turned her seat around to face the girls. "You can't tell anyone we rescued you."

Jaime looked puzzled. "Why not?"

Miranda crossed her arms. "Yeah, why not?"

Helena sighed. "The Senate didn't approve this mission. If they find out anyone of us—" she motioned to the entire crew in the back, "helped in rescuing either of you, we'll be charged with treason and sent to jail on Planet Grildoom."

"What about mom and dad? Can we tell them?"

"No, sweetie." Helena smiled. "They'll probably figure it out, but you have to deny it, okay? It's like a really good game of truth or dare…except our careers and lives are in your hands." A few of the crew members snickered at Helena's concept.

Miranda wasn't happy to comply, but she knew it was for the best. "Fine."

"Thank you," Helena stated. "Which brings me to another statement of thanks, Miranda. Thank you for this ship."

The young girl was confused. "I didn't buy you this ship. I bought you the Frigate Deluxe, Model XT 9000…" Her voice trailed off as she looked around the interior of the shuttle. "No way! You outfitted the ship I bought you? It's awesome!"

Helena smiled. "I'm glad you approve. But why don't you come fly it for a little while?"

Buck's jaw dropped. Jaime dropped the plastic cup of water given to her from Melissa, and Miranda's smile formed from ear to ear. "Yes, ma'am, Lieutenant!" Miranda sat down and pummeled Helena with questions. Jaime was content to talk to some of the crew members in the back. Buck stayed in the pilot seat, not trusting either Helena or Miranda at this point but keeping a slight smile on his face.

Suddenly, a visual com appeared, and Miranda jumped out of the copilot's seat so Helena could pretend like she had been flying the *Holliday* with Buck for the past hour. "*Holliday*, this is the *Lindman*. Come in." Nielson showed up on the visual com.

"*Lindman*, this is the *Holliday*. Go ahead."

"How was your shopping trip?" Nielson cleared this throat and raised his eyebrows twice, indicating the Presidential Security Force was listening in on the com.

"It was a great success," Helena covered. "I found two new items I'd like to show to my parents, and my shuttle flew just fine."

Nielson smiled. "You'll have to tell us all about it. You're cleared to land. Captain Tallin wants to debrief you before you show your new purchases to your parents."

Helena understood what Nielson meant: Kront came up with a way to cover for the re-appearance of Miranda and Jaime without blowing Helena and her crew's cover in rescuing the girls. "Tell the Captain I'll be there as soon as we hit the ground."

"Thank you, Lieutenant. *Lindman* out."

Nikolej wiped the most recent tears from his face. Five days since the girls went missing, and still nothing. Or had it been six days. The days and nights seemed to melt together in a mush of no appetite, little sleep, and many worries keeping him at home from work. No different story for Ida. An incoming com interrupted his musings. He cleared his throat and quietly answered as he pushed the on button. "Holley residence. This is Nikolej speaking."

"Professor Holley, this is Admiral Runhes from the Senate."

Nikolej's heart dropped to his stomach. He quickly motioned to Ida who had been sitting silently on the couch next to the spot Nikolej had occupied just previous to the com call. She quickly stood up and joined him at the com box on the wall. "Yes, Admiral? How may I help you?"

"Well, Professor, I believe it is I who can help you today. Approximately one hour ago, the Security Patrol in Grithy Village was approached by two young ladies that matched the description of your daughter and the girl from the *Grimond Wolf.* We need you to verify their names and chip ID's, please."

Ida buried her head in her husband's chest, wetting his shirt with newfound tears of hope. Nikolej could barely hold back his own tears. "Yes, sir. Um, their names are Jamie Holley and Miranda Holliday." Nikolej repeated their chip ID numbers to the admiral.

"Well, Professor, it looks like today is your very, very lucky day. We need to debrief them, but you are more than welcome to come visit them here at the Security Control Center."

"Thank you, sir! Thank you!" The Admiral turned off the com before Nikolej had finished thanking him, but Nikolej and Ida fell to the floor in tears of joy and abundant smiles. Their girls had been rescued and found. At last, all was right in their world once more.

Chapter 11. – Miranda's Surprise.

Helena ran in to the common room. On the far side, Miranda and Jaime sat in complete contentment with Professors Holley. The lieutenant smiled and began to walk toward them, but a soldier stepped in her way.

"Excuse me, Lieutenant Holley. Admiral Runhes wishes to see you."

Helena, not quite over the girls' kidnapping, immediately became defensive toward the male sergeant. "Once I've said hi to the girls."

But the sergeant shook his head. "Sorry, ma'am. If you refuse, I have to arrest you."

Helena was furious. She'd been caught, and this Admiral wanted to discuss a plea bargain with her before he reported her to the Senate. She knew it would happen, but she didn't think it would be so soon. "All right, Sergeant. Have it your way."

"Just following my orders, ma'am. This way." He motioned toward a long hallway. Helena looked toward Miranda and Jaime. The girls had confused looks on their face, but Professors Holley diverted their attention so Helena could follow these so-called orders. She marched in-line behind the sergeant for several long seconds until he walked into a room and held the door open for her. She walked inside. The sergeant sat behind a desk and clicked a com button. "Admiral, she's here."

"Good," the voice on the other side said. "Bring her in."

"Yes, sir," the sergeant replied. He came around the desk and opened a door on her right. "You may go in, Lieutenant."

She didn't answer him. She walked into the much larger room, definitely an Admiral's office. The large man behind the desk with snow-white hair and sky-blue eyes looked up at Helena. "Come in, Lieutenant Holley. I've been expecting your arrival back to Troklon for quite some time."

His tone of voice confirmed to Helena that he knew her secret. "Sir, I just want to say—"

"Sit down, Lieutenant. Let me do the talking."

"Yes, sir." She felt like a first-year student back at the

Academy.

"Rather, let me do the showing." He tossed a few printed photos her direction. One was a still of a radar scan that showed her ship landing on Planet Voplin. A second printout showed her shuttle leaving the planet. A third photo was taken of Helena sneaking away after dropping the girls off nearly a mile away from Grithy Village. The photos continued to show that he had enough evidence against her to lock her away for a long time. She gulped, hoping the Admiral would give her a chance to defend herself, or in the very least take the blame and let her crew off without charges.

"Lieutenant, do you recognize my last name?"

Helena thought it was a very strange question. "No, sir. I'm sorry, but should I?" *Okay, this is weird,* she thought.

"Six years ago, you fought in the battle of Kelont Dash on Planet Jendlas, is that correct?"

"Yes, sir. I was one of only fifty soldiers."

"And you can't remember all of their names?"

Helena shook her head. "Sir, I thought I was here to be charged with crimes of treason against the Senate."

The Admiral slammed his fist against his desk. "Lieutenant, I will do whatever I want in my office. If I want to show you pictures of my family but talk about how ducks waddle, then I'll do so. Do you understand?"

"Yes, sir." Helena was beyond confused, but she just wanted to get this over with. "Then, no, sir, I don't remember all of their names."

He leaned back in his chair. "Let me try to jog your memory. A young man named Trapper Runhes was also part of the crew of fifty. He was shot in the neck, and you ran over to stop the bleeding. You made him repeat your rank and name until the medics arrived to care for him." He paused for a moment. Helena swore he was getting choked up. "You saved his life, Lieutenant."

"I wish I could have done more, sir. That shot to his neck paralyzed him from the neck down."

"Lieutenant, you saved my son."

Helena didn't bother responding. He gathered up the photos he had tossed her direction and placed them in a manila folder. She barely opened her mouth to speak. "I'm glad I was there to help, sir."

"Lieutenant Holley, I have plenty of evidence to charge you with treason against the Senate. But," he paused as he picked up the manila folder. "This folder is all of the evidence left of your treason. Your friend, Ms. Holliday, is quite the computer...*expert*."

Helena smiled. "Yes, sir, she is."

Admiral Runhes stood up from his desk and walked over to a large machine. He turned it on and placed the manila folder through its large metal teeth. Everything in his hand was instantly shredded into millions of pieces. He turned to face her. "I suggest we mention this to no one. Understand?"

She stood up to salute her superior commander. Although she could not utter words in gratitude for his actions, he understood her tears streaming down her face. "Dismissed," he quietly told her.

*   *   *

Helena and Kront sat in the Situation Room aboard the *Lindman*. For several minutes, they had just sat in their chairs, musing over the events of the past week. Helena was first to break the silence. "Kront, you have to tell Groyt."

"I know," he said, rubbing his forehead with his fingers. "I may not like Silas, but it's still disheartening when an Admiral betrays his own allegiances."

She leaned over toward him. "What if we're wrong? What if Miranda only heard what she wanted to hear? Is it possible that she wanted to hear the Prime Commander say Silas's name if she knew your history with him? Could it be some little girl crush way of getting on your good side?"

Kront looked at Helena out of the left corners of his eyes. "Really? A little girl crush?"

Helena rolled her eyes. "You know what I mean. The Senate won't be jumping for joy in considering the testimony of an eleven-year old over an experienced and decorated military admiral. Even you know that."

"Must you continue to remind me of things I already know?"

She lightly punched him in the left arm. "How did the

investigation go, anyway?"

Kront sat up and leaned back in his chair. "There was none."

Helena's jaw dropped. "What? What happened?"

"Just what I thought would happen. It scared Silas just knowing it was a possibility. The rumors of a full-scale investigation were circulated by none other than Groyt and myself, and when it circled around to Silas, he was suddenly 'unavailable'."

"Ha!" Helena laughed in a single burst. "Unavailable, my ass! He's guiltier than shit."

Kront smiled. "I don't want revenge, you see. I just want justice, and I'll get it. Soon enough." He crossed his arms. "Is Jaime back with your parents?"

"Yes, and I felt it wise for Miranda to stay on board with us for a little longer."

Kront nodded. "I agree. No more kidnappings for a while, please and thank you." He stood up and stretched his arms. "I'm going to speak with Groyt on the visual com. Talk to Miranda and see if there's anything else she knows that she saved for our ears only."

"You bet!" Helena left the room in one direction, and Kront exited the opposite way toward his office.

"Well, of course I didn't tell them everything."

Helena dropped her head down into her hands. She sat in a chair across from Miranda in the girl's old recovery room. "Sweetie, what else do you know? And why can't you tell me everything at once? Why do I have to drag it out of you?" She picked up a glass of water to quench her thirst."

Miranda smiled. "I know how to end the war."

Helena choked on her drink. "What did you say?"

"I know how to end the war."

"But, how?"

Miranda grabbed a piece of paper and a pencil from a nearby drawer and began to draw. Helena couldn't tell what it was quite at first. The Academy student explained, "Two Handlons stood outside our cell door and discussed the Handlons' efforts to continue the war. They spoke of their joy that the clans have united; Admiral Silas Proked pays the clans 100 million Credits every six months to continue the war. The Prime Commander mentioned Admiral Proked's name when he told us we would pay for your actions."

Helena's face was serious. "That's good information, Miranda."

"Yes, but there's more! Each Handlon fortress has a secret stash of Credits and weapons since the base is built underground. On the 2nd level in a secret compartment behind the North Wall, the credits and weapons are locked away in Room 2.132. Most of their bases have 1-2 million Credits and weapons enough to arm 100 Handlons, but the reason the Handlons were so angry about you destroying their base on Planet Helgin is because that particular base has about 150 million Credits and weapons enough to arm over 2,000 Handlons." Miranda continued drawing like it was child's play from her past. "Also, I heard they have around 15,000 titanium bars and 10,000 platinum bars."

Helena couldn't believe her ears. *This information could change the war, could stop the war,* she pondered. *If any of the Handlons think that the girls' heard any of this, they're bound to have bounties on their heads…or worse…*

The lieutenant sat back and smiled. "Well, then, it's a good thing the *Vilantex* crew is stationed at the old Handlon base and won't be leaving for another four weeks."

*   *   *

Groyt flipped on his visual com. "Kront, what's so damn urgent that you must wake me from—"

"Sir, pardon the interruption, but I've got proof that Admiral Silas Proked is behind the kidnapping of Miranda Holliday and Jaime Holley."

The old man wiped his eyes with his fists to focus on the screen, grabbed his night-reading glasses, and squinted. "Did I hear you right?"

"Yes, sir. I'm sending you all of the proof now."

Groyt pushed back from his computer. "Dess! Now!"

Marshal immediately stepped into the room. "You yelled, sir?"

"Don't be cute with me, Dess! Kront's sending me a load

of documents right now. Print them up and make copies enough for each person in the Senate, and then some! We're not going back to sleep tonight."

His com officer rolled his eyes. "Of course, sir. Right on it." He left the room and closed the door behind him.

Kront pushed a few buttons and brought up an extra screen up so Groyt could read-along. "As you can see, these documents are bank account statements for the last six months. Recently, Silas sent 500,000 credits to a Handlon account on the planet Voplin. I've got testimony from both girls that they heard the Prime Commander mention Silas' name in coordination with their disappearance."

The commander shuffled in his seat. "We may not be able to use their testimonies in court, but bank account records are a great start. What else have you got for me?"

Kront nodded and switched the screen out for a new set of documents. "These documents show the Senate's annual weapons contract. Usually, the cost is 450 million credits, but for some reason they factory only received half of that amount this year. Somewhere, there are around 250 million Credits floating around." Captain Tallin switched the screen back to the original documents. "Going back for the last ten years, Silas has been paid 2.5 billion credits, but he's offered the Handlons 2 billion Credits to get the clans to join forces in order to continue the war."

Groyt took off his glasses and rubbed his forehead. "Kront, if you're right, this could end the war."

Kront didn't smile. "Sir, if I'm right, this may start a whole new war."

Chapter 12. – The Peace Treaty.

Helena stood in front of the two girls in the hallway outside the Great Hall of the Senate room. "You ladies look stunning!"

Miranda looked brilliant in a straight-line, apple-red dress of silk that met the top of her knees. Jaime shined in a sky blue halter dress that matched her eyes and swirled around her calves. But the girls agreed that Helena looked best in a cream-colored floor-length gown with an open back and silver shoulder straps. A thin scarf wrapped around her neck, giving her an air of alluring and magical beauty. Miranda kicked off her tall, black heels. "I can't wait for this to be over."

Jaime straightened the top of her dress. "Why? So you can go spend all of your new money?" she teased. "What are you thinking of getting?"

"A transporter." Miranda didn't even hesitate to answer, nor deny Jaime's teasing. After Kront delivered the news to Grillo of the hidden weapons and treasure in the Handlon base on Planet Helgin, the *Vilantex* crew found the stashes and divided up the glory among the troops of both ships. Kront shared his ship's share with Miranda and Jaime. After all, the information came from them, and it only came because they were kidnapped. Now Miranda was a huge millionaire, and Jaime had begun her own hefty savings account, from which she bought her new dress that she adored so greatly.

Helena laughed. "Well, with the money you both received for your share in the raid of the Handlon base on Planet Helgin, you could buy twenty personal transporter shuttles, and still have plenty of money left over." Music sounded through the coms, and Helena knew it was nearly time for her to take her seat. Helena hugged them. "I'm proud of you both." She kissed their foreheads and left to take her seat next to Captain Tallin in the Senate's Great Hall.

As the girls waited in the hallway, Senator Milons took center-stage. The audience clapped. Flopre raised his hands to quiet them. "Thank you all for coming here tonight. You all know why we are here. There have been several tragic events of late that have led us to this moment: the continued war with the Handlons. The desolation of Planet Dringls. The destruction of the *Grimond Wolf* and the *Helium*. The arrest of Admiral Silas Proked in connection with the kidnapping of Miranda Holliday and Jaime Holley." Flopre waited for a moment of silence as the weight of his words fell upon the crowds. "Today we rejoice for we sign a treaty of peace!" The crowds cheered wildly and shouted for joy. "May I please have Miranda and Jaime join me here on the stage?"

The girls heard their cues and walked onto the stage to join Flopre. Jaime's parents sat to the left of their eldest daughter in the front row. Kront's crew took up several rows behind them. Grillo's crew made an appearance, as well, and many of the girls' friends from the Academy. However, the girls were stunned to see an extremely large Handlon standing to the right of Senator Milons. Although he dressed in fine clothing - like that of a king - with Miranda felt on guard, and Jaime was intimidated.

Senator Milons continued, "Ms. Jaime Holley is the daughter of Professors Nikolej and Ida Holley here at the Academy. Junior Officer Miranda Holliday is a first year student that has recently broken a new record in reaching Level 10 in less than 3 months."

Kront coughed and leaned over to Helena on his left. "If she continues on this path, she'll complete the eight years at the Academy in only five years!"

Flopre smiled and brought out two medals. "The Senate is proud to honor these two lovely ladies with the Medal of Peace and Honor." He placed the medals around the necks of the girls, and everyone cheered for the bravery of the girls during the kidnapping and in relaying to Helena the information they discovered while captive. "Now, let me introduce you all to King Jhakto Davkylt of Planet Handlon 8."

The Handlon king waved to the crowd. His bodyguards moved slightly away. Jhakto shook hands with Flopre; both men sat down in the chairs at the table on the stage meant for the signing of the peace treaty. "It's a pleasure to have you here, King Davkylt. If you please, we will sign the treaty and declare peace." Senator Milons and King Jhakto signed the papers, stood, and shook hands again. "I now declare peace!"

PART 2

YEAR 2743

WORLD'S END

Chapter 13. – 6 Years Later

"Sir, you may want to see this. The scanner's picked up something unusual," Matty Dloper told his commander, Admiral Cristo Hernandez. The *Saint Triantle* had been scanning Planet Loht 9 for the last four months, looking for minerals for the Presidential Service.

"What are those?" Cristo asked. Suddenly, the thought hit him. *Those look like tunnels*, he wondered. "Get me the Senate immediately! I need the name of the best Intelligence Officer in the galaxy."

Matty turned on the com; newly-promoted Lieutenant Tony Flakes answered the call. "Hey, Matty. What's up?"

"Hey, Tony. Admiral Hernandez needs a connection to the Intel History Office."

"Sure thing. Just a sec."

Drago Hoyt ran the Intelligence History Office. He appeared on Cristo's visual within moments of the call. "Admiral Hernandez, how may my department be of service?"

Cristo pressed the transfer button, and the new scan from the planet appeared on Drago's screen. "We discovered these tunnels under the base that the *Lindman* crew cleaned out six years ago."

Drago's eyes widened. "Could it be?" he stuttered. "It's impossible..." Cristo smiled. He knew that his scanner had discovered something fantastic. Drago cleared his throat. "Admiral, I want you to stay in orbit. We need a special crew to check this out. If it's what I think, the Trikkyas will be furious!"

"I understand, sir. Whom should we send?"

"Only the *Lindman* crew is trained for this kind of mission."

Cristo frowned. He wasn't very fond of the man responsible for another admiral's execution. Cristo was sure that Captain Tallin had forged the documents proving Silas' guilt. "Sir, perhaps another crew would better suit our needs?"

Drago smiled and countered, "Cristo, we all know about

your views toward Captain Tallin. However, we know you won't let personal conflicts interfere with what's best for the Presidential Federation, will you?"

Sarcasm dripped from Cristo's voice as he replied, "Of course not, Drago, and we contacted you because you do know who is best."

Drago nodded. "Then it's final. Hoyt out." He turned to his com officer. "Get me the *Lindman* on the com."

Nielson accepted the incoming visual com. "*Lindman* here—Drago? Is that you?"

Drago smiled and laughed along with the *Lindman*'s com officer. "Nielson, old buddy, it sure is. How's life as a com officer treating you?"

"Well, I can't 'com'-plain!"

They continued in smiles and laughter, exchanging profession jokes as though their school days had not passed. Drago and Nielson graduated from the Academy the same year. That was when Drago had chosen to stay in Intelligence on Troklon, and Nielson decided on com work in Kront Tallin's Platoon.

Nielson wiped tears of joy away from his eyes, still tearing up from Drago's last joke. "Seriously, Drago, what can I do for you?"

"Well, technically, I need to speak to your Captain."

"Just one minute. I'll get him for you." Nielson turned away from the desk com and pressed the ship's com control. "Captain Tallin, please report to the Bridge." He clicked off the ship's com and turned back to more jokes with Drago until Kront came through the door.

"All right, Drago, we've had our fun, but my boss is here, so we better get serious now."

It was now Drago's turn to wipe tears of laughter from his well-watered face. "I'll try, Nielson. Man, you killed that last one."

Nielson smiled. He missed his Academy friends. He turned to his commander, standing behind him. "Sir? It's Officer Drago Hoyt from Intel History at the Senate."

Kront looked toward the visual com from a slight distance. "Hello, Officer Hoyt. How may the *Lindman* be of service?" Kront crossed his arms in slight defense. Ever since Silas was put to death for his treacherous crimes several years ago, he couldn't tell which Senators, Admirals, and others were hoping – on a daily basis – that he'd get assassinated, fall off a cliff, explode, or get sucked into a black hole.

"Captain Tallin, first, let me say that it's an honor to speak with you."

He could be sucking up to me, Kront mused. *But he seems like a friend to Nielson, and I trust Nielson's choices.* "Thank you, son. Go on."

"Second, it seems Admiral Hernandez of the *Saint Triantle* found a secret underground tunnel system beneath the Handlon base you cleared out on Loht 9 some time ago." Drago pushed a few buttons, and Cristo's picture from his ship's scanner appeared on Kront's visual com. "As you can see, Captain, the two tunnels go down about three miles. In my experience, something like this leads to a large room filled with shelves of records dating back about 500 years."

Kront's eyes widened. "Well, are you asking us to take on this mission?"

Drago smiled to him, "Yes, sir, I am. You have three months to complete, from start to finish. You must secure any and all documents recovered from the site. Preservation is of the utmost importance.

"You can count on the *Lindman.*"

"Thank you, Captain Tallin. Intel out."

Helena knocked on the Captain's door and stepped inside. "You wanted to see me?"

Kront flipped through some documents Drago sent his way after their conversation was over. He handed her a small stack as he offered her a chair. "We have a new mission.

She smiled. "Great!"

"It might start a war."

Helena's face froze. "Kront, please tell me this is a joke."

Kront shook his head. "The crew of the *Saint Triantle* believes they have found the 500-year old fortress of the Handlon's Supreme Council. If this is true, and we dare to enter and bring back the documents in the room at the end of the tunnel, the clan fighting will stop, and the real war will begin." He leaned back in his chair and sighed. "You can be damn sure we'll be attacked by the Trikkyas."

"What do they have to do with this?"

"They believe the Handlons destroyed their home planet of Trikky Talos, and that the evidence lies in the documents we are trying to recover from the fortress. They'll fight us tooth and nail if they find out where we are and what we're doing there."

Helena placed the paperwork back on Kront's desk. "Sir, I have an idea."

"Go ahead." Helena said nothing, and slightly lowered her eyes and head down, twiddling her thumbs. "Helena?" he asked. As if he could read her mind, he knew of what – or rather, whom – she thought. "No. Absolutely not. Out of the question. And definitely not *both* of them." He looked away, afraid she'd show a sad-puppy face with her gray-blue hair.

She did. "Captain, you know we need them. After all, they're the best at the Academy, the first and second best students. We can't ask for any better than that."

"Oh, yes, we can. We can count on the crews we employ, not the students who want to go on wild, death-defying adventures with us." When Helena didn't respond, he finally looked her way. "Fine! But only on one condition: we ask them, and they have to say yes. I will not order them, even if they are technically under my command."

*   *   *

Miranda ran as fast as she could; she didn't want to be late for her two tests today. If she passed these, she'd have made it to Level 90.

Only 10 more levels to go? Not bad for six years in the Academy, as compared to an average of eight years or longer, she congratulated herself. *I'm eighteen-years old, and I'm ready to take on the galaxy!*

As she neared the testing building, she began repeating different facts aloud so she wouldn't forget some of the more difficult subject matter. "The aim of the Spread Blaster must be set to one-half inch above the target for every fifty feet. If the target is at 300 feet, the aim must be set to three inches." She grumbled, knowing the Knowledge of Weapons Test would certainly not be her highest marks with so many rules to remember. *Why can't I just shoot until I hit them? It's so much easier that way,* she rationalized. "The velocity of an acid grenade in a non-gravity zone is 100 yards per second. A safe distance is 1200 yards away."

When she walked through the doors of the testing room, she stopped in mid-step as she noticed two very familiar faces standing not too far from her. "Helena? Captain? What are you two doing here?" She rushed over to hug them, all smiles and laughter.

Helena explained, "I arrived about two hours ago. The *Lindman* is in for repairs, so when I heard you had some testing today, I decided to surprise you." The smile quickly left her face. "Don't let me be a distraction, Miranda. I'll leave if you need me to leave."

"Don't be silly!" Miranda dismissed. She turned to her commander. "How's the crew, sir?"

Kront smiled. "They're fine, but test now, talk later." He grabbed Helena by the arm to pull her away to their seats. She shrugged her shoulders at Miranda, who laughed as though her two senior officers were twin siblings: sometimes they had the strongest connections, and other times they acted like silly little children.

The moment the red light bulb above the testing room's door shut off, Jaime shot through the entrance and quickly found Miranda. "So, how'd it go?"

"How else does she do but great?" a feminine voice from behind announced.

Jaime knew the familiar ring of that voice. She whipped around and bear-hugged her older sister. "Helena! When did you get here?" She pulled back and saluted the Captain. "How long are y'all staying for?"

Kront replied, "It has been around eleven months since our last stop here, hasn't it, Helena?" She nodded in agreement. He turned to face his two young recruits. "We're staying only until the *Lindman* is fixed, and then we have a new mission which we'd like to discuss with you."

Jamie and Miranda hi-fived each other just as the Professor of Testing walked in to the room. "Already celebrating without knowing the results? You must be quite sure of your studying skills, Ms. Holliday," he teased, but Miranda thought he was being quite serious.

She hung her head and stomped her right foot. "I knew it! I bombed the weapons test, didn't I?"

"Well," he began, pausing for dramatic effect. "You scored a 99% on the Intel Level 7 test."

"Yes!" she cheered, jumping in the air and pumping her fist.

"As for the weapons test…"

Jaime grabbed Miranda's hand. Even Kront and Helena seemed nervous for the super-intelligent superstar. What if the weapons test proved to be her downfall?

"You scored 98%. Congratulations, Ms. Holliday, you're now a Level 90 Academy Troklon student."

The two girls hugged and jumped in circles, hooted and hollered, and were finally stopped by other students shushing them, preparing to take their own tests. The four *Lindman* personnel left the testing room, walked down the hallway, and exited the building for some fresh air.

"Miranda," Helena asked, "how many records do you hold at the Academy?"

"Twenty-two."

Kront coughed. "What?"

"Don't worry, Captain," Jaime interjected. "She only broke eleven of your records. You're still the fastest at Weapon Assembly and Ship Maneuvering."

His face flushed red. "At least I still have some of my dignity preserved in those halls."

Jamie blushed, "Helena, I broke a record, too. Miranda and I trained for it for a long time, but I got it."

"That's great, sis!" The lieutenant smiled at the news, proud of her younger sister. The two girls looked at each other and burst out in laughter. She was beyond confused. "What's so funny?"

Miranda uttered between breaths, "Helena…it was one…of your…records…she broke!"

"But I only have two records at the Academy: Fastest on the Obstacle Course and Best Shot with the Special Sniper Blaster

XLX Precision."

Jaime blushed deeper. "Let's just say you're no longer the best shot. I beat you by 7 points in a 100-shot round."

Helena's purple hair seemed to fade as her jaw dropped simultaneously. "Jaime, are you serious?" Instantly, the color came back; tears welled in her eyes as she grabbed up her sister in a tight hug. "I'm so very proud of you. You're an amazing sister and obviously an excellent student and friend."

A loud beep interrupted the moment. Kront's visual com screen on his arm popped open. Nielson's face showed up slightly pixelated. "Captain, everything is ready, sir."

Kront replied, "Thank you, Nielson." He turned off the com and turned back to his group. "Miranda, do you know a young woman named Jamina Sonklod from the Port Center here at the Academy?"

Miranda nodded, "Yes, but she changed assignments two weeks ago."

"She sure did. She's the newest member of the *Lindman* crew."

"Really?" Jaime asked. "That's great!"

"Yes, it is. She'll be a great addition to our crew. She's marrying Nielson next week, and he wanted to know if you two ladies would like to attend."

The girls hi-fived again. "Duh," Miranda said. "It's about time they got hitched. He's the only thing she ever talked about."

Jaime ribbed her friend. "I don't think that's going to change just because she's marrying her favorite topic of conversation." Miranda grumbled and rolled her eyes.

Helena jumped in to the conversation, "Girls, is there somewhere more private we can discuss some items of business with you two?"

Miranda and Jaime led Kront and Helena to their room at the Academy. Miranda said, "We can talk in here. I've installed half a dozen security measures, so whatever you say is safe within these walls."

Kront explained, "When you two were given the Medal of Peace and Honor, you were free to choose your school and first assignment."

"We chose the *Lindman*!" Jaime proudly reminded them

all.

"Yes, which is why we're asking the two of you to join us. We've been given a personal mission, and we could really use Miranda's Intel skills and Jaime's sniper skills. I've talked to the Grand Master, and he's agreed that this mission counts as Field Points towards your next Level, and I have the pleasure to grade you."

Helena pulled out a portable 3-D unit and brought up a revolving digital image. "This is Planet Loht 9. Six years ago, we took out a Handlon base on this planet. Since then, the senate has discovered that the base was a cover up. Underground are two long pipes that go down about three miles and connect to another fortress. The Senate believes the lost documents of the Handlon Supreme Council from 7658 are down there, papers that are over 500 years old."

Jaime shifted uncomfortably in her seat and addressed her superior officers. "If this is an underground mission, you don't need me. I can't get shots three miles down."

"We need you top-side," Kront illustrated.

"How do I fit in?" Miranda asked.

"Because you're the second-best sniper at the Academy."

"I thought you needed my Intel skills?"

"We do. We need you to develop a program that allows us to open any lock we encounter, *and* stay top-side with Jaime. You each will have a Sniper Blaster."

Kront sniggered, "Yes, and God be with anyone that tries to get past them! By the way, Junior Officer Holliday, how many units of the *Lindman* Scanner have you sold since your last Senate shipment?"

Miranda opened up her personal computer and glanced at her sales statements. "It looks like just around 2500, and I just updated them all for free. Now they scan for the new Trikkyas Armor, too. Can't have them sneaking aboard ships under the protection of my scanners."

Helena shook her head in disbelief and smiled. "How did you get your hands on a Trikkyas armor?"

"Chanell Miles from the *Vilantex*," Jaime blurted out. "He sold it to her after they got attacked in the Delta Quadrant."

"And I only paid 25,000 Credits for it." Miranda's face

radiated pride in herself.

"Well," Kront concluded, "I guess the Senate couldn't be happier to have you around."

"You could say that. They gave me a brand new 400-foot Frigate Deluxe, Model TXH 9800."

"A…a wh-what?" a shocked Helena stuttered. "That's…that's the fastest civilian ship in the entire galaxy. Ever!"

Miranda reached into the pockets of her jeans and pulled out some keys, throwing them at Helena. "Yep, and she's all yours."

Helena shook her head and tried to give back the keys. "I can't. You already bought me the *Holliday*. I can't take a ship that was freely given to you for your service to the Senate."

"Helena, Jaime already bought me one the first weekend it went on the market. I named it the *Lindman, Jr.*, if that's okay with Captain Tallin."

Kront laughed, "It would be an honor, Miranda."

Chapter 14. – T-minus Four Days.

Helena was lying on her bed aboard the *Lindman*, quietly reading the mission plan, when the com sounded: "Lieutenant Holley, please report to the Hangar." She sighed, rolled her eyes, and dropped her papers onto the spot on the bed she was just occupying. *Damn,* she groaned. *I thought today would be more relaxing.* As she walked down to the Hangar, Buck passed her in a hurried jog.

"Hey, Lieutenant. You comin'?"

Puzzled, she was a little slow to respond. "Yeah, be right there." She hurried her pace, and when she entered the Hangar, she realized what all the hubbub was about: right next to her *Holliday* shuttle, she happily watched Miranda set down the *Lindman, Jr.*, Miranda's own Frigate Deluxe, Model TXH 9800. Helena smiled as Jaime de-boarded the shuttle alongside her best friend.

"Junior Officer Holliday reporting for duty, Lieutenant," Miranda saluted.

"Forget the formalities, girlfriend," Jaime dismissed. She hugged Helena. "Hi, sis."

"Hi, Junior Officer Holley and *not* Junior Officer Holliday."

Miranda's confused face showed a need for explanation. Kront happened to walk up, so Helena nudged him. "Captain Tallin, please explain to Ms. Holliday the levels aboard the *Lindman* in parallel with Academy levels."

Kront straightened his posture. "Simply put, we don't have Junior Security Officers aboard the *Lindman* above Academy Level 39. Junior Security Officers are Level 2 through 39. Level 40 to 69 is a Security Officer, and then Level 70 to 89 is a Senior Security Officer. After Level 90, your official title is Intel Security Officer, and you get a new badge."

Miranda looked at the brand new gold badge Kront handed to her. "Intelligence Security Officer Miranda Holliday," the insignia read. She saluted and then hugged her superior commander. "Thanks, Captain."

"You earned it. Plus, this means that Lieutenant Holley takes her orders from you now."

"What?" Miranda and Jaime exclaimed simultaneously.

"Don't push it," Helena warned with a wink and a smile.

"Attention on deck!" Kront announced. All crew members who happened to be within earshot immediately stood at attention and faced toward the direction of the captain's voice. "Junior Security Officer Miranda Holliday has risen to the rank of Intel Security Officer. Just three days ago, she scored a 99% on the Level 7 Intelligence exam, which means she will be placed on the Wall of Fame at the Academy as one of forty-seven students who have scored higher than 95% since the Academy first opened." The soldiers cheered and clapped.

Miranda felt so special. "Thank you, but I have chosen to live and serve so that others may also live and serve." Another round of applause thundered inside the walls of the Hangar.

"Helena, have you named your new shuttle yet?"

Helena glanced over at her younger sister lying on her bed. "No, sweetie. Do you want to help me?

Jamie looked up at the ceiling. "Sure. How about the *Slonga*, after your favorite drink?

"I'm pretty sure the company has rights of that name."

"Too bad. How about *Speedy*?"

Helena raised an eyebrow. "Really?"

"Okay, so maybe it's a little tacky," Jaime said, wrinkling up her face slightly.

The older sister spoke up after a few minutes of silent brainstorming. "How about the *Jaime*?"

Jaime shrugged her shoulders. "I like that. She's a beautiful ship, fast, elegant...sounds a lot like me!" The sisters began to laugh and couldn't stop, even when Miranda joined them in the room.

"Gee whiz, what's so funny?"

"She's naming her ship after me! The *Jaime*."

Miranda added in, "Sounds perfect."

"Come on, girls. Let's go down to the Hangar and make it official."

Jamie grabbed a bucket of paint, but Helena stopped her.

"Hey, whoa! No, we don't paint her. We laser her, burn it into the ship. Painted ships end up stolen 90% of the time and are just repainted, never recovered."

Jamie handed the bucket to a crew member passing by. "Here, take this and go put it away." She walked over the wall, grabbed the laser, and began imprinting the name onto the ship.

Miranda jumped into the cockpit and programmed the ship's computer to identify the shuttle as the *Jamie* when she showed up on radar. "Okay, Helena, the computer recognizes her now." She hopped out of the cockpit and rejoined her companions.

"May the *Jaime* serve me well for many years to come."

Miranda ribbed her commander. "If it's anything like your little sister, you might be *stuck* with it forever!" They all laughed and walked back into the main part of the *Lindman*.

"Nielson, set a course for Loht 9," Kront commanded.

"Yes, sir." He winked at Jamina on his left.

She sent him a smile and mused, *In two days, my love, you'll be mine forever. I'm so glad the day is almost here.*

Nielson loved her so much. His thoughts were scattered. He could hardly sleep or eat. Luckily, the mission hadn't officially started until today: he had wrong calculations, errors in com transmission, and a host of other – mainly minor – problems since the wedding had come ever closer.

"Nielson! Snap out of it, man! You're daydreaming!"

Nielson whipped his head around to his commander; poor Kront was laughing his head off at his com officer and wiping tears from the corners of his eyes. Even Jamina was giggling.

"What? What's so funny? Did I do something?"

"Yes and no. You were daydreaming with this stupid, lovey-dovey look on your face, and if you hadn't asked me to be your best man, I probably would've punched it off you." Kront heaved a large sigh. "And then there's the matter of your woman pummeling me to the ground if I would've touched you, too." He winked at Jamina; she blushed. "You two take off. I can handle things."

"Thank you, sir."

*   *   *

"Helena, wake up. Helena!"

Helena shot up in bed. "What? Who—oh, Miranda. What's wrong? What time is it?"

"Don't know. Don't care." Miranda sat down next to the lieutenant. "I need your help."

"Why?" Helena rubbed her eyes with her fists and ran her fingers through her hair until it met knots about halfway down.

"I forgot to have Nielson and Jamina's wedding present delivered to the ship. I contacted the company, but they think I'm joking. I need you to talk some sense into them." Miranda stood up and began pacing. "If they don't start to ship it within the next two hours, we'll be too far out for it to get here in time!"

"Calm down, Miranda. What in this great galaxy did you buy them?"

Miranda grinned. "A pink Eisen Speeder."

Helena shook her head. "Oh, Nielson's gonna love that."

Miranda started to laugh but stopped when she remembered her predicament. "Not unless you can talk some sense into that brainless, old fart who—"

"All right, all right!" Helena stood up and stretched. "But you owe me, especially for showing up to a visual com looking the way I do. Just because you wiggled your way into the Senate's heart and got our ship and crew into the Presidential Service as a shuttle-for-hire doesn't mean I have any more pull than anyone else does. I don't understand…" Helena's ramblings continued as she shuffled down the hall. The night guards that she passed dared not even look at her. She flipped them off anyway.

Miranda sheepishly ducked her head down. "Sorry, Helena." She paused for a moment before calling out after her, "Thank you!"

"Helena, thank you so much!"

Helena patted Miranda on the back as she received yet another bear hug, making a total of four or five…or so…since the moment the pink Eisen Speeder arrived a few minutes ago. "I think that's enough gratitude for one day, sweetie. Let's just focus on putting this away before Nielson or Jamina sees it."

Miranda and Jamie pushed the speeder from the backside

as Helena lowered the ramp and guided the speeder from the front, but Miranda wouldn't let the issue go. "But if you hadn't woken up and told that guy to send the present – or else – then it never would've gotten here in time!" Miranda stopped pushing and grabbed Jaime in a big hug. "You're sister is awesome!"

Jaime pulled away. "Yeah, I know. Come on, I want to go take a nap before the wedding."

Miranda couldn't stop smiling. She was going to keep giving for as long as fate, destiny, and life seemed to bless her with so much, including a grateful heart. Suddenly, she frowned. At what point might she not meet expectations? What if she failed? What then?

*   *   *

Buck grabbed Nielson by the shoulder. "Nielson, stop fretting. You're acting like a damn woman."

Nielson wiped the sweat from his head with a spare handkerchief. "It's more than nerves, man. I can't go through with this."

Buck's grip tightened on his friend. "Nielson, don't play with me. It's cold feet, and nothing more. You love this girl, right?" Nielson nodded. Buck continued, "Does she love you?"

"Yes." Then, he gulped. "Wait, what if she's changed her mind? What if she's getting cold feet about me right now? What if—"

"Dude," Buck interjected, "Don't make me send you to your wedding with a black eye."

Nielson smile was nervous, but he straightened his posture. Buck released his friend from his grip. "You have nothing to worry about. You two are in love, and you're about to marry the woman of your dreams who loves you so much that she transferred her job to a freighter-for-hire in the Presidential Service just so she could be with you." Buck nodded at the groom. "That's one hell of a woman if you ask me."

The groom and his best man stood in front of the platform, upon which stood a fifteen-foot visual com screen, specially ordered for Nielson and Jamina's wedding occasion. Jamina wanted a traditional wedding but refused to burden the *Lindman* with traveling all the way to Lhiesto to have a priest conduct the ceremony. After all, the two choices for galactic marriages included the traditional method involving a priest – but they were found only at the Monastery on distant planet of Lhiesto – or by utilizing the powers of a shuttle Captain under the service of the Presidential Fleet. The com screen was the answer they were looking for.

Nielson knew that the ceremony would start at any moment. Jamina had chosen a simple ceremony. No flower girl or ring bearer; no bridesmaids or groomsmen. Just Nielson and Jamina, and Nielson's best man, Kront, since he had allowed them to marry on his ship. Kront acted more like an adult ring-bearer anyway.

The prelude music softened and stopped, and the processional music began. The audience rose to its feet, and the doors at the back of the large room opened, revealing the most beautiful bride. At least she was according to Nielson.

With Juliet sleeves and an open back, her plunging V-neck and lightly-glittered veil of lace struck every man in the room with awe. The ladies hugged and cried. She was a stunning sight. In that moment, Nielson had never been more sure of his love, for he focused on nothing but her face, keeping his gaze locked to hers in a bonded connection of love.

Kront leaned over to the groom and whispered, "You lucky bastard." Jamina took the last three steps up to stand next to Nielson, and they turned together – hand-in-hand – to face the priest on the visual screen.

The priest smiled upon the couple and began his usual wedding speech. "Dearly beloved, we are gathered here today....."

Miranda's eyes were filled with tears. "I love weddings. They're always so beautiful."

Helena smiled. "I couldn't agree more."

"One day, it'll be you up there, girlie!" Jaime ribbed her teenaged companion. Miranda wrinkled her face in disgust and turned back toward the happy couple. However, Miranda couldn't help but think of her future in that moment. *I wonder if I ever will get married*, she pondered. *Am I meant for marriage? Could I ever feel that special feeling that so many people feel?* She looked at

Jaime and Helena. *Easy for them: they're beautiful. I could see them getting picked up easily.* She thought of herself. *I don't know about me. Maybe I'm just not marital material. Maybe not now...maybe not ever...* She shook her head and focused back on the wedding.

"For as Tyler Nielson and Jamina Sonklod have consented together in wedlock and have witnessed the same before this company, by the authority vested in me by the Presidential Senate I now pro...." The transmission cut off in the middle of the priest's sentence.

"What happened?" Nielson turned to Kront.

"Probably just a computer glitch." He jogged over to the control monitor, rechecked the cables and settings, and tried to restart the screen, but it remained a black picture. "Let me check the ship's radar. It might be passing interference." Nielson held on to his bride's shaking hands.

Miranda's eyes widened. "I've got a bad feeling about this."

Helena nodded. "Me, too. Get ready."

"I hope not," Jaime added.

Kront slammed his fist on the desk, seeming much angrier than a computer glitch would make him. "Damn it! Battle stations! We're under attack!"

Jamina began to cry and sunk down to the floor. Miranda jumped over several seats and ran down the aisle as Helena and Jaime followed behind her.

Miranda knelt down next to the bride and groom. "Nielson, go with Kront. Jaime will take care of Jamina. She's the best sniper at the Academy. Nothing can get by her, right?" She looked to her companion for agreement.

"Right," Jaime nodded. "Jamina, don't worry. Come with me." The two left the room for the main part of the ship. Other troops and crew members ran through different exits to their various stations to prepare for battle.

It pulled at Helena's heart strings to see Nielson and Jamina pulled from each other moments before the finalization of their ceremony, but a battle was waging. Nielson, Miranda, Helena, and Kront were the last ones to leave the large room. They quickly found their seats at the Bridge and joined the fight.

Kront ordered, "Miranda, get on the scanner and radio."

She hurried over to a console on his right and began scanning. "Captain, we have two very large Chase-class Trikkyas ships approaching from the rear, speed at Hyperspace +1."

Kront restated, "Chase-class?

Miranda nodded, "Yes, sir." She turned back to her radar screen and yelled, "Plasma charge! Impact in eight seconds,"

"Nielson, we need an evasive maneuver, now!"

Nielson pulled the steering rod as hard as he could.

"Hold on, everyone," the Academy student warned. "It'll be a close—" The plasma charge exploded and shook the ship as though it had an onboard earthquake. "Plasma charge missed, Captain, but it was too close to not have damaged the ship."

"Thank you, Officer Holliday. Lieutenant Holley, did we get those shields repaired?"

"Yes, sir, but max capacity is only 80%."

Kront frowned. "That'll have to do. Shields at maximum capacity, Lieutenant."

"Shields online, Captain."

Miranda turned up the strength knob on the scanner. "Captain, the Trikkyas have a new kind of armor. I'm detecting four Fly-Class Trikkyas ships, coming in full-speed from above."

Kront pushed the com button. "All squad leaders, open fire on all Trikkyas Fly-Class ships. Repeat: open fire on all Trikkyas Fly-Class ships. Shoot them down!" Kront returned to the conversation in the room. "Miranda, how quickly can you adjust the scanner to temporarily include the new armor types?"

Miranda pursed her lips together and used a nearby calculator to run some numbers. "Captain, I need two minutes."

"Make it one minute."

"Captain," Nielson reported, "two of the Fly-Class ships are down, but we're taking a beating, sir. They're much faster and lighter than this ship."

"There goes another!" Helena added.

Kront's voice turned toward his last hope. "Miranda?"

"Just a few more seconds, Captain." Then, Miranda made the happy announcement. "Sir, it's done. The scanner's picked up eight more Fly-Class ships inbound, light armor, easy targets. One of the Chase-Class ships is heavily damaged. A simple ion blast would take care of it."

Kront nodded. "Nielson? Fire away."

"Firing ion blast," Nielson repeated. The ire in his voice was only part of the anger and frustration he felt in the ruination of his wedding day by this Trikkyas battle. "Success!"

"Sir, the Trikkyas are pulling back," Helena stated.

Kront hung his head. "Thank goodness." He pushed the ship's com button. "All stations, report."

"Engine room: no damage."

"Mid-section: small hull breached. Repaired. One sent to the Medic Center with small burns."

"Front section: no damage."

Kront was ready to celebrate until the last section's report came in. "Rear section: hull breach. One dead."

The Captain couldn't believe his ears. Helena stood up and joined him. She pressed the com button. "This is Lieutenant Holley. Name of the casualty?"

"Ma'am, it's Moniqé Nastas. She got hit in the head from the blast of the plasma charge. She went quickly. Probably didn't feel a thing." Helena looked at Kront; he slunk down to his seat. She pressed the com button again. "Battle stations, stand down. Everyone report to the Hangar." She used her hand to motion for Nielson and Miranda to leave the room so Helena could talk to Kront. Once the two were alone, Helena knelt down beside his chair. "Captain?" He didn't respond. "Kront? We need to address the crew."

He didn't blink. He didn't really move much at all. "Helena, I…I just…another casualty…"

She wrapped her arms around him. "Sir, I can't use tears or words to take away the pain or grief you feel. But I can remind you of the importance of our mission." She stood up. "Just like all of the others, Moniqé would want you to continue, sir. That's all we can do."

"As you all know, Moniqé Nastas lost her life today when we were attacked by the Trikkyas," Kront said, barely above a whisper. "Most likely they attacked because they discovered our mission." He raised an eyebrow and scanned his troops. "There must be a rat somewhere in our ranks. Only a handful of people outside of this ship know what we're doing."

Helena took over the conversation. "We're starting an internal investigation. Intelligence Officer Miranda Holliday and Specialist Jaime Holley will do the questioning. If you do not cooperate, you will be arrested and immediately deported to the prison on Planet Grildoom."

Miranda exchanged glances with Jaime. Neither of them knew of this plan; both were quite surprised at the extreme actions. Helena walked over to the girls after dismissing the troops, Kront at her heels with his head slightly lower than usual. "I know you both may be confused, but we need your help. Miranda, use the lie detector you built. Jaime, assist Miranda in whatever she needs. Question the crew, and find the rat."

Miranda nodded. "Okay. If you don't mind, we'll use your room since it's sound proof. We'll set up a visual recorder and patch it through to the Captain's quarters Captain and you can look for any nonverbal clues we may miss."

Helena nodded. "Thank you for doing this." She turned to Kront. "Have no fear, Captain, the girls are here."

He half-smiled and let out a deep, sad sigh, a sigh that brought more worry to the girls' faces. Helena stopped walking away as she and the two Academy students watched Kront trudge his feet along the path that would lead him back to the Bridge. He passed by Jamina and Nielson, hugging and crying near the entrance to the Control Center. He didn't stop to say a word, but patted Nielson on the back and closed the door behind him as he entered the main part of the ship.

At that moment, Miranda was determined more than ever to make a smile come back to Kront's face. *Whatever it takes*, she swore to herself. *Whatever it takes…*

* * *

Kront held his head in his hands. The only person on the Bridge in the middle of the night, he tempered his voice so as to not raise alarm within the confines of the *Lindman*. A secret meeting with the Handlon Prime Commander wouldn't look good on his resume, peace treaty or no peace treaty. "I'm begging you, Prime Commander, release the Trikkyas king. It's bound to cause more damage than good. Who knows what the Trikkyas people may be planning as we speak!"

The Prime Commander sneered. "Captain Tallin, I'm surprised that you would doubt our efforts to...*persuade*...the Trikkyas race to end their war against your people. Without a king, they have no leadership by which to run their forces." He smiled. "Have no fears, Captain. All will go according to plans."

"I hope you're right."

Chapter 15. – Truth Be Told.

"I'm ready. Bring in the first crew member," Miranda asked Jaime. Jamie nodded and walked over to the door of Helena's room that Miranda and she temporarily occupied as the Lie Detector room. Miranda sat down behind one side of Helena's desk and went over the machine's settings for a fourth time. She glanced over her list of questions and reviewed the interrogation tactics she learned from classes at the Academy.

Before Jaime opened the door, she called out to Miranda. "Hey." She waited until Miranda looked up at her. "We know they're all innocent."

"We hope," Miranda corrected her friend." Jaime didn't say anything; she just opened the door. Helena stepped into the room. The Academy students were stunned.

"I know what you're thinking," Helena started, raising her hands in her defense, "But Kront and I believed the crew would cooperate more if they say me participating, too."

Miranda looked to Jaime who only shrugged her shoulders. She closed the door and sat down next to it, showing Helena her seat across from Miranda. The Level 90 student situated the five sensors on Helena in various locations. "I'm going to ask you a series of yes-and-no response-type questions. In order to find a baseline, I need you to purposely answer 'yes' to the first four questions. Do you understand?"

Helena nodded. "Yes, ma'am."

Jaime stifled a laugh. Miranda shook her head. "I'll never get used to that. Question number one: is your name Helena Holley?"

"Yes." The line on the paper didn't budge.

The interrogator marked the result on the printed paper. "Have you ever been selected as Queen of Troklon?"

"Yes." The line spiked.

Miranda marked the answer again. "Are you a crew member aboard the *Lindman*?"

"Yes." Again, the line didn't budge.

"Are you married?"

"Yes." For the second time, a spike appeared on the detector.

Miranda marked the spike. "Thank you, Lieutenant, but now the real questions begin. You must answer with the truth. Understand that anything you say can and will be used against you if you are found guilty of any crimes against the *Lindman*, the Senate, or the Presidential Federation. Do you understand and accept your rights?"

"Yes, I do," she replied.

Miranda nodded to Jaime who nodded back. "First question: have you ever killed a crew member of the *Lindman*?"

"No."

The lie detector's line didn't budge from a straight path. "Second question: have you ever conspired with an alien race to attack the *Lindman* or any other galactic ship, shuttle, planet, or race?"

The lieutenant's eyes widened. "No." *Damn,* she thought to herself, *these are some serious fucking questions.*

Again, thankfully, the detector showed no spikes. "Have you ever been questioned by an alien race about the *Lindman* or any other galactic ship, shuttle, planet, or race?"

"Yes."

Miranda shot a quick glance toward Jaime. Her friend's widened eyes and raised eyebrows were a clue that the two felt the same: the news came as a big shock that sunk into the pits of their stomachs. In addition, the lie detector showed it wasn't a lie. "Have you had inappropriate contact with an alien race? Examples include spying for the enemy, stealing valuable information, etc."

"No." No spike on the screen.

"Last question: did you know about this morning's attack on the *Lindman*?"

"No." No spike.

"Phew," Miranda sighed. "Thank goodness. You're all clear, Lieutenant Holley."

"Thank you, girls. This is very important to Kront and me." She turned to leave the room. "I'll send in the next person."

A knock sounded on Kront's door. He knew exactly who stood at his door. "Come in, ladies." Helena, Miranda, and Jaime crossed the threshold into his office. They took a seat and looked around as he closed out of a few programs and windows on his monitor and turned it from their view. "I just spoke with Captain Grillo of the *Saint Triantle*. It seems they had a traitor aboard who overheard our plans for the recovery of the Handlon fortress items. So, what's your report?"

"After an exhaustive eighteen hours of interrogations—" Miranda began.

"—and only one lunch break—" Jaime chimed in.

The interrogator mockingly sneered at her friend. "Captain, I'm happy to report that there are no traitors aboard your vessel."

Kront rested his head in his hands, propped up by his elbows on his desk. He ran his fingers through his hair and messed up his crew cut, but he could care less right now. "That's such a relief to my mind." When he looked up, he noticed the ladies weren't smiling. "What's wrong?"

"Sir," Helena mumbled, "There's something else we need to discuss."

"A *few* something else's," Jaime explained, crossing her arms.

Miranda pulled her notes out from her folder. "Captain Fonty Dlags from Alpha Squad admitted to stealing 250 Titanium bars from the cargo brought back from the raid on the Handlon base on Planet Helgin."

Kront frowned. "It's not treason, but it's not acceptable behavior on my ship or as a member of my crew." He turned toward Helena. "After this meeting, I want to talk to him." She nodded in response.

"In addition," Miranda continued, "Captain Blake Jameson went on a solo mission after the Handlon War was over. He raided two abandoned Handlon bases, finding and keeping over 25 million credits and enough weapons and armor for 400 troops."

"Again, it's not illegal, but I'm actually offended he didn't ask us to join," he tried to joke. "Helena?"

"Say no more. I've got it." She knew he wanted to talk to Blake, as well.

*   *   *

The shuttle began its descent over Planet Loht 9. "T-minus two minutes to touchdown. Snipers, prepare to position upon landing." Buck turned off the com. He and the rest of the S.S.A.U. team finished gearing up, including a new member to cover Moniqé's position: Jens Nessau.

Miranda took a deep breath. *Okay, it's time. I can do this. I can do this,* she tried to convince herself. Suddenly, the Sniper Creed of the Old came into her mind. She had first seen it during her fourth year at the Academy. It was a wall-hanging in one of her weapons' classrooms. It read:

> "May your shots be precise,
> May you stay clear and cool,
> May the wind guide your bullet to its target,
> and May you stay invisible to the enemy."

Its format read somewhat similar to Irish blessings given by the Irish people on Planet Earth. She had read about some of the cultures on earth in a book she found during one of her meanderings in the Academy's library. Earth people were a weird people.

The bumpy landing of the shuttle shifted her from her wandering thoughts and brought her back to the present moment. Within a split second, the two Academy students exited the back of the ship to their first position. It was a small shelf on the north side of the mountain that faced the abandoned Handlon base; small enough to hide them, but just big enough for both of them to fit with their weapons, they scurried to the area, built a small stone wall to protect them from enemy fire, and made two small holes in the wall for the barrels of their guns.

Miranda called back to Helena on her personal com, "Team Foxtrot in position. Over."

"Roger that, Foxtrot. Team Bravo entering the base; keep an eye out on our backs."

Jaime grabbed the com from Miranda. "How about four eyes?"

"Roger that. Bravo out."

The girls could tell that Helena snickered when she heard

Jaime's comment. The younger Holley sister opened the weapons bag and took out the two Sniper Blasters, handing one to her companion. "Did you bring your scanner?"

"Hell, yeah, I did!" Miranda stated confidently.

"Good," Jaime nodded. "Keep an eye on the radar so we don't get our asses kicked while trying to save Helena's fat ass." The girls laughed, feeling like school girls at the same time feeling like trained assassins. Jaime reached back into the bag. "By the way, fat-ass got us a little gift." In her hands were two silencers. "They're Classic Blaster Silencers, but Helena had Reggi upgrade them to fit our Sniper Blasters. Problem is we only get twenty-five shots apiece, so let's hope there aren't more than fifty Trikkyas troops today."

Blip-blip, the radar sounded off. Miranda studied the radar. "Speaking of which, we've got company." She punched in some numbers and brought up an additional screen. "Looks like thirty Trikkyas. Call it in."

"You got it." Jaime turned on the com they shared. "Bravo, this is Foxtrot. We've got company. Looks like thirty Trikkyas headed your way. Standard two-by-two formation. Approximate distance is 1900 feet away. Standby for update."

"Foxtrot, this is Bravo. We're almost to the underground fortress. Happy hunting. Over."

Jamie turned off the com and tucked it away. She adjusted her scope and looked towards the target location indicated by the scanner. "Let's do this." Her friend nodded. Jaime took the reins and led Miranda in weaponry. Miranda may have had the brains, but Jaime trained hard – very hard – to become an expert in dealing with weapons, and now as top student, she wanted to prove her skills on the battlefield: she wanted to be more than a great shot; she wanted to prove her skills as a leader, too. "You take the right side, and I take the left," she explained. "We shoot the back rows first, leading up to the front. Shoot at the same time, like we are one shot, so they think there's only one sniper."

For several minutes they waited as the Trikkyas marched closer: 1900 feet, 1800 feet, 1700 feet. At 1700 feet, the Trikkyas were close enough, but the girls couldn't risk making a single mistake. They wanted to be absolutely sure…1600 feet…1500 feet…

"Here we go," Jaime whispered.

Miranda placed her eye comfortably against the scope, took a deep breath, and adjusted for wind. She followed her first target step-by-step as he walked closer to the base's entrance where Team Bravo had disappeared.

"Ready...Aim...Fire." The two Sniper Blasters fired, and the two Trikkyas in the back line dropped to the ground. "Reposition...Ready...Aim...Fire." The newest last row dropped to their knees and fell over dead. Now the troops numbered four less but marched only 1200 feet away.

"We're not going fast enough," Miranda realized.

Jaime swiftly agreed. "We take out two more lines, and then we take out the front line, remove the silencer, and let loose." By repeating the "ready-aim-fire" process twice, the girls had dropped four more Handlons in less than ten seconds. "Front line focus. Ready...Aim...Fire." The front line dropped, and the remaining twenty Trikkyas brought up their weapons, searching the area for enemy soldiers and moving targets. One of them heard a noise and shot at a rock nowhere near Miranda and Jamie.

"Time to have fun," Jaime smiled as the two girls removed their silencers and repositioned themselves into the ground. With only a second or two between shots, the students shot off an assault of bullets directly at the surviving Trikkyas troops. Four of them tried to run toward the base's entrance, but Miranda shot them down. Another three Trikkyas tried to run back to where they came from, but they panicked as they came across the bodies of the back-line troops. The Academy girls didn't stop firing, and Trikkyas bodies didn't stop falling dead. Eventually, only two Trikkyas remained. The situation stunned them; they hit their knees, threw their weapons far from them, and interlaced their fingers behind their heads. Miranda and Jaime pulled their faces away from their scopes, surprised by the lack of desire to die for the Trikkyas cause in protecting the Handlon base and its contents.

Miranda and Jaime stealthily crept from their hiding spot. As Jaime covered for Miranda, the latter pulled out and turned on their com unit. "Team Bravo, this is Foxtrot. Top-side is clear. Twenty-eight down, two in custody."

"Foxtrot, this is Bravo. Roger that. Package secure. All clear on our end. We're about to surface. Keep watch, and great job. Bravo out."

Chapter 16. – Let's Go Home.

Kront smiled as the hostages were brought to their knees in front of him. "Jindso! Tena! Take our...*guests*...to their new quarters." The two crew members saluted as they took the Trikkyas soldiers into the main part of the ship. "Now, let's hear all about this mission report, shall we?" He motioned for Teams Bravo and Foxtrot to enter the Conference Room. "Please, take a seat."

"Sir, I don't believe Jens and Mason need to be de-briefed on this mission," Helena offered. Kront nodded and dismissed them with his hand. They stood, saluted their leader, and left the room, closing the door behind them.

Team Foxtrot gave their report to Kront. He smiled and swiveled his chair to face Helena. "Your report, Lieutenant?" Kront asked.

"Of course, sir." Helena smiled. "Team Bravo entered the Handlon base after Team Foxtrot was set up. We cleared the area and searched for the tunnel entrance. At first, it was not easy to find, but Mason noticed a small difference in one of the walls. It turned out to be a cover—a fake. We made our way behind the fake wall and down the three-mile-long path to the room found on the scanner by Captain Grillo's crew. We encountered no enemy targets, so we entered. We found four large shelves covered with dust. On one of the shelves was a small wooden chest. It took Jens nearly ten minutes to open it. We verified the contents, took our leave, and reported back here." She pulled out the disc. "It's all here, sir. This disc contains all of the records of births, deaths, weddings, wars, planet ownerships, and secret mission of the lost Fortress of the Handlon Supreme Council."

Kront shifted in his seat. *Something doesn't feel right,* he pondered. *This feels too easy, like we were set up to find this disc. Like they were busy planning something while we went on a witch hunt.* His eyes darted around with his head lowered, and his fingers twitched a little.

Miranda nudged Jaime. Both of them were catching on to

Kront's uneasiness. "Captain?" Miranda asked. "Something wrong?"

"Probably nothing. I just…never mind. Don't worry about it."

Helena smiled. "Well, Captain Tallin has given me permission to grade your skills in the battlefield. Officer Holliday, you are now a Level 92, Intelligence Level 8, Sniper Level 4. Specialist Holley, I advance you to Level 87, Intelligence Level 3, and Sniper Level 4. Congratulations, both of you!"

The girls leapt up from their seats and hugged their Captain like a favorite uncle. He pushed them back, straightened his uniform, and saluted them. "Ahem, ladies. Congratulations are in order, most definitely." His serious face broke a wide, toothy grin. "In addition, Specialist Holley, Helena has mentioned your interest in finding employment. Perhaps you could be of assistance to my crew as Nielson abandons us temporarily for someone called his wife?"

"Are you serious?" Specialist Holley inquired. "You're not kidding me, are you?"

"Nope," Helena chimed in. "It'd be an honor to finally have you both on board."

Jaime and Miranda hugged each other and jumped up and down. Kront rolled his eyes. His best lieutenant just laughed and shook her head. She finally stopped their bouncing when she said, "Ladies, we still have a wedding to finish. Miranda, please inform Corporal Dlags to set course for Troklon. After his stunt with the Titanium bars, he's on pilot duty for the rest of the trip, or I'll kick his ass into space myself."

*   *   *

Nielson and Jamina stood in front of the large visual com screen again. The priest appeared and smiled. "Are we ready?" Nielson nodded. "All right, then. I now pronounce you Husband and Wife. You may kiss the Bride."

Nielson grabbed Jamina by the shoulders, pulled her close, and forced his mouth onto hers. For several intimate seconds, the audience cheered. The Academy students blushed. Even Helena was shocked at Nielson's behavior. Finally, Nielson pulled back from an apple-red Jamina and wrapped his arms gently around her for a second, more compassionate round of kisses. "I'm sorry, Mrs. Nielson, but I couldn't wait any longer, and I wanted you to feel a smidge of just how much I love you."

Jamina diverted her eyes for a moment. "Mr. Nielson, you can make me feel like that all you want for the rest of our married life." Her response brought another round of applause from the wedding attendants. The com turned off – on purpose, this time – and the crew members settled into their seats in the large room in preparation for a small reception. Jaime and Miranda couldn't wait to give the newlyweds their present, so they ran up to the happy couple.

"Mr. and Mrs. Nielson? Miranda and I have a special wedding present for you," Jaime said.

"It won't fit in the Common Room with the other gifts, so we brought it in here for you!" Miranda walked over to a small side room and opened the double doors. There sat the pink Eisen Speeder.

Jamina screamed in joy. Nielson hung and shook his head. "Oh great," he mumbled.

Kront walked over and slapped his friend on the back. "I think it's definitely your color," he joked. Nielson took a swing at him and nearly love-punched his best man. Kront laughed. "Your poor manhood."

Jamina ditched her groom and ran toward the Speeder. "It's adorable! I love it!"

Neilson walked up behind Miranda and Jaime. "Ladies, thank you, but I think I'll let Jamina have this one solo. It was a nice idea, though."

"But, Nielson," Jaime taunted, "pink is so your color." She winked, and sure enough his cheeks matched the color of his wife's new toy.

"Specialist Belland, report to the Situation Room," Jaime called over the com. Not even an hour after the reception was over for Nielson and Jamina's wedding, the two Academy students were hard at work making sure others got a chance to fall in love, too. As Miranda walked down the hall to the very room mentioned in the com call, she grabbed Buck's arm as he walked toward Officer Holliday. "Sergeant Cypher, let's walk and talk, shall we?" She pulled him into the room from one side; Adriahna entered the other. "Both of you, please have a seat." Using her interrogation skills, Miranda invited an air of tension into the room. Adriahna sat upright and perfectly still while Buck leaned forward on his elbows on the table.

"Officer Holliday, did we do something wrong?" Buck asked.

"No," Miranda answered. "It's the wrong that *could* happen if things are not resolved between the two of you." The two extra parties wore puzzled expressions on their faces. "Buck, recall the hour in which I interrogated you in Lieutenant Holley's quarters."

"Yes, ma'am?"

Miranda smiled, "*Buck* up, man."

Buck looked at Miranda, then at Adriahna, and then back to Miranda. "With all due respect, ma'am, I don't think I—"

Miranda leaned forward on the table, centimeters from his face. "If this tension is not resolved, you might continue making mistakes while on the job. Instead of fixing an electrical error that leads to a shortage, you might electrocute someone or send our ship plummeting down in to the blackened depths of space. Is that what you want, Sergeant?"

He swallowed and straightened his posture. "Specialist Belland…Adriahna…I've been in love with you for the past two years." Adriahna's eyes widened, and right before she could reply, "I've never had the courage to say anything, so here goes: when we land on Troklon, will you have dinner with me?" He lowered his head, waiting in shame for her response of hideous decline. His ears couldn't stand the silence as he knew she would stomp out and tell the crew of her embarrassment.

Instead, he heard a quiet voice say, "Sergeant Cypher, I've been waiting for you to ask me. I'd love to go on a date with you."

Buck raised his head and smiled. The two love birds couldn't keep their eyes off each other. Miranda crossed her arms, highly pleased with the outcome. "My work here is done. Keep it appropriate so long as you are on this ship," she warned them before exiting the room and closing the door behind her.

Miranda went up to the Bridge. "Reporting for duty, Captain." She winked at Jaime who giggled. Kront heard the female noises and looked up from his work station. Jaime turned back to her com station. Nielson and Jamina were busy packing for their honeymoon, so Kront had Jaime hard at work already. "Miranda?" he inquired. "What's so funny?"

Helena joined everyone on the Bridge. "Sir, have you seen Sergeant Cypher? He's not in the Engine room where I thought he'd be."

Jamie started to laugh again. "You might want to check the Situation Room."

"Or Adriahna's or his quarters," Miranda mumbled under her breath.

Helena smiled. "Are you two playing matchmakers again?"

Kront rolled his eyes and smacked his forehead. "If you two keep this up, everyone will be married off, and I won't have a crew to run my ship!" They three ladies busted up into fits of laughter. Miranda walked over to her station and sat down. She realized her radar was showing activity. "Captain, something large just appeared on the long-range scanner."

The laughter died off, and a more serious atmosphere returned to the shuttle's Bridge. Kront looked down to his screen. "Well, what is it?"

"I'm not sure, sir." Miranda squinted and cocked her head slightly. "It's moving quite fast and is still growing, almost like..."

Helena prodded, "Like that, Miranda?"

"Like a bomb went off," she quietly uttered. For one long moment, the crew members on the Bridge didn't move.

Kront negated, "A bomb? That's highly irregular. Which direction is it coming from?"

Miranda increased the scanner's power by turning the knob all the way to the right. "It's definitely a blast wave of some kind. It's at approximately 200,000 miles and growing." She punched in some numbers and gasped when the answer appeared on her screen."

Jaime looked over at Miranda. "What's wrong?" She caught a glimpse of her friend's screen. "No...no, it can't be. That's can't be right."

"What the hell is going on?" Kront demanded. "Officer Holliday!"

She gulped and replied, "Sir...it's Troklon...it's gone."

*   *   *

"But… my p-parents," Jaime stuttered, "all of our friends, the Academy—the Senate!" Tears streamed down her face. Even Miranda felt the waterworks hinder her vision.

Kront's heart raced so fast he was sure it would burst inside his chest, if not from the speed then from the pain and grief of this latest emotional blow. He grabbed the ship's com and slammed on the button. "All squad leaders, report to the Bridge, now! All crew members, report to the Hangar immediately!"

"Officer Holliday, test a sample of the blast," Helena directed. "We need to know what kind of explosion occurred, natural or designed."

Miranda nodded, "Yes, Lieutenant." She turned to her monitor, fingers flying across the numerous keys and dials.

"Specialist Holley," Kront commanded, "get Frigal on the com. I want to know what's going on."

"Yes, Captain. Right away." She sniffled and used the sleeve of her shirt to wipe away the tears from her face as anger began to set in. She set up a com call to Frigal. "Frigal, this is the *Lindman*. Emergency contact from Captain Kront. Please accept immediately."

Marshal's face popped up on the screen. "Specialist Holley, is this about Troklon?"

Jaime's jaw dropped. "You know?"

Kront and Helena repeated. "They know?"

Miranda questioned, "But how?"

Marshal interrupted the nonsense. "Yes, we know. Commander Hellond," he called over his shoulder, "it's Captain Kront."

"Jaime, transfer this com to the big screen"

"Yes, Captain Kront." Jaime sent a few commands to a program on her computer. The visual com disappeared from Kront's individual monitor and appeared on the large screen at the front of the room.

Groyt appeared on the screen. "Kront, you've heard?"

"No, sir. Our radar picked it up. How did Frigal find out?"

Groyt shook his head, "Professor Nikolej Holley informed the Senate."

The room aboard the *Lindman* fell silent. All eyes turned

toward Jaime and Helena. "Our parents?" Helena asked.

"Yes, Lieutenant Holley. But I'll explain later. Right now we need to focus on the survivors."

"Survivors?" Miranda stood up from her seat. "How did anyone survive that explosion?"

Groyt appeared to answer, but the sound didn't accompany his voice. Suddenly, the entire screen turned white: the picture had disappeared. A bad feeling stirred in the room as each person felt the same thing. "Jaime," Kront nearly whispered, "retry the connection to Commander Hellond.

She pushed the buttons on the com unit. "Sir, the call won't go through. The signal numbers won't lock." She looked toward Miranda, meeting eyes that feared the same fate as Troklon.

Helena looked to a white-faced Kront. "Sir?"

His eyes did not leave the large screen where Commander Hellond's face was last seen. "Miranda, check the radar for Planet Frigal."

The Academy student gulped. "Sir, the radar indicates another explosion. It's Frigal."

Kront lowered his head and took several deep breaths. Then, with the air of his full command and experience, he stood up, gripped his hands, tightened his expression, and took back control of his ship. "Specialist Holley, inform all Presidential Fleet ships of the situation." She nodded and began to contact the com officers for each ship in the service. "Officer Holliday, what have the scans determined about the blast compounds?"

Miranda shook her head. "You're not going to like it, Captain."

"I haven't liked a single thing that's gone on the past several minutes, Officer Holliday. What I need is the truth, and all of it."

"Attention!" Helena's voice carried through the Situation Room. The squad leaders saluted as Captain Tallin entered through a side door, accompanied by Nielson and Jamina. It was obvious she had been crying, but with such a tense environment at bay, no one spoke up to ask. A transmission carried the discussion from the room to the soldiers in the Hangar so all in the ship could hear it.

Kront stood at the front of the room. He stood at attention

but paced the room. "The information I am about to divulge is Classified Top Secret. It may be hard to hold back any reactions, reservations, or other remarks you may have, but I demand that you hold your tongue until I am done speaking." He paused for two seconds before continuing. "About thirty minutes ago, the *Lindman Scanner* – developed by Officer Holliday – detected a large explosion in space. At first we could not identify the wave of blast material. Was it natural? Was it chemical?" Again he paused, including his pacing around the room. "Was it designed? We discovered that Planet Troklon had been destroyed."

Loud riots of noise erupted from the Hangar: yells, cries, shouts, and tears. Some soldiers fell to their knees; others hugged their neighbors in an effort to find solace. Kront just let them get it out. Then, he raised his hands, and the commanding officers in the Hangar were able to get silence in the echoing room.

"The whole planet is gone. We made contact with Planet Frigal. Commander Hellond was explaining the situation to us and telling us of survivors when…when we lost the signal. Frigal is gone, as well." The second round of noise was more desperate. The realization that two very beloved planets were demolished had set in to the hearts and minds of the troops under Kront's command. "The *Lindman Scanner* identified the blast material as a chemical compound known as Triktysol, a common element found in bombs made by the Trikkyas people. We do not know if the Trikkyas race is behind this, but we are not excluding them as suspects. We need to focus on the next steps we must take in moving forward. First Pilot and Mrs. Tyler Nielson, please step forward." Tyler and Jamina walked up to the front of the room and stood on Kront's right side. "First Pilot and Mrs. Tyler Nielson are risking their lives in order to help the survivors of Planet Troklon. They are flying to Planet Earth to ask for help."

Buck interrupted. "Sir, that's a suicide mission!"

Helena's eyes burned holes into Buck. "Sergeant Cypher! Captain Tallin gave a very specific order—"

"But he's right," Drenge interjected. Helena lost her will to argue and looked to Kront. The Captain listened to the pleas of his squad leaders. "Earth is 23.8 billion miles away. It'll take them six months to get there, and another six months to get back."

"Not to mention the Asteroid Belt and the Black Hole of

Aramea," Michael chimed in.

John sat forward in his chair. "No offense, Captain and Lieutenant, but the Earth people are known for being extremely selfish people. What if they refuse to help? What then?"

Miranda couldn't take it anymore. She slammed her hands down on the table and stared into the faces of the squad leaders. "And what if the Presidential Fleet is next? And what if we survive and are taken as hostages, sent to wander the deserts alone on the Handlon Planet of Wrisjok?" She stood up to her full height, though much shorter than the men. "Should we not try? Tyler and Jamina volunteered. Give them a chance! Give Earth a chance. Give the survivors of Troklon a chance…If you're not willing to send them, then you can go in their stead!" She stormed out of the room, and Jaime followed, tears streaming down from her face.

"As I was saying," Kront picked back up, "we've made contact with the other 24 Presidential Cruisers. We twenty-five Admirals are the Acting Senate until we can get help. You must continue with your jobs as best you can. Seek counseling when you need it. Do not act as though you have been unaffected by this tragedy; it was only serve to worsen the symptoms. Alpha Squad?"

Sigu stood up and saluted at attention. "Sir, yes, sir!"

"I want your squad to report to the Handlon base on Planet Helgin. I've contacted them, and they've granted up temporary stay for the survivors. We don't know how many were able to escape before Troklon was destroyed. Hope for the best…but expect the worst…"

Chapter 17. – The New Order.

For two hours non-stop, Miranda stared at the radar on her screen, hoping for traces of any life form after the explosion on either planet. She shook her head in frustration. "Captain, I'm just not getting anything."

"I wasn't expecting you to find anything," he replied with a sigh. "Time to change our focus, Officer Holliday. Program your scanner to search for the explosive Triktysol. We'll fly to as many planets as possible, scanning for bombs and dismantling any we find before they go off." Kront turned to Jaime's direction. "Specialist Holley, send out an intergalactic message for all survivors to head to Planet Helgin."

Her forehead wrinkled in confusion. "But, sir, won't the Trikkyas hear that, too? What if they try to attack Helgin?"

"I'm not worried," he stated bluntly. "With the war over, the Handlons are a much more peaceful people, and King Davkylt – among others – has assured me the assistance of his soldiers and shuttles if we just ask, especially with this tragedy." Jaime nodded.

"*Lindman*, come in. This is the *Holliday*." Jamie looked up at her visual com screen. Nielson was smiling at her. "Hi, Nielson. How can we help you?"

"Please get Captain Tallin on the line, will ya?"

She called over her shoulder for Kront. "Nielson demands your attention, Captain."

Kront smiled. "Thank you, Jamie. Patch him through." Nielson's face transferred from Jaime's screen to Kront's monitor. "Yes, Nielson?"

"Incoming scan, sir." His radar sent a still image to the large monitor aboard the *Lindman*. "As you can see, we're approximately four million miles from Troklon space. Only a few minutes ago, we discovered several blips on the screen: over 200 small Trikkyas fighters are headed your way. At their current speed, they'll arrive in twelve hours. After that, they may try to attack Helgin…and the survivors."

Miranda spoke up, "Sir, at that speed, they're most likely Fly-Class Speeders."

Kront nodded in agreement. "Specialist Holley, get *Vilantex* on the com. We need backup. Helena, have the Squad Leaders prepare their troops for battle. They're coming in fast and hard. We'll take sleep-shifts tonight. When they get here, we'll be ready."

Buck stopped in his tracks, trying to catch his breath. He had spent the past hour running around the *Lindman*, giving orders to everyone in preparation for their next intergalactic battle. He placed his hands on his hips, and inhaled and exhaled slowly. He noticed one of Delta's squad members sitting on the ground. "Greddy!" he called out. The young man didn't seem to hear him. He walked closer toward the crew member. "Greddy, are you okay?"

Greddy Monk from Delta Squad faced toward the direction of Buck's voice. He immediately stood up and stood at attention, saluting his superior. "Sergeant Cypher, sir! I was just—I was...you know, resting, sir. I h-haven't slept well..."

Buck placed his hand on Greddy's right shoulder. "Greddy, don't make up excuses. Just tell me the truth."

Greddy's shoulders slumped forward; his voice went hoarse. "Sir, my grandmother raised me to be a good man, a right and just man. Frankly, sir, there's no way that woman could've made it off Troklon. She's in a wheelchair, sir."

Buck stepped back as the downhearted soul walked past him and began filling up the shuttles with ammunition. His words stuck with Sergeant Cypher the rest of the day.

*   *   *

"Lieutenant Holley, report to the Bridge."

Helena laughed. It was still weird for her to hear her sister's voice in place of Nielson's in making the com calls on the *Lindman*. She made her way up to find Jaime. Miranda was sitting at her station, waiting for her next order from Kront. "Yes, Jaime?"

"Oh, hey, Helena. The *Vilantex* will arrive in about eight hours. Seems the Fly-Class Speeders hit them about four hour ago. The crew reports heavy damage, but they are still willing and able to fight."

Helena smiled, unable to hold it back any longer. "Good to

hear. By the way, I have some good news for the three of us. Jaime stared at her sister and leaned forward in her chair. Miranda was all-ears, as well. "I just received a com call…from Mom and Dad." Her younger sister's eyes began to water. Miranda leaned over to hug her Academy friend. "They arrived alive and well at the base on Helgin."

Jaime sniffled and wiped away some tears. "How did they get away? How did they know about the bomb?"

Helena smiled, "We can thank Miranda for the answers to both of those questions. They escaped in the SHX 2000 Personnel Transporter that she bought them 6 years ago which was equipped—"

"—with the *Lindman Scanner*!" Miranda interjected. "I taught them how to read it, but I never expected it to pick up anything like a Trikkyas bomb."

"Well, it did," Helena pointed out, "and it saved many, many lives."

The three girls hugged in silence for a few moments before Kront entered the room. "Sorry to break the girlie moment, ladies, but we've got work to do. Officer Holliday and Specialist Holley, are you ready to graduate?"

The jaws of the two students dropped to the floor. "Captain?" Miranda asked.

The lieutenant laughed. "Before the Professors took off, they were able to save several other students. All in all, of the 800 students and 35 teachers, most of them survived because of the scanner you implemented into their shuttle. They got word to the Academy, and the teachers volunteered to shuttle students to safety on their personal vehicles."

"In addition," Captain Tallin stated, "the remaining teachers agreed in a conference a few moments ago that all students Level 85 and up are automatically upgraded to level 100." The girls looked at each other, and then to Helena and Kront. "In other words, you two are full-time members of my ship. Welcome to the *Lindman*."

*   *   *

"Attention all *Lindman* crew members," Jamie announced

over the ship's com system, "I have uploaded to the computer the list of survivors from the Troklon explosion. As a reminder, no one survived the Frigal explosion. Our hearts go out to you, the family members and friends affected by these tragedies. Captain Tallin reminds you to seek counseling when appropriate, and do not be afraid to discuss your concerns with your superiors if you believe they are affecting your ability to function properly in your position aboard this ship. God be with you." As she turned off the com, she noticed an influx of crew members sign in to the computer system to check for names. They nearly overloaded the system in the first few minutes. She sighed and hung her head; she knew that only about 30 % of the crew would find familiar names on the survivors' list. Too many were lost on Troklon. All were lost on Frigal. Kront entered the room, and Jaime whipped around in her chair. "Captain, request permission to suit up and fight the Fly-Class Speeders."

Before he could answer, Miranda stood up. "Captain, request permission to accompany Specialist Holley."

Kront stared down at his newest, full-time crew members. "Before you decide on revenge, research the terrain and come up with a plan that I can approve. I want you to prove you're doing this with your head and not your gut."

"Already done," Miranda stated. She handed Kront a few papers in her hand. She winked at Jaime as though she had read Kront's mind ahead of time.

He nodded. "Permission granted. Ask Sergeant Flort where to find the titanium-tip bullets. He says they go straight through the cockpit glass to hit a bull's-eye on each pilot." He shrugged his shoulders. "Don't take my word for it, though. You might need to…ahem…go test try them for him." He winked at the girls, and they took off to find Sigu. He wasn't leaving until they'd had a good word or two with him about these awesome bullets.

"So, what's the plan?" Jaime looked at her companion; they stepped out onto the hull of the *Lindman*.

"No idea. I just printed something out for Captain to look at." Miranda smiled. "You're the best sniper. You've got to pick the good spot and set us up for success."

"Thanks," Jaime responded with sarcasm. She quickly

scanned the rear of the ship and pointed to an area on their right. "There's a small rounding in the hull over there. If we lie down in it, we can shoot from it unnoticed since our suits are the same color. Like camouflage. It's perfect."

"Sounds great!" Miranda's usual nerves were building up, but this time the feeling was different. It wasn't just revenge. The Handlons were paid to fight them, so it wasn't really a battle of hard feelings between them. This was definitely a different story: the Trikkyas had to pay. As the two girls settled into position, Miranda called over the com system, "What's the status on those fighters, Captain?"

"E.T.A. in about twenty minutes. Clear shots about 3,000 feet out."

"Roger that. When can we expect the fighters?"

"Approximately 4,000 feet out."

"Copy that. Foxtrot out."

Jaime ribbed her sidekick. "Here they come."

Miranda radioed in, "*Lindman*, this is Foxtrot. Trikkyas Fly-Class Speeders at 15,000 feet, eighty miles per hour. Estimate thirty seconds to range."

Kront jumped up in his fighter, buckled up his seat harness, and turned on his com. "Attention all squad leaders and shuttle pilots: the enemy has arrived. Let's give them a warm welcome." The cheers from the pilots of the thirty-two fighters could be heard echoing throughout the Hangar.

"Speeders 5,000 feet," Miranda warned.

"Move out!" Kront directed.

Helena turned on her com. "*Vilantex*, this is the *Lindman*. We are on the go!" Looking at the *Vilantex* on the radar, she watched as its 58 fighters soared off into the blackened sky of space toward the 250 enemy ships. Meanwhile, at the rear of the *Lindman*, Miranda took a deep breath and aimed at the nearest ship. She moved her scope up to aim at the cockpit, squeezed the trigger, and fired the first shot. The bullet flew in a perfect line towards its intended target; she smiled when the cockpit's glass shattered and the pilot's head exploded. Jamie simultaneously shot her Sniper Blaster. Another Fly-Class Speeder went out of control. Adjusting the scope, taking aim, and firing became their process for the next twenty minutes as the girls assisted in this battle against evil. They grinned when they saw the thirty-two fighters from the *Lindman* twirl, scoop, soar, and rocket past them. Miranda followed one particular Fly-Class ship that seemed to evade everyone's bullets. The pilot consistently spoke into his headgear set. *He must be one of the leaders,* she wondered. She aim and took fire, but missed. Repositioning her scope, she calmed her frustration at a complete miss, and watched and waited before taking a second shot. The opportunity came, and she took it. She didn't miss this time: the Trikkyas Pilot's head blasted backwards, a thoroughly blood-stained spot in the middle of his forehead.

"All right, ladies," Buck called over the com, "Which one of you took my shot?"

"She did," Jaime immediately answered.

Miranda ribbed her friend when she was sure Jaime wasn't making a shot at a Trikkyas speeder. Miranda smiled, "Sorry, Buck, but he was asking for it." Buck could only laugh.

Helena had followed the fight from the Bridge. Unfortunately, she had witnessed the fall of Heidi, Tom, Adam, Regan, and Mort. After a thirty-three minute fight that seemed to last for hours, the fight was finally over. The *Lindman* had lost five crew members, and the *Vilantex* had lost eight.

"Lieutenant Holley," Jaime called in, "Team Foxtrot returning to base. All clear."

Helena smiled at the sound of her sister's voice. "Great job. You two really gave them hell."

Miranda laughed. "We did, didn't we? They put us through hell, so we might as well send them there."

*   *   *

Kront stood at the Platform. He looked down at his troops, feeling the loss of five more members of his crew. "Let's take a minute of silence in memory of Heidi Kalt, Regan Drogly, Mort Klav, Tom Raven and Adam Pander. Their great sacrifices were certainly no less than other missions they have accepted or paths they have taken. May they live on in our memories." The crew bowed their heads, and after two minutes, Kront raised his head to break the silence. "Thank you all for your time and attention, diligence and dedication. We must continue to move forward. We have more work yet to do."

Chapter 18. – Hostage.

Greddy Monk was helping two small children when Buck called him on his com unit. "Greddy, can you please report to Camp 2? We need your help over here."

The young man looked over at Adriahna. "Miss, would you mind covering for me? Sergeant Cypher needs me in Camp 2." She nodded, a slightly dreamy look in her eyes when he mentioned Buck. He wasn't sure why, but he shrugged it off as she walked over to the kids he was watching and took their hands in hers as they continued looking for the little girl's doll and the young boy's baseball cap. Greddy found Buck in Camp 2 and looked around. "Sergeant Cypher, excuse me for saying so, but it looks like y'all have things under control over here. Why do you need my help?"

Buck smiled, "Because one person in particular says only you can help her out." Sergeant Cypher pointed behind Greddy.

The young man turned around and gasped. "Grandma?" He knelt down to her level and hugged the elderly woman. "I can't believe it. You're here. You're okay! But how did you escape? When did you get here?"

"Slow down, Greddy," his grandmother warmly stated. "Let your commander answer your questions. I'm very tired." She took his hands in hers. "I'm just glad we found each other."

"She and forty-five others were on an unmarked shuttle," Buck explained. "They arrived just two hours ago. Their com unit was busted, so they couldn't send out any messages, but they were able to hear the ones we sent out, and thank goodness, too!"

*   *   *

"Captain, we have an unmarked shuttle on the radar," Miranda noted. "It's heading this way."

Kront stood behind Miranda at her station and looked at the radar image on her screen. "Turn on the scanner. I want to know everything about that ship. We don't need any surprises."

Miranda turned on the scanner, increased its power, and changed a few others settings and dials. The report flashed onto her screen. "It can't be."

"What is it?"

"Sir, it's the *Holliday*."

Kront uncrossed his arms. "That can't be. Check again. She's supposed to be 600 million miles away."

Miranda rescanned the shuttle but found the same results. "Sir, it's definitely the *Holliday*. She's severely damaged, and I read only one life form...not two..."

"Jaime, I want all squad leaders and Doc in the Hangar now!" He stormed out of the room, Helena fast on his heels.

Jaime turned on the ship's com. "All squad leaders report to the Hangar exit for a shuttle emergency. Doc Trad, standby for possible medical emergencies." She turned off the com and took over Miranda's spot as her friend joined the others at the outside of the *Lindman* ship.

The called-in crew members shielded their eyes from the evening sun, waiting for the ship to arrive. Michael joined Kront at the front. "What's the word, Captain?"

The commander of the *Lindman* stood with arms crossed, gun at the ready at his side. "The *Holliday* is back." Michael gawked and looked back at the other squad leaders, echoing Kront's message to them.

Sigu shook his head. "But how can that be?"

John rested his hand on his weapon on his left side. "Be prepared. We may not like what's coming."

The *Holliday* landed hard on the Helgin ground very close to the *Lindman*. The shuttle door opened, and a battered and bruised Nielson fell onto the ground. His friends and superiors rushed to his aid. They quickly examined him, but his voice stopped them."

"Quiet!" Helena commanded. "He's saying something."

Kront leaned closer to Nielson to pick up on the man's hoarse voice. "What is it, Nielson? Tell me."

"Jamina...Trikkyas..." Kront pulled away from Nielson's breath to see tears trickle down the husband's face. "Jamina..." Suddenly, his eyes rolled back, and his body went limp.

Drenge grabbed Nielson's wrist for a pulse. "He's going fast, sir. He needs Doc, now!"

"Take him! Go!" Kront directed. Drenge, Michael, Sigu,

and John lifted Nielson's body, carefully maneuvering the group huddle into the *Lindman*, down its hallways, and into Doc's surgery room. Helena cradled Nielson's head and gently laid it down on the patient bed as Doc entered the room, unprepared for the sight before him. Kront came in and closed the door behind him. Although it was a larger than usual room aboard a shuttle, Captain Tallin dismissed the squad leaders until further notice.

Frank examined Nielson, clicking his tongue in concern. "He has a blast wound on his lower back, blade cuts on his legs, and probably has internal bleeding from a bad beating." He typed some instructions into the wall monitor; the x-ray scanner came down from the ceiling. After another minute of waiting, the light ceased its test and returned to its place inside the ceiling. The image appeared on the wall monitor. "Kront, he's lucky to be alive. His nose, right hand, and six ribs are broken. One bone is fractured in his left leg, and he has a punctured lung." He began to push the remaining crew members out of the room. "I need to call in my assistants; I must start surgery right away, or we'll lose him. I'll keep you updated." He nodded to Kront before closing the door on Captain Tallin's face.

Helena stood beside Kront but turned to walk down the hallway leading toward the outside and the spot where the *Holliday* landed. "Helena?" Her walk turned into a jog. "Helena, where are you going?" He began to follow her. Her jog became a run. "Helena!"

"The black box, Captain!" she yelled into the air. "The *Holliday's* flight data recorder!" She exited the *Lindman* and found the *Holliday*. She began rummaging through its cockpit pieces, hoping the Trikkyas hadn't found it while busy internally and externally damaging the shuttle. "Where is it?" she asked aloud. Kront had finally caught up to her. He stood behind her, hoping the same things. "Found it!" she announced after a few more moments of scrounging through the ship's physical contents.

"Let's take it to the girls," he suggested. "They'll be able to decipher it."

The two superior commanders walked onto the Bridge together. "Officer Holliday," Helena began, tossing the device to the girl in discussion, "I need you to decode it."

"Right away, Lieutenant." She found the cords that plugged

the box into the ship's mainframe and downloaded the content onto a temporary hard drive, in case the Trikkyas had found the box and uploaded a virus onto it. *I'm so glad these things aren't as heavy or awkward as they used to be, or even anything like the ones they have on earth,* Miranda pondered as they worked. She had read in a library book that the Earth version of the so-called "black box" had been made with heavy frame so it could withstand fiery airplane crashes; great minds previous to her had laughed at the silly Earth people. They had created a lighter, damage-proof, titanium-alloy frame that weighed in at a total of 2-3 lbs. for shuttles the size of the *Holliday*. Miranda focused back on her work; Jaime did her part by separating the files: text into one folder and video into another. While Miranda focused on the video, Jaime translated the text.

"Almost done, Miranda," Jaime said.

"Me, too," Miranda commented. Little by little, the pieces were coming together. "It's not much yet, but the *Holliday*'s radar picked up on a large ship coming at the *Holliday* from the rear." Helena wrung her hands and paced the floor; it was Kront's turn to stand still with his arms crossed and patiently wait for the girls' full report. She pushed a few more buttons. "It's a Trikkyas ship, Draglon Class. Identity: *Revenges*."

"Trikkyas," the lieutenant mumbled. "Again, Trikkyas."

Kront pressed the com on his wrist unit. "Buck and Sigu, contact your squads. I want as many volunteers as can be found, including civilians. John, talk to the Academy students Levels 80 and up."

Jaime threw off her headgear. "Captain, we've got it!"

Kront jumped down the few stairs to the lower level of the Bridge, a few feet from his own station. He joined Helena behind the girls, and watched and listened as the black box pieces came together.

Jamina and Nielson sat in the cockpit of the *Holliday*. Although they had just been married, their nerves were strained and emotions fragile. A caring Nielson stroked his wife's hand. Jamina didn't look toward her husband, but he saw a silent tear and a loving smile on her face. Suddenly, an alarm sounded.

"Jamina, we've got contact on the radar. Call the *Lindman*."

Jamina tried the com button several times. "*Lindman*, this is the *Holliday*. Come in. Is anyone there? Hello??" She glanced at the radar, trying not to panic. "Tyler, it's not going through. The incoming ship must have a transmission blocker."

Nielson changed several dials and settings, and steered the ship straight up, trying to make a quick loop to escape the enemy. "Don't worry, dear. I promise we'll be fine."

Jamina tried to believe him, but her heart raced as the ship released several smaller speeders to surround them. "Tyler, it's a Trikkyas ship!" A large thud shook the ship; Nielson and Jamina put on their P.S.A. suits, and an explosion sounded off in the background. The pilot and copilot whipped around, pulling their guns from their seats, but they weren't quick enough. A bright flash of green and blue filled the screen. They'd been hit by a stun ray. The black box video turned off.

The squad leaders watched in horror and disbelief as the two com officers fell prey to the Trikkyas troops. "That was just the beginning," Helena warned to the crew member gathered in the Situation Room. "This next part is much worse." She nodded to Miranda; the latter ejected from the disc player the first of two discs onto which she burned the black box video and sound recordings. She input the second disc and pressed play.

A few seconds of blackness quickly disappeared as the picture of the inside of the *Holliday* came into view. The shuttle door opened; two Trikkyas troops entered. They kicked Nielson's body and stomped on his face and chest. One of them took out a big knife and slit the com officer's legs, randomly sticking the stunned man's legs like a toothpick into slices of fruit. The other Trikkyas lifted Jamina's body of the floor and took her away until she wasn't in the picture anymore. He called out to the other, still busy hurting Nielson, "Leave him. He needs to be alive when he arrives. Program the shuttle to fly to Helgin, and give them the message."

The Trikkyas beating Nielson obeyed – kicking Nielson once more – and programmed the navigation system of the *Holliday*. Then he bent down over the visual recorder. "Give us the record disc from the Lost Fortress of the Handlon Supreme Council by the end of the 21st week, or your friend dies."

Kront went in to a rage in front of his troops. "Damn Trikkyas! One thing after another!"

His squad leaders all stood. Drenge spoke up. "Sir, we stand behind you, whatever the call."

Kront placed his hand on Drenge's shoulder. "Thank you, but I think I need to handle this one personally. I'm tired of being responsible for my soldiers getting hurt and killed because I make the call." He turned to Helena. "Lieutenant, I've got a plan." He motioned to Miranda and Jaime. "And I need your help, too." The girls smiled. The older Holley sister grinned.

Captain Tallin smacked the table with his fist. "It's payback time."

*   *   *

"Team Foxtrot in position. Ready at 1700 feet on your 2 o'clock," Miranda radioed in to the Captain and Helena. Jaime nestled herself in some tall grass while Miranda took her gun sling from off her back so she could take a similar position next to her friend. She reached into her pocket and grabbed a portable ship communicator. Pressing a button, she watched as the *Lindman, Jr.* went into stealth mode by camouflaging itself. She smiled and turned back to the work at her front. She shook her head and whispered, "Jaime, it's just not right. I know Captain and Helena are great at what they do, but seriously? The two of them all alone down there?"

"I know. They could've at least brought John or Sigu," Jaime chimed in. They quickly attached the silencers to their Sniper Blasters and prepared for another mission.

Miranda turned on the portable scanner. *Blip, blip.* She turned on the com unit, careful to keep her voice low. "Seven life forms approaching from the front." Miranda and Jamie turned their sniper scopes towards the direction of the Trikkyas troops. "Confirm," Miranda continued. "Six Trikkyas troops and Jamina. She's walking, but looks like facial bleeding possible broken left arm, and slight limping in her right leg."

The six Trikkyas troops walked towards Kront and Helena but stopped fifty feet away. One Trikkyas member stepped forward from the front. "Do you have the disc?"

Kront pulled it from his front pocket and waved it at the thugs. "The agreement was two from each side. Apparently you can't count.""

"Apparently, you're too trusting." The Trikkyas leader laughed. "We have another forty in shuttles ready to attack if you back out on your word."

"Apparently, we shouldn't trust your word, so why keep ours?" Kront took one step back to test the enemy.

The leader leaned forward but stopped; instead, he raised his left hand in the air and snapped his fingers. The two Trikkyas crew holding Jamina pushed her to the ground; one of them placed his heavy boot on her back, and the other put the barrel of his gun to the back of her head.

Helena cried out, "Don't hurt her!"

The leader smiled. "Don't test us."

Kront fisted his other hand. "Let her go, and we won't have to hurt you."

The leader shook his head and laughed. "I believe we have the upper hand here. Remember? Fifty of us to only two of you? That means we keep the prisoner *and* retrieve the disc."

"Should I snap my fingers, too?" Kront raised his eyebrows. That was the signal. The Trikkyas leader pulled his blaster, but Miranda and Jamie were faster. Their Sniper Blasters fired, and two Trikkyas fell to the ground, including the leader. The remaining four Trikkyas troops stared at their dead comrades.

"What say you?" Kront asked.

One of the Trikkyas who had stood to the leader's right side stepped forward and took charge. "I will send the girl." He nodded to the troops behind him. They lifted up Jamina from the ground and tossed her toward the new leader.

Kront mentally sighed, glad this would soon be over. "Once she is over here, I give you my word that I'll put the disc on the ground and walk away. If you try anything, just remember what happened to them." His glance toward the dead bodies sent shivers down the spines of the remaining Trikkyas troops.

The leader none-so-gently tossed Jamina forward, but she stayed on her feet. She limped toward Helena and her captain, nearly falling into their arms. She burst into tears though she didn't know how she had any more stored up inside of her to give out.

Helena took the young girl's face in her hands. "Jamina, easy, it's okay. Breathe."

"Hele...they...I couldn't..." Jamina fell into another round of uncontrollable sobs. Helena pulled her away as Kront placed the disc on the ground.

"You held up your end of the bargain. I hold up my end." Kront walked away. "It's all there on the disc."

"It better be," the new leader warned. He walked forward to claim the disc, but the tears of the hostage got the better of his loose mouth. "By the way..." Kront turned from looking at Helena and Jamina to hear the leader's words. "A new bride is always more fun than a used one."

His sickening words hit Jamina's heart; he licked his lips and made kissy faces toward Tyler's wife, but she fainted from too much emotional exhaustion. The other Trikkyas troops joined in the teasing. Helena's face sent a plea to Kront to do something. Captain Tallin knew revenge was not the answer, but in this galaxy where evil seemed to come at them from every angle, a few less bad guys didn't seem like such a bad idea. He raised his left hand. The leader stopped smiling, as did the other Trikkyas men. Kront snapped his fingers.

Chapter 19. – Brilliant Idea.

Nielson had barely come out of surgery when his wife and the crew from the *Lindman, Jr.* arrived back at the mother ship. She broke down at his bedside. Nielson's body resisted his motions to grab his wife and hold her tight. Instead, the pain, stitches, slings, restraints, and bandages pinned him down to prevent movement from further harming his condition.

"My love," Jamina cried, "I was so lost without you. I didn't know where I was. I couldn't find you!"

Nielson shushed her concerns. "Don't worry. We're together. Just focus on that." The couple continued a much more hushed conversation, including the rape, as far as Kront could tell, since Jamina cried, and Nielson clenched his fists and tried to punch his bedside. Instead the man broke down into tears and kissed the top of his wife's head. "I love you. Don't you ever forget that. I'll never look at you differently because of what they did to you."

"What did they want from us anyway?"

"The disc we retrieved from the underground fortress on Loht 9."

Jamina eyes widened. She looked at Helena, standing on the opposite side of Nielson's bed. "But…did you…do they have it now?"

Helena smiled, "No, we gave them something better."

Nielson turned his eyes to his superior officer. "What do you mean? Did you give it to them or not?"

Kront spoke up from the shadows, coming toward what little light shown over Nielson's body from an overhead lamp. "Miranda copied the disc several times over and made some slight adjustments. Anytime they open the disc, we will have access to everything: their computers, their ships, their plans, videos, conversations—everything."

Jamina smiled. "So you can stop the Trikkyas?"

Kront and Helena were no longer smiling. "From what?" Helena prodded.

"From whatever they're doing with a Usinde against the Handlons."

Captain Tallin sighed and lowered his head. "Usinde means 'planet killer' in the language of the Trikkyas people. I thought they might have used it on Troklon and Frigal." He looked at the married couple. "All you two need to worry about is recovery. Doc should come in soon with some news for you, Jamina. We'll leave and give you two some privacy."

As they left the room, Jamina grabbed Helena's hand. "Lieutenant, please?"

Helena looked to Kront who nodded and shut the door as he left the room. Helena held Jamina in her arms as Jamina stood next to Nielson's bedside. Doc walked in and turned to his wall monitor, pressing some buttons to bring up various medical reports.

"Well, Mrs. Nielson," Doc began, "I need a sample of your blood to conduct a full medical report on you. Your husband is healing just fine after his numerous surgeries, but he needs lots and lots of rest."

Jamina held out her left arm. Doc pulled a sterilized needle out of an unopened package, popped on a small container, drew her blood, and connected the container's data chip to the wall computer. Within seconds, statistics, charts, levels, numbers, and other medical data flew across the screen. It was making Helena dizzy looking at it, but she figured that Doc was obviously accustomed to it.

"Good news and bad news, my dear," Doc frowned.

Tears welled up in her eyes. Nielson clenched his fists until they shook. "Just tell us doc."

"Well, I'll just come out and say it. Jamina, Nielson knocked you up."

The jaws of the married couple dropped to the floor. "Are you sure, Doc?" Nielson asked.

"Would you rather it be by someone else?" he retorted. "Of course it's you! Jamina may have been raped, but she's already seven weeks along. Congrats, young man. You're going to be a father." Helena hugged Jamina, and as the wife turned back to her husband, Helena winked at Doc and quietly slipped from the room, receiving a wink in return in his approval of her comforting Jamina in her time of greatest need.

*   *   *

Miranda was programming as fast as her fingers could fly across the numerous keyboards and touch-screen monitors. *It's a great idea! Exactly what the Trikkyas would fall for,* she convinced herself. *I've just got to build the blueprint of it and persuade the others of its success.* No one had noticed what she was working on. In fact, no one was at the Bridge with her. "Okay, now, if this part goes here, that leaves room for this piece…no, wait, I have to turn—yeah, that'll work. Then, this part goes over there and…yes! I've got it!" She pressed the upload button, grabbed the disc the moment the computer ejected it from its wall system, and ran down to the Situation Room. *Where is everybody?* she wondered. Then, she slapped her forehead. *Duh, I forgot to make a com call!* She laughed aloud and pressed the ship's com button from inside the Situation Room. "Attention, Captain Tallin, Lieutenant Holley, Specialist Holley, and all Squad Leaders. Please report to the Situation Room immediately." As the individuals shuffled into the room over the next few minutes, she smiled and greeted them nonchalantly.

"Miranda, what is this all about?" Kront asked.

"Yes," Helena chimed in, "why did you call us here?"

Miranda turned a knob to activate the 4D Model-Maker in the room. The computers whirred and buzzed, and blue lights appeared above the center table to bring to life the blueprint of her plan of success—and of attack. "This is a model of a special satellite I designed that has the ability to travel Hyperspace 5+. It can hide from any radar that isn't programmed to find it, but will automatically reveal itself to Planet Earth's radar when it arrives at the edge of the Milky Way Galaxy."

Kront looked at her. "It sounds great, Miranda, but the Trikkyas are expecting us to do something. They'll be looking for anything out of the ordinary, including this."

"That's right," John spoke up.

"How can you guarantee it'll ever make it?" Sigu argued. "Not even two of our own troops could make it without great harm and distress?"

Helena interrupted, "Hold on, everyone. Miranda's smarter than this. I'm sure she already has our questions answered." She turned back to the Academy student. "Don't you, sweetie?"

Miranda smiled. "I sure do," she replied to the woman in orange and black hair. It may not have been Halloween time, but they were about to scare the daylights out of the Trikkyas people with some serious wartime efforts. "We are going to build two of them. This one will be exactly as it is. The other will be slightly less perfect. The Trikkyas will find it on their radar; it may have a computer malfunction, but we won't make it too easy because we don't want them to be suspicious."

Michael cleared his throat. "How long until it gets to Earth?"

"Four months or less," she grinned.

Drenge crossed his arms. "I like it. Sounds good to me. We'll find the parts and start construction immediately." He looked up to the Intel Officer. "If there's one thing I've learned, it's that you haven't been wrong, yet."

Buck pushed the com button. "Miranda, would you please come down here to the Hangar?"

Miranda opened her eyes and looked at the red glowing light of her alarm clock. *Are you fucking serious? An hour's sleep, and now this?* she complained. Another long night of working on the satellites led her to an early-morning bedtime. She pushed the com button to reply. "I think I'm going to kill you when I get down there, Buck."

He laughed. "Only after you see what we've done, okay? As in, the satellites are done."

Miranda's eyes shot open. "I'll be right there!" She slipped on some jeans and a sweatshirt, threw on some shoes, and noisily ran down the empty hallways until her mind jogged itself awake. She approached the two satellites with caution as Buck and the other engineers stood back to gaze at their work. "Well, I think you all have done a great job. Leave the rest to me."

Buck dismissed his engineers and looked over to Miranda, busily sitting at a nearby workbench and laptop. Hands on his shoulders, he cocked his head. "I thought you were going to kill me."

"Don't wake me up when I haven't slept, and I won't."

Buck threw his hands up in the air in defeat. "I promise! I promise." He smiled and walked away.

Just then, dozens of reports flashed onto her screen. Jaime's voice came over the ship's com. "Officer Holliday, report to the Bridge immediately. Like now, please."

Miranda rolled her eyes. She knew what was going on. Jaime didn't need to freak out about it. She joined Jaime at the Bridge and was met with a huge hug. "It works, Miranda! It works!"

"I know!" she said half-enthusiastically. She meant to be happier, but her hour's worth of sleep had long left her body and mind. "I think I'll take a look at it after I take a cat nap."

"No, you need to look at it now!" Jaime dragged Miranda to her own station and sat her down. She pressed the com button. "Captain Tallin, report to the Bridge immediately!"

In less than two minutes, Kront came running up to the Bridge. "What's going on?"

Jaime bounced up and down, happily repeating, "It works! It works!"

"What works?" A puzzled expression crossed his face. "And will you please calm the hell down?"

"Sorry, sir. Miranda, you tell him. It was your program and idea, anyway."

"Miranda?" Kront looked to the other student with bags like ocean liners under her eyes. "Maybe you should get some sleep first."

"No, sir, she's right. I need to at least take a look at it before I catch some z's." Miranda pulled up some reports onto her computer screen, duplicating the images onto Kront's computer and the large wall screen in front of them. "The disc has been accessed by the *Revenges*. The program I installed as a backdoor is sending us tons of information."

Kront smiled, "Good job Miranda, now we can start to mess with them,"

She shook her head in the negative. "Sir, I think it would be wiser to wait patiently on this one. They may send it to their other ships or bases."

He nodded in agreement. "Okay, keep me posted. Anything

else?"

"Buck and the other engineers have finished building the satellites, and I completed the programming prior to coming up here. They're ready when you are, sir."

He pressed the com button. "Lieutenant Holley, please join Captain Tallin at the Bridge." As Kront and the Academy students continued discussion of the backdoor program and the satellites, Helena came bouncing into the room, a tall mug with a dark, warm drink in her hands.

"Helena reporting for duty, sir!" she saluted. Miranda gave a cocky grin, realizing she wasn't the only one with little sleep. And that Jaime got her crazy, early-morning bounciness from her older sister.

"Damn, Lieutenant," Kront remarked, "how'd you clean up so fast?" He looked at his watch. "You only got about three hours of sleep after a forty-eight hour shift."

"A little splash of water in the face, and a lot of coffee down the hatch." She took a sip of her drink and winked at her little sister, drinking in her own tall brew of warmth and jitters.

Kront shook his head. "What's our next step, Officer Holliday?"

The woman in discussion turned to her numerous monitors and examined the statistics and reports still flooding her screens. "If my numbers are correct—"

"—which are never wrong," Jaime interjected.

Miranda smiled to her friend. "The hidden satellite has the best chance of reaching earth by taking a different trajectory toward Earth, albeit a slightly longer one, out of the way of the Trikkyas path. Remember, the Trikkyas expect us to take fast and easy, so when they find our not-so-camouflaged satellite, it'll boost their ego and reduce their worries of another satellite actually making it past their defenses."

"Well, let's go send out some satellites."

The crew members of the *Lindman* ship stood in front of their shuttle and gazed into the distance at their hard work for the last two weeks: a satellite made for contact with Earth, and one made just to be destroyed. Alpha and Charlie Squads had just returned from hauling the satellites several miles away to an agreed-upon deserted area that the Handlons had allowed Captain Tallin to use for satellite deployment.

"It's a tragedy, it is," Sigu dramatically sighed. "That one should make it to a far-off, exotic destination while the other must die in the name of survival." John rolled his eyes; Drenge and Michael playfully jumped Sigu in a temporary man-brawl before they were called to attention. Captain Tallin entered the scene.

"Officer Holliday, run one last diagnostics test. Sergeant Cypher, check the engineering. Everyone else, standby for liftoff." Kront stood at attention, Lieutenant Holley at his right side and Specialist Holley at his left. Miranda and Buck nodded to each other and stepped back from the laptop computer on the makeshift stand from the Hangar.

"Sir, Satellites Red and Blue are ready to go." Miranda saluted to her commander and smiled.

"Countdown, everyone," Kront announced. "Ten... nine... eight... seven... six... five... four... three... two... one..." He slammed on the launch button, and a ground-rupturing rumble started. The two small rockets took off with tails of heat and flame. Somewhere around 50,000 feet in the air, a small blast occurred, and the satellites broke free from the rockets.

"Now they're on their own," Helena stated. She gazed up at the parallel trails of orange fire streaking across the morning sky. *A lot like me,* she mused. *A lot of fire and passion, but all alone.* The *Lindman* crew returned to work, but Helena chose to spend her afternoon with the survivors of Planet Troklon. The children had little with which to play: a few balls, an old toy car, a doll with only one arm, or nothing at all. Many of the older ones had bare feet because they gave their shoes to their baby siblings. *Something has to be done,* she demanded. She pushed the button on her personal visual com unit. "Captain, can you spare a moment's time?"

Kront's face showed up on her visual. "Of course. What do you need?"

Helena looked up and saw a little boy sitting on the ground, moving a rock around like it was a car. "Since you asked, technically I need five assistants and eight million credits."

"Um," Kront stuttered, "what was that?"

She didn't want to sound whiny, but maybe whiny would

get her what these kids needed, which is what she wanted to get for them. "I want to make an arrangement with the Handlons to get toys, shoes, and clothing for the survivors. I know the Handlons are helping out with food, but other essentials may help these people feel less like fugitives."

"Way ahead of you, Lieutenant. I've already called the Handlon Senate and explained to them our situation. Remember that small cache of weapons we found six years ago? We've made a deal to exchange it for toys, shoes, and clothing for approximately 3,000 children."

"How big is this small cache of weapons?"

"About 20,000 weapons and 15,000 pieces of armor. We have a peace treaty with them. It's the Trikkyas I'm more concerned about."

"Yes, agreed, but still it seems they're on the losing side of the bargain."

"Well, we're also giving them a copy of the disc and 1 million credits."

Her eyes widened to the size of cantaloupes. "Are you sure, sir?"

"Yes. Miranda has placed the same backdoor program on it, just in case they decide to break the treaty on us."

Helena smiled. "All right, I'm ready to go. When do we leave?"

Kront shook his head. "Sorry, Helena, but I can't have you going over there. Many Handlons know your face. Treaty or no treaty, you killed their family members, and they won't hesitate to take revenge."

Chapter 20. – The Thirty Usindes.

"*How many* Usindes?"

Miranda gulped, afraid to say the number again in fear her captain might lose his mind. "Um, thirty?"

He fell backwards into his chair. "Where are they?"

"Three apiece on ten different planets."

Kront shook his head. "Any good news in this bomb you've dropped on me?"

Miranda winced. "Not a good pun, sir."

"You're right. Sorry."

"My scans indicate that eight of the planets are unguarded, so we can easily go and disable them."

"What about the other two?"

Miranda looked back at her screen. "Those two are Jesiget and Handlon 4."

Kront's eyes widened. "Those are both Handlon worlds."

"Uh-oh," she whispered.

He grabbed his desk and pulled himself closer to his work station. "Jamie, get me the Handlon Council on the com."

Jamie had been sitting contently in her chair near Miranda, reading over the Communication Skills Level 8 book; at his bark, she nearly fell out of her chair. "Yes, sir! Right away!"

*   *   *

"Land here, Miranda," Helena directed. "The Usinde should be just around that hill, one mile out." She stared out the window at the deserted landscape. No people, troops, or developments as far as she could see. Just barren, wasted space. *What's the point of placing a Usinde out here?* she wondered.

Miranda slowly landed the shuttle down. "I'll be waiting. Good luck."

Helena nodded, "Let's go, Jaime." The two Holley sisters wore full body armor but as Jamie reached for her Sniper Blaster, Helena stopped her. "You won't want that out here." She reached to her left and grabbed a weapon of similar, but smaller build.

"Here. Try this. It's a Sonic Semi-Blaster. It holds fifty rounds, and you can use the scope to take out targets up to 600 feet away."

Jamie accepted the new weapon. "Thanks. I appreciate lighter weaponry." Together they stalked the hill, checking for Trikkyas and traps. Right as Helena was about to round another corner, Jaime pulled her sister back. "Helena, stop!" Helena froze; Jaime pointed toward a small clump of dirt, right where Helena's next – and last – step would have been. There laid a small, anti-personnel mine.

Helena gulped. "Good eye, sis. Missed that one." She kneeled down to disarm it. Slowly, she dug around it to free up enough space to open it. "It's a Trikkyas Slasher. It carries only one pound of explosives, but it's loaded with sharp metal spikes that cut through every kind of armor." Jamie kept watch as her older sister took the side lid off the mine. "Damn!"

"What?"

"It's double-wired." The lieutenant stood up and began walking away. "We have to shoot it out around 200 feet. I'll give you the shot, but once you take it, duck down."

"Yes, ma'am!" Jaime saluted and laughed, running to catch up to Helena. Once they were back far enough from the booby trap, Helena hunkered down, and Jaime prepared her single shot. Kneeling down, she leveled the Sonic Semi-Blaster on her sturdy knee, placed her eye against the scope, adjusted for wind, and pulled the trigger, falling down for quick cover.

The sound of the explosion echoed for miles. Miranda jumped forward in her seat and slammed on the com button. "Foxtrot, report! What's going on?"

"We're fine, Miranda," Jaime assured her friend. "We took out a booby trap that Helena nearly stepped on."

Miranda smiled. "Gotta be more careful, Lieutenant."

"Shut up. I know where you sleep," Helena threatened. "And I've been playing tricks on the *Lindman* for longer than y'all have been alive."

Jaime abruptly stopped laughing. "Helena, get down!"

*   *   *

"Captain Tallin, how may the Handlon Council assist

you?"

Kront stood up straight, hoping he had pressed out all of the wrinkles in his best uniform. "Council Member Gastvolk, I'm actually calling to help you. We have reason to believe that Trikkyas forces have hidden Usindes on Planets Handlon 4 and Jesiget, possibly three bombs apiece. We can give you the exact locations and disabling methods for each bomb." Kront pressed a few buttons, and the information appeared on Gastvolk's screen.

"Captain, this is a serious claim against the Trikkyas people. In light of recent events, it would not surprise me."

Kront nodded. "We are in the process of disabling and removing twenty-four other Usinde bombs located on other planets."

Gastvolk shook his head. "Captain, we greatly appreciate your help. We will take immediate action. Once we have the Usindes, we will contact you again. Handlon Council out."

* * *

Miranda squinted at the radar. Out of nowhere, ten Trikkyas troops appeared. "Foxtrot, there are ten targets at your eleven o'clock. Take cover!" Several long seconds passed by. The Trikkyas soldiers moved closer. "Helena, Jaime, can you read me?" Again, no response. "Shit!" she said aloud. "Those damn Trikkyas must have communication blockers!"

A faint scratching noise on the com added to her fear levels. Then, a voice came on the com with constant interference. "Miranda, we …pickup Jamie…help…" Miranda jumped over to the controls; she started the engine and blasted the shuttle over to her friends' position. She settled the ship down, noting many dead Trikkyas lying on the surrounding grounds. She grabbed her own weapon and stepped outside, already prepared with full body armor in preparation for an incident like this, although she had hoped it wasn't going to happen. But her worst fears were true: Jamie was lying on the ground, bleeding, and it didn't look very good. She ran over to Helena, cradling Jaime's neck in her hands. "What happened? Where was she hit?"

Helena wiped her tears away with her shoulder. "They came out of nowhere. We got 'em all, but one. He must have snuck up on us from behind. I turned around just as he got Jaime…right in the neck…"

Miranda ran back to the shuttle and brought back the stretcher and first aid kit. They bandaged her neck and carried her in to the ship. "Helena, fly her back to the *Lindman*. Get Doc ready before you're anywhere near landing time."

"What about you?"

Miranda shook her head. "If this Usinde isn't disabled, we've failed the mission. Jaime's important, but that's why you're here, too. Get here to safety." Helena looked at Jaime and then back at Miranda. "Please don't make me give you an order, Helena."

Tight-lipped, the lieutenant nodded. "Fine, but take care of yourself. Look out for the mines. Use your scanner, and mark it. Don't blow it up."

Miranda took one last look at Jaime. "Jaime, take it easy, okay? See you soon." She grabbed Jaime's Sonic Semi-Blaster and ran to her companions' previous position, the direction opposite the shuttle. Helena closed the shuttle doors and took off for the *Lindman*.

The Academy student watched only until she could no longer see the *Lindman, Jr.* well enough to make it out clearly against the evening sky. She pulled her head back down to the ground and continued the mission. In one hand she held her weapon; in the other, the portable scanner. Two hours later with a few marked booby traps and no Trikkyas troops, Miranda reached a small building. "According to my scanner," she quietly said aloud, "the Usinde should be in here." She checked the door for traps. Clear. Gradually, she shifted the door open. She peeked inside, noticing a shaft in the ground with a ladder. She rolled her eyes.

"Damn it! There could be a hundred Trikkyas down there!" She pulled down her infrared goggles and searched as far as she could without actually climbing down the ladder. *It looks clear,* she surmised. *Of course, so did the area my friends cleared before they were ambushed. Maybe I should toss down a stun grenade.* Not wanting to take chances, she pulled out a single stun grenade from her side bag, pulled the tap, dumped the grenade down the shaft, and closed the door. But there were no screams of pains. No writhing bodies against the floor or guns accidentally shooting off. She opened the door and slid down the ladder until her feet slammed against the ground beneath her. Before moving, she listened for noises. Still, no sounds. She began walking down the long underground passage until it suddenly stopped at a bolted door.

Quietly, she placed her ear against it. She heard shuffling, only slight movement, but no voices, no talking. "Here goes," she whispered. Miranda took a step back, jumped forward with her right foot to the door, and kicked it in. She tucked and rolled across the floor, stopping in front of an elderly man with a rope between his lips. Like a prisoner. She put her weapon away and stood up. Looking around the room, she counted twenty-three people hostages with their arms and legs tied up. She grabbed a knife from her armor pack and freed each one.

"Thank you so much," one of the freed men stated. "We've been here for weeks."

"Glad to help, but now I need your help." She hated to say her next words, but she had to pick survival over the possibility of more fear in their eyes. "I'm looking for a Usinde bomb."

"I know where it is," a little girl spoke up. "One of those ugly men hid it."

Miranda walked over toward the little girl and held her frail hand. "Can you show me?"

She pointed to a distant corner of the room. "Over there." As they walked, the little girl opened up. "I watched them press a button. It opened up, like the wall has magic in it."

Miranda could see the button; she pushed it, and the secret compartment opened. Miranda kneeled down next to the Usinde and spoke aloud to herself. "Red and white, blue, green, yellow and orange, black, white, orange and brown...eight wires." Miranda thought back to her days at the Academy. *Every color represents a number,* she contemplated. *Most bombs are built and disarmed by basic mathematics. White is the most basic color and represents the number 1; yellow is 2. Blue is 3, green is 4, red is 5, and orange is 6. Brown is 7, and black is 8.* After some quick calculations to figure out the numbers for the multi-colored wires, she smiled, hoping her teacher would have been proud of her.

Miranda looked down at the little girl still standing next to her. The child's dirt-smudged cheeks couldn't change her angelic features. "What's your name, sweetie?"

"Mona Johnson, miss."

Miranda laughed. "Well, Mona, I need your help, but you have to call me Miranda, not miss, okay?"

"Okay, Miranda. What should I do?"

"I want you to remember two numbers that I tell you. Three and four."

Mona nodded. "Three and four."

The Academy student pulled a small computer from her pocket; she attached the connectors to the Usinde bomb. "Mona, what was the first number?"

"Three." Mona smiled, unaware that Miranda remembered but very aware that she herself was very happy and not as afraid anymore.

"Thank you!" Officer Holliday typed in the first code number, quickly followed by the next two code numbers. "Three...five..." She looked to Mona. "I forgot the other number. What was it?"

"Four!" she smiled so bravely.

"Right! Great job, Mona." Turning back to the computer, she continued the work. "Four...eight, one, six...seven..." She pressed enter and closed the computer. "That should do it. The bomb will shut off soon." *Or blow up in our faces,* she thought to herself. She looked over Mona's shoulder and saw the man that had thanked her. In his eyes, she saw what she, too, felt in her gut: this bomb could go either way.

Chapter 21. – Jamie's Revenge.

Helena steered the shuttle over the hill and landed it in the place she last saw Miranda before taking Jaime back to the *Lindman*. She pressed the com button. "Miranda, this is the *Lindman, Jr.* Can you read me? Over." The silence on the com system increased her fears. *Oh, I hope she's okay*, she worried. She threw on her armor and grabbed her weapon. When she opened the rear hatch, she found herself looking Miranda straight in the face. "Whoa!" she screamed, jumping backward and clutching at her heart. "I don't need a heart transplant. Call me on the com next time."

"Sorry, Helena," Miranda shrugged. "I would've, but my friend accidentally broke it." She nodded her head toward a young child holding her hand.

"Oh?" The lieutenant smiled at the little girl, and then she saw the other twenty-two people standing behind. "Oh my," she gasped as her eyes roamed across the dirty faces and life-squelched beings. "You made some friends, I see."

The Academy student grinned. "Yup! They're waiting to rejoin their families." She raised her eyebrows and gave Helena 'the look.' "Let's get going before the Trikkyas find their hostages missing."

"You don't have to tell me twice." Just like that, Helena popped back into the pilot seat. "Buckle up and hold on!" She closed the rear door from the front control panel, and the *Lindman, Jr.* soared back into space. Miranda joined Helena after assuring herself the passengers were okay.

"So...speaking of getting back to family members..." she began but couldn't finish.

Helena grabbed Miranda's hand. She knew of whom she referred. "Jaime's fine. No nerves were hit, and she'll be on her feet in a week or so."

The copilot let out a big sigh. "Thank goodness."

"What about them back there? What's their story?"

"The little girl helped me find the Usinde and disarm it.

They've been held hostage for five weeks in a room underneath a random building two hours southwest of the gunfight with the Trikkyas."

Helena shook her head. "Five weeks…wait, that means they don't know about—"

"Nope," Miranda interrupted. "But since we have time in the flight right now, I think I'll go break the news." Helena nodded and handed her a portable digital display unit. Miranda could access the survivors list from this tablet. She walked over to the men, women, and children in the back of the shuttle. "If I could have your attention, please. I know you all have been through a great deal in the past five weeks, but I need you to hang on to a bit more sad news. Please bear with me, okay?" She heard an audible sigh and several women begin to sniffle. Their emotions couldn't take any more beatings. "While you were held captive, the Trikkyas planted Usinde bombs on Planets Troklon and Frigal. Although many people escaped from Troklon, not all had the chance to leave. No one survived the Frigal explosion."

A few people began to mourn the potential loss of loved ones, but the first gentleman that Miranda had freed – the one who had understood her look in hopes the Usinde was disarmed and not detonating – was the first to stand up and step forward. "My name is Captain Soren Plickart."

Miranda extended her hand to shake his in a formal introduction. "I'm Officer Miranda Holliday." She typed his surname into the survivors' list and found three people. She breathed a sigh of relief. "Captain, are you looking for family members or friends?"

"Family," he promptly stated. "My wife, Doris, and my two children, Mark and Missy." He gulped. "They were living on Troklon when our ship was attacked by Trikkyas troops."

She smiled at him. "Captain, your family is alive and well on Helgin. I need you to assist these others in finding their family members and friends. I'll show you how to do the first one, and you can do the rest. Is that all right?"

Soren saluted her. "Yes, ma'am." He grabbed her hand. "Thank you again for saving us."

Miranda blushed. "Sir, thank you for not giving up on being found." He smiled as tears rolled down his cheeks, aged with experience. She bent down to Mona's level, and Soren sat next to the young girl. "Mona, what's your last name?"

"Johnson."

The copilot blanked. "Um, what's your mom's first name?"

"I don't know. Did my mommy die?"

Miranda cleared her throat and looked to Soren. "Did you know her mother?"

"I met her briefly before we left Troklon. She was supposed to come with us, but she became very ill and was not cleared for flight." He rubbed his chin with his left hand. "I believe her name was Lizzy."

Quickly, she typed the first and last name into the system. One single result appeared, and it seemed to match the search data. Miranda beamed at the little girl. "Mona, your mom is waiting for you."

*   *   *

Doc Trad ran down the hallway to the Bridge, pushing past other Soldiers in his way without excusing himself. "Captain!" he yelled as he approached. "Captain, Specialist Holley's gone!"

Helena muttered under her breath, "She's probably hiding from you, Doc." Miranda ribbed her friend; they giggled, but Doc ignored their antics.

Kront looked up from his computer screens. "What do you mean gone?"

"I mean exactly what I said," he stated in an irritated voice. "I check on her once an hour, but just now when I checked, she was gone. She's supposed to have assistance to go or do anything when out of bed, but no nurse or assistant of mine has seen her anywhere."

As the atmosphere in the room rose from no concern to a level of worry for Jaime's health and safety, com calls were made to the squad leaders, ship departments, and various survivors' quarters of Helgin to find the missing soldier. With no inbound reports of a younger Holley sister running around rampant as healthy as a newborn chick, the *Lindman* crew became increasingly worried. Captain Tallin focused his stare on Miranda and Helena. The ladies exchanged glances.

"Do you think—" Miranda began, but before she could finish Helena whipped around and ran towards the Hangar, the Academy student close on her heels. When they arrived, Helena grabbed the nearest soldier and threw him against the wall, pinning his shoulders in order to conduct a fierce interrogation.

"Have you seen Specialist Holley?"

"No ma'am!" The young man with night-black hair and emerald-green eyes shook his head and held up his hands in his defense. "It's just been me down here, but I've been in and out of the Hangar, helping families out and all."

Miranda and Kront found Helena and pulled her away from harassing the young man. "Lieutenant, get a hold on yourself!" Kront demanded.

"Damn me!" she cursed. "How could I be so stupid?" She looked to the young man. "How could you not see a wounded troop take off in a shuttle?" She shook herself free from the grasp of her friends and stormed off, heading back to the Bridge.

"Captain Tallin, sir?" the young man spoke up.

"Yes?"

"I did see Specialist Holley take off in the *Jaime* an hour or two ago." He gulped as he continued. "I swore I would've stopped her, sir, except she threatened to take away my rank, and that's all I have right now, sir. My rank and my little sister. The rest of my family didn't survive Troklon, sir."

Kront clapped the young man's right shoulder with his left hand. He let go, nodded for Miranda to follow, and ran to the Bridge to join Helena.

The lieutenant was already tracking her younger sister's life signature. "Found her, sir."

Miranda joined her friend at her station. "It looks like Jaime is two million miles out. Somewhere in Section Delta, Grid Alpha 3...damn it!"

"What?" Kront asked.

"She's only 200,000 miles away from the Trikkyas ship *Spitfire*, Draglon Class." Miranda shook her head. "There's only one reason she'd go after a ship that big."

Jamie steered the *Jaime* shuttle straight towards the *Spitfire*. Its scramblers were turned on full power, and she had taken out the transponder before departing the *Lindman*'s Hangar. *There's no way they can see me,* she convinced herself as she slowly maneuvered the shuttle into position at 15,000 feet from the *Spitfire.* Jamie put on her suit and picked up her Sniper Blaster; she opened the shuttle door and stepped out in space. She loved the feeling of floating in space just as much as Helena. They were meant to be Freedom Fighters.

She pushed herself forward by pressing the throttle button. "8,000 feet… 7,500… 6,000… 5,500…" Jamie heard a small scratching on her radio, but the communication was severely hindered by the Trikkyas ship's radio blocker.

"Ja… D… Sto…" If the person continued to send a signal, the Trikkyas would find her position, and her mission would be compromised. She turned off the radio and hoped the transmission would stop. That *she* would stop.

"Okay, just a little bit more, and I'm in range," she said aloud. She let go of the throttle button, and her personal thrusters turned off. "Perfect." She pulled out her Sniper Blaster and placed her eye against the scope. "Fuel cells…engine…electrical…come on!" Jaime cried in frustrated tones. She glanced over the ship from her position several times over. "Give me something I can blow up to send these bastards to hell!" Then, she found exactly what she was looking for…and something she wasn't. Suddenly, two small speeders raced toward her from the rear of the Trikkyas ship.

"Shit!" she cursed. "They found me!" They shot at her, bullets whizzing past her as she defended herself with her own sniper. She took out one pilot, and the speeder exploded near the *Jaime,* the blast waves sending her ship spiraling out into deep space. She screamed in rage and turned back to take on the other pilot, but he was faster. His bullets pierced her suit, and she felt her blood pouring from the wounds in her stomach, chest, and right leg. Just as the lights were going out in her eyes, she gathered up the reserve energy in her body, lifted her gun, took aim, and pulled the trigger. She watched as her bullet flew in a straight line past the Trikkyas speeder towards its intended target on the mother ship. The Trikkyas speeder shot her again…and again…Jaime swore she heard her name being called. She thought she saw the speeder explode, like a shot from another sniper. "Just like Miranda's sniper," she spoke barely above a whisper. Though only half-conscious, she was fully aware that blood now dripped from the corner of her mouth. As she let her eyes close upon her world, she felt her arms being pulled; she couldn't tell if the devils below dragged her down, or if the angels above pulled her to safety, but she was so glad to be done with this life.

"Jaime, stay with me!" Helena screamed. She had pulled her younger sister's lifeless body into the back of the *Lindman, Jr.* just in time to escape the explosive fireballs from the destroyed Trikkyas ship. Jaime's bulls-eye hit had demolished one of the most powerful Trikkyas ships. Their revenge would be swift and sure, but for now Miranda and Helena had to grab Jaime and get back to the *Lindman* as fast as possible.

Miranda shoved the hyperspace control forward. "Hold on!"

Helena took off Jaime's headgear; she searched for a pulse on the com officer and expert sniper as the tears from the lieutenant's eyes splattered onto the specialist's pools of blood below. "Jaime! Wake up!"

Miranda placed the shuttle on auto-pilot for Helgin and ran to the back. She helped Helena remove the rest of Jaime's space suit. They used several first aid kits to try to ease the blood loss, but soon they realized Jaime wasn't going to make it this time. Miranda pulled the oxygen mask from the shuttle's wall and placed it on Jaime's face. The specialist's eyes fluttered open and closed twice. "Jaime?"

Helena searched for a pulse again. "Her pulse is getting weaker. She doesn't have much time. We've got to go faster."

The Intel Officer shook her head. "Helena, we won't get there in time." She placed her hand on Helena's which laid on Jaime's chest over a largely wounded area. "We're gonna lose her this time."

She couldn't believe it. She wouldn't believe it. She held her little sister close. The labored breathing she heard beneath the oxygen mask gave witness to Miranda's words. *But she's my little sister,* Helena argued in her mind. *I can't lose her…not now…*

Jaime coughed and blood filled the mask. Helena removed it, and Miranda wiped the girl's mouth, but Jaime tried to grab

Miranda's hand. She wheezed and inhaled blood, sputtering as she tried to speak. "I'm...sorry..."

Miranda's eyes filled with tears; she wasn't afraid to hold them back in front of her two sisters-in-arms. "I forgive you, but I'll kill you if you try it again."

Jaime's half-smile nearly killed Helena, watching her little sister fight to stay alive long enough to apologize for her stupid actions. "Oh, Jaime, why'd you do it?" Helena complained. "I would've gone with you. Why couldn't you just ask? Why do you have to be so reckless sometimes?"

Jaime half-smiled again, followed by another blood-filled cough and wheezing inhale. It was enough to make the healthy ladies feel as though they couldn't breathe, either. "I love... you... sis..." She closed her eyes and coughed again, but this time she couldn't cough it out. Her hand dropped. Her pulse stopped. Helena cradled the dead body of her younger sister for hours after the ship had landed in the Hangar of the *Lindman*.

*   *   *

It had been two weeks since Jaime's burial, but Helena stayed in her room on the *Lindman*. No one could make her come out or eat, not even her own parents.

"I wouldn't worry, Captain," Nikolej reassured Kront. "She'll come out in her own time."

"But I am worried," he retorted. "That silly woman hasn't colored her hair since Jaime died. It's weird seeing natural colors on her head." His remarks got a smile from Ida. She placed her hand on Kront's arm and kissed his cheek, but walked away without a word. Kront raised his eyebrows to Nikolej.

The father shook his head. "The Holley women suffer in silence. That's what they do."

Kront shook the man's hand, and Buck escorted them out of the *Lindman* and back to their campsite. Meanwhile, Kront meandered down the hallways of his shuttle, purposely ending up at the lieutenant's room. He knocked on the door and let himself in. Helena lied on her bed, facing the door. She knew it was Kront.

"Hi."

"Hi," he responded. He took a seat at her desk and crossed his arms. "I need you, Helena. We need you on this ship."

"Don't lie to me, Captain." She rolled over and turned her back to him. "My little sister is dead. I can't go on anymore. She gave up her life to kill over 1400 Trikkyas troops on that ship, and what does she have to show for it but a grave and a tombstone?"

Kront stood up and opened the door to leave. "Fine. Rot in your bed. You'll have less to show for it than she did. But the Little Sister is waiting for you…and she's just like Jaime." He closed the door behind him and walked to the Hangar, knowing his words would pique her interest. Sure enough, as soon as he got down to the Hangar to meet Buck about a new weapon, Miranda called his personal com. He pressed the button his wrist com. "Yes, Miranda?"

"It worked, sir," she smiled. "She called me on the com as she was dressing and brushing her teeth at the same time…although I don't know how she was able to do that."

Kront laughed. "I don't know either, but send her down here. We're ready."

"Roger that, sir. Miranda out."

Within seconds, a very angry Helena stormed down the stairs leading from the upper floors of the ship down to the Hangar bottom. "What's the meaning of this?" she yelled from side opposite Kront and Buck. "How dare you use the phrase 'little sister' in front of me in as a joke!"

Buck started to say something, but Kront slapped him in the chest to stop him. "I wasn't joking, Lieutenant," the commander negated. "Sergeant Cypher has created the Little Sister in honor of Jaime, a weapon that literally has her kind of temperament: nice and kind looking but with a nasty thirst for revenge."

Helena's eyes popped open so wide Buck was afraid they'd fall out. Of course, he was afraid his own eyes would leave their sockets: he'd never seen Helena's true hair color before. "Lieutenant, your hair…"

Just as she was about to threaten Buck, Kront intervened, took the weapon from Buck and wrapped his left arm tightly around Helena to drag her outside the *Lindman*. "How about we take this little beauty for a test drive, hmm?" He placed the weapon in her hands and searched the horizon for a decent target. He pressed the com button on his wrist visual. "Miranda, find me a target approximately 17,500 feet southwest of my exact location, please."

"Yes, sir," she replied. "There is an abandoned metal building that would make fine target practice. Area is cleared for the Little Sister. No life signatures within a three-mile radius any direction. Have fun." She signed out, and Kront turned off his com.

"All right, Lieutenant. This weapon is just a prototype, and its power is nowhere near the maximum capacity, but its range is accurate, so go ahead and give it a shot."

Helena didn't move. "I don't understand, sir."

He formed fists at his hips. "Helena, you've been stuck in your room for two weeks. Jaime's dead. She did the Service proud, but she was also very stupid, and you know that. Now, you can choose to mope around in your room, and I'll take away your rank and kick you off my ship. You can spend your days moping around Helgin for all I care, or you can get up and act like one of my crew."

She straightened up. "Yes, sir. I'm sorry…I just really miss her, sir. You know…"

"I know, Helena." He dropped his fists. "Buck made this prototype based on a weapons blueprint from Miranda who got the idea from Jaime's…escapade. It should help us clear out some Trikkyas ships from 17,500 feet away. It's an upgraded form of the Sniper Blaster with some modifications. Like I said, it's got Jaime's personality, so we dubbed it the Little Sister."

A tear escaped Helena's eye. "Thank you, sir." She quickly wiped it away, held up the gun, aimed at the target through the scope, and fired. "Score one for the Little Sister."

Chapter 22. – A Fight for Justice.

During the next week, Helena and Miranda each took on a single, solo-soldier mission to destroy a Trikkyas ship in order to test the Little Sister weapon in a real-time environment. Of course, that's what they claimed. Everyone knew it was a little more than that, especially with Jaime's death still so fresh on their minds and in the air. Helena flew the *Jaime* and found the *Hauling Drum*, another Trikkyas ship in the Draglon Class. Miranda set her eyes on a higher prize, the biggest ship in the Trikkyas fleet: the Store Class Fortress *Proud Trikk*. She barely escaped on the *Lindman, Jr.*, for the explosive fireball the Trikkyas ship had become nearly overtook the speed of her shuttle, but she had marked her distance and calculated her numbers correctly, leaving the scene of the crime with only a singe on the wings and tail of her speeder.

She called over the com system as she headed back to the *Lindman*, "Captain, tell Buck to make about 100 more of these Little Sister guns. I like 'em!"

Kront laughed in response. "Helena already called in to demand the same thing. Don't worry; Buck's engineers will be quite busy for the next several days."

"Roger and amen to that!" With a more serious turn in her voice, she continued. "Captain, I'm seeing a distress call from Loht 9. Can that be right?"

Kront checked the radar and scanner himself at the Bridge. "It could be, but I'm not sure if you should check it out. It could be a trap. I'm not seeing anything from here. No one else has reported a distress signal coming from there."

"Captain, I don't think anyone else is picking up the signal but me." She punched some numbers into her ship's computer and read the results. "Sir, I believe that someone rigged a signal down there so the closest, non-Trikkyas ship could receive the signal. Something about the Trikkyas Shuttle *Gribbon* threatening to kill them if they try to escape the planet."

Kront sighed, "Just don't make the same mistake Jaime did, okay?"

His comment immediately humbled Miranda. "Yes, sir. I understand. I'll continue running a report on it. If it's a trap, I'll hyperspace out; otherwise, I'm going on a rescue mission. *Lindman, Jr.* out." She pushed forward the throttle for hyperspace and set her course for Loht 9. She turned her scramblers on full-strength. Weapon loaded, the Academy student suited-up for the mission as the signal continued to come in from a remote location on the planet guarded by another Trikkyas ship.

"Please be a little one. Please be a little one," Miranda hoped aloud. As she rounded the planet, her hopes plummeted when a large Trikkyas fortress came into her view. "Damn it!" she cursed aloud. She exited the ship with her suit, gear, and weapon to clear her head.

"Calm down, Miranda. You can do this." Formulating a plan in how to use the remainder of her ten sniper bombs to destroy a 24-pack of fuel cells, her mind turned toward Jaime. She wondered, *What would you do, Jaime? I'm stuck.* Suddenly, she thought of a time in class back at the Academy when they had to answer a prompt with a similar situation: "In using limited resources to either disarm or destroy an enemy target, which weapon would be best and why?" surprisingly, Jaime had the only different – and correct – answer out of everyone. She chose a weapon that would simply disarm the ship enough to create the havoc necessary for the enemy to destroy itself. Miranda sighed. *Of course,* she remembered. *It doesn't matter if I actually blow it up. If I disarm its fuselage enough, the combination of an oxygen leak, lack of pressure, and rapidly decreasing elevation will cause the ship to overheat and blow itself up all on its own! Genius!*

She aimed for several weak spots in the Trikkyas ship and fired away, using up all of her sniper bombs. *Hope I don't come across any more enemy troops before I get back to Helgin,* she prayed, crossing her fingers. Her bullets flew straight, but she didn't stay to watch the fireworks show. She floated back to her ship, slammed the door shut, jumped into the cockpit without taking off her suit, and shot straight toward Loht 9. She focused on her radar as the signal of the *Gribbon* shuttle *blipped, blipped,* and then faded from view.

Kront sat in front of his computer at the Bridge. He heard a noise at Miranda's computer, took the few steps leading down from the top level to her station, and woke her computer out of sleep mode. A message lit up across her screen. His eyes widened. "It can't be," he whispered. "No fucking way." He ran back up to his station and punched in the information, only to find his concerns confirmed. "Damn!" He pressed his personal com unit on his wrist. "Nielson, are you there?"

"Yes, boss," Nielson replied, his head filling Kront's tiny visual screen. "What's up?"

"Do you feel okay enough to open the com to the entire galaxy?"

"Um…the entire galaxy?" Kront would've laughed at Nielson's confused face if not for the seriousness of the situation. "Are you sure?"

"Yes, can you do it?"

"Yeah, just give me a second." Nielson disappeared from the screen and returned a moment later. "It's up. Ready when you are, sir."

Kront smiled. "Attention. This is Captain Kront of the Presidential Space Ship *Lindman*. I am calling for the surrender of all Trikkyas troops. King Seriten Avar has been released as a hostage of the Handlons. Sign a peace treaty with us. We want this war to end. I repeat, King Avar has been released, and we ask for a peace treaty between the Trikkyas and humans. *Lindman* out."

Captain Tallin turned off the com and returned to Nielson. This time, Nielson's face was shocked. "Sir, is this real?"

"Yes, it is." He said nothing more, arising curiosity from Nielson.

"Sir, did you know anything about the king's capture prior to this moment?"

"Please get Miranda on the com."

The captain's non-answer was all the answer Nielson needed, but he knew that whatever the Captain had done, it was always in the best interest of the human race. He'd never question his commander. "Yes, sir. Nielson out." At the same moment, Buck called up to the Bridge from the Hangar. "Sir, Miranda has returned…with some extra cargo…Did you know about that?"

"Yes, I did, Sergeant. No worries." Kront started toward the Hangar, wiping the guilty sweat from his brow. "I'll be there momentarily. Kront out." He turned off his com and stepped down the stairs, meeting Miranda halfway across the hangar as she walked over to salute him.

"Sir, mission success, and I brought back hostages from Loht 9."

"So," Kront stated, "the signal was real."

"Yes, sir, and it was sent from this young man." She pointed to a young man around twenty-years old standing near her at the front of a large crowd of people. "This is Preston Henson."

Kront shook his hand. "You're very talented, young man. Making a signal reach only the closest, non-Trikkyas ship? What is your profession?"

Miranda suddenly felt feelings of jealously prick at her heart. She'd never felt this before, especially since she always had the great ideas, but now for a *guy* to come into the scene and have great ideas, too? Preston cleared his throat and stood at attention. "Sir, I'm a Level 93 Com Officer from Academy Troklon."

Kront shook his head in the affirmative. "You may have known one of our own. She recently passed away due to an unfortunate incident…Jaime Holley?"

Preston's eyes met Kront's. A sad shade of blue filled his eyes. "Yes, sir. I vaguely remember sitting near her in one or two classes. Of course, that was before Troklon blew up. My family—," he motioned to the others around him, "—and I were on vacation when it happened."

"Sir," Miranda interrupted. "Preston is grandson of the late Christian Henson, Admiral of the *Grimond Wolf*. He wants to work as a com officer aboard the *Lindman*…if you have need of him."

Kront's eyes flipped back and forth between Miranda and Preston. A grin tugged at the corners of his mouth. *Oh, sweet revenge,* he thought. *To finally play matchmaking in Miranda's life instead of having her play matchmaker for everyone else!* Kront looked down at the floor, up at the ceiling, and paced the room for a moment. Then, he nodded. "Officer Henson, you'll have to pass the Lie Detector Test before I make my decision."

"Understood," he answered. "Thank you for even giving me the chance, sir."

"Miranda, please call Helena on the com," Kront directed. "Have her report to the Conference Room with the Detector. Escort Officer Henson to the room when she's ready. I'm going to help these fine people get situated in the campsites."

"Yes, sir." Miranda called Helena over the com as everyone cleared the Bridge except for the two Officers. She finished the call with Helena, looked Preston over once, and then sat at her station, leaving Preston standing alone until Helena called in ready for the test. Miranda and Preston walked down the hallway to the Conference Room. He stared at the back of the head of the cute red-head and smiled like a dumb, love-struck puppy. She whipped around, and they nearly collided. "Officer Henson, the test will be conducted in this room. Good luck. You'll need it," she haughtily remarked.

"Oh, yeah?" he taunted. "Why's that?" He raised his eyebrows several times in a flirtatious effort.

Her cheeks flushed, no matter how much she wished she could control her emotions. "Because I made the test. And I'm never wrong." She turned around and walked back toward the Bridge.

Preston knew he was testing his luck, but he whistled out a catcall. Miranda looked back at him with a shocked face and stormed off to her station, muttering curse words not-so-quietly as she went. He snickered until he realized the door to his right was opened, and a woman with blue and white hair stood in the doorway with her arms crossed. He slowly pivoted his feet until he faced her. "Ma'am?"

"Officer Henson?" She arched one eyebrow.

"Yes, ma'am." He gulped.

"I'm Lieutenant Helena Holley. Please, do come inside," she half-sarcastically stated. After administering the test, he sat back and sighed in relief. She smiled. "There's nothing to worry about. You passed. I'm sure Captain Kront would be more than happy to have found another com officer."

"I heard about Specialist Jaime's passing. I knew her in school. I'm sorry about your sister, ma'am."

Helena's eyes teared up, but she cleared her throat and kept her emotions in check. "Yes, well, she was haphazard and didn't always make the smartest decisions, but her dedication was true, and she did a hell of a good job being a com officer, so you better keep up to her standard."

"I plan to, ma'am," he smiled. He stood up to leave. "Am I dismissed?"

"One more thing. Do you like Officer Holliday?"

Bright pink filled Preston's cheeks. "Is this part of the test, Lieutenant? Because I think if I give you the correct answer while employed on this ship, the lie detector will find me out."

She laughed. "Preston, just answer the question."

"Love at first sight, no, but I think she's beautiful, smart, and a temperament that I'd like to see out to its full extent just for fun." He grinned like the Cheshire cat playing a game.

"Would you consider taking her on a date?"

"Most definitely."

She leaned closer. "I think you should lay off the catcalls and just do it, soldier."

His cheeks turned a slightly darker pink as he straightened to his full height. "Yes, ma'am. Mission accepted." He saluted and left the room, closing the door behind him.

Helena smiled. "This is going to be lots of fun."

Chapter 23. – Preston's Plan.

"Okay, calm down and tell me about your dream," Helena persuaded Jamina. "Let's analyze it together."

The pregnant woman looked at her husband; he nodded, and she took a deep breath. "Each night for the past three nights, my dream starts out the same. Bravo Squad is patrolling on Planet Trikk. Everyone is in high spirits, laughing at each other's jokes."

Helena smiled. "Sounds pretty normal, so far." Internally, Helena was waging warfare of heart versus gut. *Pregnant woman can have premonitions about things, and they're generally right,* her heart argued. But her mind countered, *That may be so, but you never hope for the bad dreams to come true...* Jamina's most recent nightmares were definitely not for the faint of heart. The younger woman touched Helena's hand, shaking Helena from her own thoughts. "Go on."

Jamina sighed. "It seems normal, yes, but then things go wrong. An explosion blasts Buck down the hill. He's dead. Trikkyas soldiers surround you all, and there's no place to hide. They kill the whole squad in seconds, cut off your head, Helena, and send it back to Captain Tallin."

The Lieutenant's eyebrows rose in amazement. "Is there more?" *Please tell me no. Please tell me no, and please don't come true,* Helena wished to herself.

She nodded. "Kront sends out the other squads, but the Trikkyas launch an attack and kill them all, then Captain and the crew, and all the survivors on Helgin."

Helena shook her head. "Jamina, we don't have any patrols on Trikk, so I'm pretty sure this is just a bad dream." Though statistics were against her words, she couldn't risk upsetting Jamina more than she already was.

Jamina sighed. "I hope you're right."

"Me, too." The Lieutenant sighed. "Me, too."

*　　*　　*

Miranda scanned the area around Helgin. No Trikkyas

ships in the area. *Maybe I should boost the scanner and increase the search radius*, she thought. She stole a glance Preston's direction. He was "reading" the com manual, staring at Miranda over the top of the book and grinning from ear to ear when he caught her looking at him.

She put her nose up in the air and snooted.

He snickered, and just as she was about to make a snide remark, his monitor displayed an alert. He jumped forward in his seat. "Miranda, I've got a message alert, no visual."

"Sure you do," she caustically stated without looking his direction.

Preston leaned back. "Fine. Don't believe me."

Tight-lipped, Miranda reneged. "Fine. Send it to me. Probably just one of those dumb chain-letter stories anyway." Preston sent the message to her monitor and watched as she opened it up, still muttering under her breath. The words didn't quite come across as a typical chain-letter story.

> *Humans, we received your message over the galaxy com. Did you think that would dissuade us from destroying you? We have sent out 200 ships to find and destroy your planet, your fleet, and your entire race and civilization. If you surrender yourselves to the Grand Ruler of the Trikkyas Empire, we will not kill all of you. You have 24 hours to respond.*

Preston gulped. Miranda shook her head. "Call the squad leaders on the com. Get them and Captain and Helena to the Situation Room, now!"

"You got it!" Preston did as he was told, and Miranda sent a copy of the digital file to the computer in the room down the hall. She left her station as Preston was finishing up the com calls. "Miranda!"

She stopped and turned around. "Yeah?"

"Now you believe me?" A slight smile tugged at his mouth.

"Not now, Henson." She stormed off, and he could tell that he was pressing all of the right buttons when it came to Intel Officer Miranda Holliday.

"Conduct a deep scan of space," Kront directed to Officer Holliday. Everyone had been in the Situation Room for over an hour trying to figure out the next step in dealing with the latest Trikkyas news. "I need to know their distance from us and how long until they arrive."

"The scanner indicates the nearest ship is nineteen days away."

He lowered his head and ran his fingers through his hair. Standing up, he placed his hands on his hips and addressed everyone in the room. "Okay, we have nine days. Let's get to work. I want ideas and plans. I want volunteers. I want to be prepared for anything and everything until we can figure more of this shit out." As the room cleared out, Kront, Helena, and Miranda returned to the Bridge. Preston stood up at his station and saluted.

"Sir?"

Kront looked over to Preston. "Yes, Officer Henson? What can I do? Although as you may not know, this isn't really a good time. The Trikkyas just sent—"

"Yes, sir. I know about the ships and 24-hour deadline," he interjected. "The message first came up on my screen, at which time I informed Officer Holliday."

"Oh, is that how it happened, eh?" Kront eyed a very pink-faced Miranda as she excused herself to her station. Helena smiled, visually hi-fiving Preston. "What did you want to say?"

"Well, sir," he began, turning around to his computer and bringing up a rough blueprint on his screen. "I drew up a weapons design for a new missile, and I wanted to know your opinion on it. We could use it to defend ourselves against the Trikkyas in this new attack."

Helena and Kront looked over the designs at their own computers. "Preston," the lieutenant said, "this doesn't look any different than our other missiles in the Armory."

"That's right, ma'am. The physical features are the same, but the guiding system has been altered. It's designed to locate and wipe out a specific signature."

Miranda's curiosity was now piqued. "Let me see." She bumped him over from his computer, took over his keyboard, and ran program after program in order to find a hole in his new toy. Unsuccessful, she returned to her seat without a word.

"Well, Miranda?" Kront asked. "What do you think?"

She turned around in her seat and crossed her arms. "It's good, but I'm sure there's a flaw somewhere. I haven't found it yet, but we don't want to send an imperfect missile against the Trikkyas."

Kront pondered for a moment. "Explain the entire idea to us, Preston."

"Sir, every ship has a different signature. If we program the missile to locate the ship, but target its fuel cells, that would start a chain reaction. We'd need to use a missile that's fast enough to avoid being taken out before accomplishing the mission, *and* needs to be hidden from radars and scanners with a scrambler." Preston looked at Miranda with admiration. "But from what I've heard around here, I believe someone has already accomplished this task."

Miranda blushed and turned to Kront. "Captain, it's worth a try. It's an idea to consider."

"Good," Helena stated. "Since you'll be working together non-stop to fix all the kinks in the plan, better get accustomed to each other. Be prepared to present in 48 hours." She took Kront's arm and led him down a hallway leading away from the Bridge, leaving Miranda with her mouth gaping open as Preston slid his arm around her shoulders and waved.

"Helena…" Kront started.

"Kront, don't," she interrupted. "You and I both know what she needs is someone of the *opposite* gender right now." She stopped their walk. "She needs to stop focusing on the loss of Jaime and start focusing on her own life. She needs a guy in her life to spice things up—shake things up a bit. Give her a little scare and a little magic at the same time."

Kront smiled and pushed a few strands of her red and yellow hair from her face. "You know I wish I was little younger."

She hugged him. "I know, Kront."

Helena walked in to the Hangar; she watched Miranda and

Preston talk as they worked on the missile. She tiptoed around some equipment so she could get closer to hear their conversation better.

"Miranda, when we finish this project, would you like—" Preston began.

"—to get the hell away from you? You bet!" she answered.

Preston laughed. "Not quite what I meant. How about dinner before you ditch me?"

Miranda sat up straight. Her eyes narrowed into a hawk-like look as she tried to pierce her gaze through his head. "What is it you're really after?"

Preston threw his hands into the air in his defense. "I'm a typical guy and won't lie about that. But my mom would come back from the grave and kill me if I tried to get you in bed before at least going on a few dates."

"One dinner does not constitute a few dates."

"But one dinner could lead to several more."

Miranda shook her head. "Preston, I'm not the dating type."

"Maybe it's because you won't let yourself be the average type." Preston's words hit her in the chest like a rock. "And that's not a bad thing. I really like it. I don't want to see you settle for someone whose intelligence, attitude, or passion for talents isn't matched by your own."

Miranda leaned over and leaned close to his face. He could hardly breathe. She was so beautiful. He reached up to touch her hair. She was literally a breath away from kissing him. Just as their lips were about to touch, she grabbed his hand from her hair, pinned him to the floor, and whispered in his ear. "Dinner. Nothing else." She released him as she stood up and walked away. Preston sat up and smiled, knowing he wasn't imagining a slightly more enticing shake in her rear rhythm as he watched her backside.

Oh, yeah, Helena thought, smiling to herself. *This is going to be so much fun...*

Chapter 24. – We Can Do It.

It was a unanimous decision that the *Lindman* would best serve the survivors on Helgin by remaining in space instead of trying to protect them from the ground. Before entering space, Sergeant Cypher's engineers and a few civilian volunteers relocated the newly-finished missile to a remote launch site. Now, Captain Tallin, Lieutenant Holley, and the squad leaders stood at the Bridge. On the large screen before them, they watched the first completed missile prepare for its launch into space. Officers Holliday and Henson sat at their stations, checking and re-checking for any last-minute glitches.

"This is the first of many missiles," Kront began. "Can we survive a war against the Trikkyas? They have the means to defend their threat, and we need the means to defend our people." Several nods and military shout-outs sounded from the individuals standing near him.

Miranda called over her shoulder, "Captain, the missile is clear for launch."

Helena suggested, "Why don't Officers Holliday and Henson launch the missile, sir? After all, it was their combined ideas and planning that got it to this moment." She nudged Kront in the ribs.

He nodded in agreement. "Officers Holliday and Henson, you have my permission to launch."

Miranda looked to Preston; he smiled, but there was something more than just friendship glinting off those pearly whites. Miranda blushed and shyly smiled in return. *He's not so bad once you get to know him*, she conceded. She placed her hand on the launch button, and he placed his on top. They counted down, "Five…four…three…two…one…" Together, they pressed down, and the missile's engines roared to life, burst into fire and flames, and pushed the missile off the ground and into the air. Although the moment called for celebration, only an air of serious contemplation filled the Bridge.

"Impact in 13 hours and 22 minutes, sir." Miranda looked up to the countdown on the visual screen, but as she removed her hand from the launch button, Preston kept his on top and held firmly to her hand. Not wanting to catch his glance, she didn't look his direction as a lighter pink blush covered her cheeks, but she didn't pull away, either.

I'll take every moment I can, Preston thought to himself. *Every moment…*

"Officer Henson?"

Preston dropped Miranda's hand. She pulled her hand to her lap, feeling oddly that she missed it being held in the warmth of his grasp. "Yes, Captain?"

"The Lieutenant and I will take the first watch. Buck and Adriahna will have the second," he stated. "I believe you two need some sleep."

Miranda sighed. "I couldn't agree more, sir." She got up to leave, Preston quick on her heels, but Kront stopped him.

"Preston, I need to warn you." Kront put his arm around the young man in a fatherly fashion. "I have come to love Miranda like my own daughter. I treat her like she is, so I expect her to be treated by others as such. Am I clear?"

"Yes, sir." Preston nodded. "Very clear."

Kront whispered into Preston's ear. "I have cameras everywhere. Stay in your own quarters." He pulled away and turned back to face the large visual screen. "Dismissed."

*   *   *

"Officer Henson, please report to the Bridge." Helena turned off the com and settled into the seat next to Kront at the Bridge. "Tell me again, why I just did that?" She looked up at the screen. "We only have thirty minutes until the missile hits its target."

Kront leaned back with his fingers laced together behind his head. "Just watch. You think you've got these love birds figured out. I want to have some fun with them, too."

Preston came running to the Bridge. "Ma'am? Sir?"

The commander jumped to his feet, turned red in the face, and yelled at Preston. "Soldier, I told you to stay in your quarters! You disobeyed a direct order from a superior officer—and your commander, at that!"

Preston went white-faced. Helena was shocked, as well, but

knew she had to trust Kront in the matter. He was known to pull all kinds of gags on his soldiers. Preston backed up to the wall behind him as Kront neared him. "Sir, I swear I didn't—"

"Do not lie to my face, Officer Henson!"

"Sir, should I get the Detector?" Helena interjected, playing along with Kront's scheme.

He backed away from Preston and crossed his arms. "Yes, I think so." Just then, Miranda rounded the corner with the very machine in her hands.

"Miranda?" Kront asked, eyebrows arched in question.

"Go ahead and scan him," she dared. "He's telling the truth." She crossed her arms and stood toe-to-toe with Kront. "He didn't go in my quarters."

Preston sighed in relief. "You see, sir, I—"

"—I went in his," Miranda continued.

Preston and Helena gawked at Miranda's boldness. Kront and the Academy student looked like they were having a father-daughter argument about how late she could stay out after prom was over.

"And what do you have to say for yourself, Officer Holliday?" Kront arched an eyebrow.

Miranda grinned from ear to ear. "I'd say he likes green boxer-briefs the best, although I imagine blue is more his color." She turned around and gazed at him from head to toe several times before walking away.

Helena and Kront busted out laughing; within seconds, they were grabbing at tissues to wipe the tears from their faces. They sat in their chairs and clutched at their sides. Preston grabbed his very red face and slunk to the floor in embarrassment.

Kront wiped another tear and stuttered between laughs and gasps for air, "Is...that t-true...Preston?"

Helena fell to the floor. "Green...or...b-blue?" Her laughter turned into cackles and snorting. Preston shook his head. Then, something green that was too close to the same shape and size of his own boxer-briefs came strutting down the hallway on a figure that should never wear a man's piece of clothing.

Miranda Holliday.

Helena and Kront, near the end of the first bout of laughter, erupted into more chuckles and chortles as Miranda put on a red-carpet catwalk displaying a pair of Preston's green boxer-briefs over her uniform.

"That's it!" Preston yelled. He stood up, grabbed Miranda by the sides, and threw her over his left shoulder. Turning to face Kront amidst Miranda's demands for release, he asked, "Permission to return to my quarters, sir?"

Kront could only shake his head in the affirmative. Helena watched on her hands and knees as Preston walked away with a red-faced Miranda over Preston's shoulder. She saw them round the corner and disappear from sight. She waited…waited…and then she heard the slam of a door which she surely thought was Preston's. "Good thing that boy's as smart as Miranda," she commented aloud.

Kront stopped laughing and, somewhat seriously, looked at Helena with his head slightly cocked in response to her awkward comment. "Why's that, Helena?"

"Well, sir, he took her into his room, but he's programmed the door so only he can open it." She smiled at Kront. "I don't think she'll be leaving for a while…or at least until they figure things out between them." At that, they both started laughing all over again.

*   *   *

"Impact in thirty seconds," Miranda announced. "Still no indications that the Trikkyas have seen the missile." Miranda and Preston watched their monitors closely—the radars, the scanners, the reports…nothing disproved them, yet. "Impact in ten seconds." Kront moved to the edge of his chair as Miranda counted down. "Five…four…three…two…one…Impact!"

For a split second, everyone on the Bridge held their breath. Just as they had hoped and expected, both the missile and Trikkyas ship disappeared from the screen.

"Yeah!" Preston jumped up from his seat and punched the air. "We did it!"

"We did it," Miranda echoed, a large grin spreading across her face. "We did it!"

Preston grabbed the red-headed woman into his arms and planted a huge kiss on her lips. "*We* did it, ma'am." He winked as he set her down; she grabbed his left arm, her senses off-balance after such a surprise. Sigu and Michael pointed at Miranda and laughed; even John smiled, a rare feat, indeed. Drenge hi-fived Preston on his accomplishment in taming the woman of wild temperament.

Kront and Buck shook hands, but Helena grabbed Kront in a huge hug. "It worked, Kront!"

"I know! But now we need to make a lot more." He turned back to Buck. "What do you say, Sergeant?"

Buck pursed his lips in thought. "Give me one week, and we can have enough smaller ones to knock out all of the other ships."

Kront's eyebrows pushed together in confusion. "How so?"

"Chain reaction, sir. Traveling in such a large group as they are, they're too close together to not be affected by a chain reaction of explosions."

Kront nodded. "Get started as soon as you can. Helena, find volunteers among the civilians to help us move the missiles into position when they're ready."

"Yes, sir."

"Miranda, how many ships are left in the Trikkyas fleet?"

Miranda sat down at her station, finally recovered from the surprise attack on her lips by Preston. She pulled up the report of the last scan. "572 ships, sir."

Kront frowned. "That will still leave 372 after we launch the missiles onto the approaching fleet." He ran his hand through his hair. "Until they figure out how to find, read, or avoid our missiles, we have to hope we can keep using them for our defense."

"Sir," Preston addressed the commander, "we have an incoming com from the Earth vessel *Protector*."

Kront jumped up from his chair. "Earth vessel? But the satellites are still three days from its orbit. Is it possible we miscalculated?"

Preston shrugged. "I don't know, sir, but I'm sure it's the *Protector*."

"Patch it through."

"Yes, sir." Preston accepted the call and transferred the

visual to Kront's station at the higher level at the Bridge. "*Protector*, this is the *Lindman*. I'm Captain Kront Tallin. How can we be of service?"

A beautiful woman with dark brown hair and dark red lips appeared. Her chocolate brown eyes seemed to draw Kront into the visual with a little more intensity than he was prepared for. In a sultry voice, she stated, "*Lindman*, this is the *Protector*. I'm Commander Angelina Francis."

"Angelina?" Kront recognized the woman as the pilot of the flight to Troklon from Earth. For the past five years, she had piloted the flights, and they had met up while she stayed on Troklon until her return to Earth. Unfortunately, it had been two years since the last flight to Troklon, and two years since they had last seen each other.

"Kront. It's good to see you, too," she replied," but I believe that it is you who are seeking our help, am I correct?"

Feeling slightly put back into his place, he nodded. "Yes, indeed. We weren't expecting the satellites to pass into Earth's orbit for another three days."

She smiled. "We were in the area. Update me on your current situation."

"We've launched a counterattack and have successfully taken out several Trikkyas ships and a few fortresses, as well. They're sending another 200 ships our way, but we've developed a missile that could set off a chain reaction to destroy all of the ships in that fleet. If it works, it may convince the Trikkyas to sign a peace treaty."

"If not?"

"Then, at least it'll keep them at bay until we have more firepower ready to deal with them. I'd give it another month."

"How did you develop the weapons and technology to defeat the Trikkyas with so few survivors and such a small fighting crew?"

Kront beamed. "I have a few secrets, Commander. My squad leaders have been exceptionally heroic in their missions aboard various ships and planets. My second-in-command, Lieutenant Helena Holley, is unmatched by any other I know. Three recent students from Academy Troklon have proved especially fruitful in their talents and endeavors: Intelligence

Officer Miranda Holley and Communications Officer Preston Henson…and the late Specialist Jaime Holley, the lieutenant's younger sister."

"I'm sorry for your loss, Kront. I'd like to meet these individuals," Angelina requested. "The Earth militaries could learn a great deal from such talented young people."

"I don't see why not," Kront shrugged. He turned to Preston. "Officer Henson, send the *Protector* our coordinates, please."

"No need, Captain," Angelina interrupted. "We'll be onboard shortly."

Miranda's screen alerted her. "Captain, an unknown ship is approaching the *Lindman*."

Kront suddenly felt slightly suspicious of Angelina's intentions toward Miranda and Preston. *How did she get past our radar and scanner? How did we not see her coming?* Kront asked himself. *I don't like the feeling of this, but Angelina's a friend of mine. Surely I can trust her…can't I?* Quickly, he glanced down to his monitors and pulled up the screens that accessed the video cameras all over the ship. He verified they were recording and minimized the screen.

"Sir?" Miranda interrupted his thoughts.

"It's all right," Kront reassured his com officers. "It's just Commander Francis and the *Protector*. Prepare for them to dock and enter."

"So you two are the brains aboard this ship?" Angelina stood at attention and paced the floor in front of Preston and Miranda. Numerous soldiers from her ship had accompanied her onto the *Lindman*. Kront had given them permission to search the ship – a regular rule in the protection of high-ranking officers in intergalactic communications – but he didn't remember allowing them to stay on the ship. He also didn't remember seeing so many of them at one time; there seemed to be too many of them to be a simple protection detail.

Miranda smiled. "Yes, ma'am. Officer Henson had the idea to use the missile design."

Preston stood up a little straighter. "That's partially true, Commander. Officer Holliday installed her scrambler to hide the signature from the Trikkyas radars and scanners, and she used a replica of the engine from the satellite we sent to your planet to power it out into space at a fast speed."

Angelina spoke to Kront but kept her eyes focused on the couple before her. "Captain, you have a fine team, but I wouldn't mind having them aboard my own ship. We could use some new blood."

Kront smiled, "Commander, with all due respect, Miranda is family, and Preston's family is located on Helgin, so I believe that it's in his best interest to serve on a ship that is nearest his family, especially since the loss of Troklon and Frigal are still fresh on our minds."

Angelina frowned. Miranda didn't like the goose bumps that crossed her flesh or the chill that shot up her spine. The commander's eyes pierced her soul like a cold, steel sword straight through her heart. "Well, then, have it your way. By the power invested in me by the Senate of Earth, I order Officers Miranda Holliday and Preston Henson transferred to the service of the *Protector*."

Preston stepped forward, matching Angelina's eyes with his own furious glare, though kept in check. "Ma'am, I am a civilian. No rank. No military papers. I am a volunteer. Therefore, your power over me is void and null." He stepped back in place. Even Kront was astonished by his remark. Preston noticed Miranda's nose tilt a little higher in the air, proud of his ability and confidence in standing up to an Earth Commander.

Angelina lowered her head to the ground. "Captain, I'm sorry, but you leave me no choice." She raised her head and snapped her fingers. Her accompanying protection detail took out their weapons and pointed them at the individuals on the Bridge of the *Lindman*. Kront, Helena, Miranda, and Preston had pulled out their own weapons, but were quickly disarmed. The squad leaders hadn't had a chance to get their hands away from their sides before being overtaken.

"Angelina!" Kront roared. "What's the meaning of this?"

She walked over to him and smiled, trailing a long, painted fingernail over his cheek and chin. "Kront, I always get what I want, and what I want is what Earth needs right now. We deserve the best, and we do what it takes to get it. They're the best, and I want them. Earth needs them."

"You strut around acting like you own everything, as though you can command anyone and everyone—" Helena interjected.

"Oh, but I can, Lieutenant." She coyly smiled. "Who do you think convinced the Handlons to kidnap the Trikkyas king to force a treaty with Earth?" No one answered, but all eyes gawked and stared at the bold woman. "Who persuaded the Trikkyas to leave Loht 9 so you could retrieve the documents? Do you think they're smart enough to do that on their own without their king? Ha!"

"You bitch." Kront's comment was enough to earn a gasp from even the most bold of speakers, like the red-headed personality of Miranda.

Angelina slapped Kront hard and walked away, turning before she left the room. "Don't try to save these two, or there'll be plenty more of this." She snapped her fingers a second time, and one of the members in the protection detail shot Sigu in the chest four times. He fell to the floor, blood dripping from his wounds.

"No!" Helena screamed.

John, Drenge, and Michael tried to wriggle free of their captors, but Buck yelled, "Guys, quit! Don't fight them."

Preston chose this moment to try to free himself. He threw his head backward, slamming his captor's head and knocking the man back. Using his right foot, Preston kicked the man in the stomach, but he didn't see the other man in black come from the left, raise his weapon, and slam it down on the back of Preston's neck. He collapsed to the floor and moaned, half-conscious until he fully relented to the blackness.

"Preston!" Miranda cried. Already she was crying over Sigu, but now the one man she had cared about aside from Kront was being beaten before her eyes.

Angelina walked back into the room. "Don't hurt him any further! I need him alive and well. Both of them. Let's go." The protection detail in charge of Miranda and Preston left. Miranda looked to Helena and Kront. Helena's tears of sympathy and Kront's look of fatherly revenge gave Miranda comfort and hope, but she knew it was up to her to disable Angelina from the inside.

The soldiers remaining at the Bridge took the captives to

the Situation Room and locked the door from the outside. They returned to the *Protector*, and the ship took off from the *Lindman* with Miranda and Preston aboard.

No one saw it when it happened, but the long range scanner alerted Miranda's screen: the great fleet of Trikkyas ships – all 200 shuttles, speeders, and fortresses – had mysteriously disappeared from view.

PART 3

YEAR 2744

WE ARE OUTLAWS

Chapter 25. – Never Leave A Man Behind.

"Ohh," Preston moaned. Miranda rushed over to help him sit up. He rubbed a sore spot on the back of his neck. "What happened?"

"You were hit in the back of the head when you tried to escape," Miranda explained.

Preston had never seen Miranda cry before, not ever. Not only was it really weird, but it was also very humbling to know Miranda could still be in-tune with her emotional side. "Honey, I'll be all right. It just hurts quite a bit." He looked around the confines of their environment. "Where are we? It looks like a prison cell."

Miranda nodded. "We're aboard the *Protector*."

"I'd rather die than work for that bitch. What was her name…Angelina?"

"That's right," a voice sounded from the shadows. Angelina stepped into the dim light of the room. "And if you don't want to work for this bitch, then we'll have no problem arranging your funeral for you."

"I want an explanation," Preston demanded. "Who do the hell do you think you are, anyway?"

"Easy now, boy," the woman warned. Two of her soldiers materialized from the darkness at her side.

Miranda's man was not so easily swayed. He stepped forward and grabbed the bars of the prison. "What you've done is illegal. The Senate will remove you from your position for your treachery, and you'll be nothing but a bad taste in the back of their mouths when they're done with you."

Angelina frowned. "We're over four million miles away from the *Lindman*, and even farther from the militarized Senate formed from the remnants of the previous policymakers." She stormed forward until her nose nearly touched his, and he could smell the whiskey on her breath. "Do you think they care about two young people when they have entire cultures and civilizations to care for? There's no way they'll send anyone out to rescue either of you or imprison me for doing my duty."

Miranda stood up and joined Preston at the bars. "Commander, I don't know what you expect, but we won't work for you willingly. Even if you make us, what's to stop us from rewiring your ship for failure or uploading a virus to cause multiple hardware malfunctions?"

Angelina stopped smiling. She hadn't thought this far ahead. Her plan had included the couple's eagerness to take on new agendas as members of her renegade team. "No more talk." She walked toward the door to leave. You have one day to change your mind; otherwise, you both will be killed." She snapped her fingers, and the two men in back disappeared back into the shadows as the door slammed shut behind her.

*   *   *

Helena looked up from her computer. "Forty-six hours away, sir. There's no way we could catch up to them before they reach Earth."

Kront lowered his head. "I've failed them. The two people who have done the greatest good for this fleet in using their brains instead of their brawn, and I let them get taken because I was taken for a fool."

"Sir, you can't blame yourself," Helena consoled her commander. "Sigu gave his life. He wouldn't have done it unless there was something worth fighting for, so you haven't failed them. We're just taking a little longer to come up with a solution."

"And I've got your solution right here," Buck announced as he walked into the room.

Kront looked to his senior engineer. "Show me what you've got."

"Captain, Lieutenant, remember the engines Miranda designed for the satellites?" Buck asked.

Helena nodded. "Yes, but they aren't strong enough to use on the *Lindman*."

"Unless you make it bigger," he retorted."

"A *lot* bigger," Kront added, his eyebrow arching in Buck's direction.

"No problem, sir. My people are already working on it." Buck grinned. "We'll be done in about twelve hours."

Kront nodded and clapped the man on the shoulder. "Good job, soldier. Dismissed." Buck returned to the Hangar; Kront faced his second-in-command. "Helena, I want stun and jamming missiles that use Preston's signature design. We want to disable the ship so we can get onboard and rescue those two wisecracks."

Helena smiled and saluted. "Yes, sir."

Kront looked down at the radar on his screen. "Hold on, you two. We're coming."

* * *

"So, have you two made up your minds?" Angelina walked through the door to the prison cell holding the couple kidnapped from the *Lindman*. They stood up to address her, but not out of respect for her rank.

"On the condition that you'll free us after we have finished our services aboard your ship, we'll work for you," Miranda committed.

"We won't give you any inventions," Preston added, slumped over in the corner. His wound was healing slowly, but his head still spun too quickly when he tried to stand up for too long. "But we will help you make the weapons you already have better."

Angelina smiled. "Now, *that* is a deal I can work with. What do you need?"

"I guess we'll both need computer access," Miranda suggested.

"I'll bring laptops." Angelina crossed her arms. "You two are not leaving your cells for work on this ship. You use your brains."

"Okay, that will work." Miranda looked over to Preston and then back to Angelina. "We could use some better food and water, and some bandages for the wound on his head."

The commander from Earth rolled her eyes. "I'm not running an infirmary, but if you insist..." She snapped her fingers, and a soldier left the room. "He'll return with the extra things you need. I'll bring the laptops and other essential items."

"What about system access?" the Intel Officer asked. "Without it, I can't upgrade anything."

Angelina shook her head. "I'm not that dumb, cookie.

You'll do as you threatened and rewrite my programs to screw with my crew and shut down my ship."

"You've got to give me something to work with!"

Angelina stared at the younger woman for several seconds. "Your computer access will be strictly monitored. Any hanky-panky with the coding, software, hardware – anything – and you're dead, he's dead, and we leave your bodies in the open space to bloat up like a balloon and burst like a firework for New Years. Am I clear?"

Miranda squinted her eyes into a hawk-like glare. "Like crystal."

*   *   *

"Sir, we have the engine and the missiles ready," Helena reported from her station.

Kront turned around and nodded. "Tell Buck to fire the missiles and start the new engine."

"Yes, sir." She called over the ship's com. "Bridge to Hangar: missiles are a go. Sergeant Cypher, start the engine."

Buck smiled, "Oh, this is going to be lots of fun." Buck slammed his fist onto the launch button. The missiles took off in the direction of the *Protector*. "Find your target," Buck said aloud, "and prepare the way for us to rescue our friends."

Kront smiled. "They'll never know what hit them."

Helena nodded. "All of their systems will suddenly go black, and they'll be dead in space." She stood up. "Sir, I'll go prepare squads." He nodded, and she left for the Situation Room.

Chapter 26. – The S.S.A.U. Mission.

Miranda and Preston sat at the portable computers, fingers flying and programs coding to upgrade the systems aboard Angelina's ship. "Miranda, how do we send for help?"

She leaned over and kissed Preston on the cheek. "We don't have to. Captain's already on his way."

"How do you know that?"

"I just know," she answered simply. "And because the radar showed me." She opened a window with a scanner showing the *Lindman* approaching at rapid speed.

Preston smiled. "Let's buy them a little more time. I'll write a code for a timer for several hours from now. When the *Lindman* is within range, it'll shut down the *Protector*'s computers and erase the ship's memory. All of the upgrades will be deleted."

Miranda whispered to him, "You're a genius, sir." She leaned back and looked at him. "I think I love you."

"You *think* you love me?" Preston dramatically grabbed at his heart and fell to the floor. "She *thinks*! She doesn't *know*!"

"Hey, you two!" a voice shouted from the darkness. "Get back to work! Stop horsing around."

The couple sat up, and Miranda grabbed Preston's hand. "Okay, I *know* that I'm in love with you."

He grinned, showing off his pearly whites. It reminded her of the first time she saw his full smile, the feelings it started in the pit of her stomach. "If we survive this, we're getting married."

Miranda's jaw dropped. "You're not even going to ask me?"

"Nope. If I asked you, you'd play hard-to-get with me." Preston shook his head. "No, I have a feeling that telling you what's going to happen is exactly what you want to hear."

"You know me too well, Officer Henson," Miranda admitted, arching an eyebrow in his direction. "Let's get to work."

*   *   *

Nielson fixated his gaze to the screen before him. "Sir,

engines are at 70%."

Kront nodded. "Give it a few more minutes, Nielson. Start them at 90%."

"Yes, sir." He didn't move his eyes from the red thermometer indicating the increasing status. "Engine is now at 85%." He was ready to push the button. "88%…89%…90%, sir."

"Nielson, start it up."

Nielson pressed the sequence of buttons that started up the engine. "Engine is running, Speed at Hyper +4…Hyper +6…Hyper x2…Engine is running at Hyper x4, Captain."

"Here we go," Kront said to himself. "Nielson, turn on the scrambler."

*   *   *

"It's gone. The *Lindman* signal is gone."

Miranda looked at her screen, too. "But, that can't be. It was just here a moment ago."

"Either they got blown up or they used your scrambler," Preston whispered.

"I'm sure they're all right," Miranda convinced herself. Worries nagged at the back of her mind that a Trikkyas ship escaped the bombs they sent off before they were kidnapped, and sought after the *Lindman* for revenge. "The nearest ship is 1.6 million miles from Helgin compared to them."

Preston scooted closer to the Academy student. He wrapped his arm around her shoulders and squeezed her tight. "I'm sure they're all right, too. But we need to be prepared. We'd better give Angelina something the next time she comes in here, or we may not live to see our own rescue."

*   *   *

"Helena, what does the scanner say?" Kront asked of his second-in-command. "How long until our missiles impact the *Protector*?"

Helena sat in Miranda's seat and analyzed the student's custom-built scanner. "Sir, forty-five minutes to—wait! They're not moving. Recalculating impact time." Helena punched in some numbers, and read the results aloud. "Missile will impact in less than twenty minutes."

"Somehow they got Angelina to stop the ship," Kront stated. "Nielson, how long until we arrive? We need to be there shortly after the missiles arrive."

"An hour, sir, but if we use a little more juice, we can get there in half the time," Adriahna's fiancé reported.

Kront commanded, "Helena, get the S.S.A.U. Squad ready: full armor and loaded weapons. Take out any resistance like they took out Sigu."

Helena saluted, "Yes, sir."

*   *   *

Preston lied down on the floor. He couldn't shake off the awful pain in his head, and it felt like the room was continually spinning. "Ohh," he moaned.

Miranda crawled over to him. "Honey? Are you ok?"

He clutched at his head and noticed she was doing the same. "Yeah, but what's wrong with you?"

She lied down next to him and cuddled. "My head is killing me. It feels worse than any migraine I can imagine. Did Angelina come get the update?"

"Yes, sweetie, she—"

Out of the blue, the entire ship shook, thundered, and rumbled. A great "CRASH" sounded through the hallways. The alarms went off in every room and hallway. Crew members ran everywhere trying to figure out how to get the lights and computers back on. Even the laptops in the prison cell turned off.

"Honey, what happened?" Miranda asked, but there was no response. "Preston?"

*   *   *

"Everyone ready? We go in thirty seconds." Helena and the eleven members of the S.S.A.U. stood on the outer hull, waiting for the *Lindman* to attach to the *Protector*. "They have no power at all. They don't know we're here. Our mission is to rescue Officers Holliday and Henson." Mason Jung stood in front. He was ready to

204

jump from the *Lindman* over to the *Protector*. "Mason, in five." He winked at her, and she smiled. "Go!"

Mason jumped and landed with ease next to the hatch. He grabbed on to the handle tightly and pulled the hatch open. Buck threw in a stun grenade; immediately after the big blast, Helena jumped through the hatch and down the tunnel that led to the lower levels. The other members cleared the surrounding areas, staying close to the lieutenant. They all came back with puzzled faces, making remarks on the emptiness of crew and member.

"Where is everyone?" Helena asked.

"Maybe they got a heads-up?" Buck suggested. He shrugged his shoulders.

"Let's just find the Officers and get going," Mason nodded.

Door by door, they searched until they found the brig aboard the ship. Helena peered through the glass window in the metal door. "Two guards," she whispered.

Buck kneeled down and prepped his Stun Gun. "I can take 'em." The rest of the team backed away. He fired two shots, and the guards dropped to the floor as unconscious bodies. "All clear." The team ran down the hallway to the last door in the corridor. The lieutenant searched the dimly-lit cell through the tiny window in the door. "I see them, but they're lying on the floor."

Buck grabbed the handle, but Mason stopped him. "Wait, it could be a trap."

"Mason's right. I think I see something," Helena commented.

Buck looked at her, "What is it?"

"I see a fine wire from the door to the cell, like some kind of booby trap."

Mason stepped over to the door. "Helena, let me see." He looked through the window, conducting his own analysis of the situation.

Helena smiled; she liked Mason. Always had, always will. He was the best in the service, aside from Kront. Helena shook her head. "What was that, Mason?"

"I said it's a trick wire," he repeated. "When we open the door, the wire snaps and pulls the airlock release. It'll kill them and anyone who tries to get in to save them."

"Well, how do we get them out?" Buck asked.

Mason smiled. "Leave it to me." He pulled a long knife out of his boot. "Stand back and watch how it's done, children." Everyone moved back, guns at the ready and still watchful of the immediate area. In a split second, he yanked the door open and threw the knife, severing the string attached to the airlock handle and jamming itself between the wall and the airlock door.

The squad entered the room; Helena shot off the lock and kneeled down to Miranda and Preston. She tried to find a pulse on either body. "Buck, quick! Something's wrong with them!"

Buck whistled, and Jens Nessau ran over and took off the bag from her back. "Here's the Medic supply." He kneeled down next to Miranda. "Her pulse is weak, and her skin feels like it's on fire." He reached over to Preston. "He feels the same."

Buck opened the pack and pulled out two syringes filled with a clear liquid. He handed on to Helena who kneeled next to Miranda while Buck moved closer to Preston. "Give her this shot in the chest."

"What is it?" she asked.

"Adrenaline."

Helena cautiously accepted the syringe. "Are you sure about this?"

"Do it, or we won't know what's wrong before they die." Buck lifted Preston's shirt and shot the liquid into his body. No reaction. "Damn. Try it on Miranda."

Helena lifted Miranda's shirt and placed the syringe close to the young woman's chest. "Okay, here we go." She pushed the needle in and injected the adrenaline. Miranda gasped for air. Helena began to cry. "Miranda! I was so worried!" She helped her sit up. "What happened? What did they do to you?"

Miranda looked around, very dizzy and dazed. Her gaze fell on Preston, lying still on the floor. Miranda's own tears began to fall. "Preston? Are you okay?" She grabbed him by the front of his shirt and shook him. "Preston!"

Helena released Miranda's hands from Preston. "Sweetie, we need to know what they did to you so we can save him."

Buck felt for Preston's pulse. "You'd better hurry. He's slipping fast."

"It was Hepro-toxin."

"Are you sure?" Helena asked.

"Yes," Miranda confirmed. She pulled a small bottle from her pocket with the label that read of the same deadly title. "The guards gave it to me to taunt me when Preston was getting really bad. They've been slipping it in small doses in our food, but started increasing the doses recently, and they put more in Preston's food than mine because Angelina wanted to…make me pay…" She hung her head. "There's no cure, is there?"

Helena wanted to push Miranda over as a joke. "If there wasn't a cure, how did we get you back to life?" Helena smiled. "Don't worry; I know how to fix this. I was poisoned by that same drug doing the Handlon War,"

She turned to Buck. "Give me all the salt and sugar in the bag, and your water jug." He handed over the ingredients; she mixed them together, reused the syringe with the new mixture, and gave a shot to Miranda. "Let's hope this works on Preston, too." She used a vein in his left arm and emptied the needle.

Buck stood up and called Mason over. "Help me carry him back to the ship. Let's get going, everyone."

"It's so good to have you back, Miranda." Kront hugged the student for a long time and didn't want to let go. As he had told Preston, she was like a daughter to him.

"Thanks, Captain." She pulled away after few more moments in the embrace.

"How's Preston?"

"He'll survive, but he was pretty poisoned from the Hepro-toxin."

Kront shook his head. "On a better note, my dear, the bombs you two created were a huge success. The most recent scan shows the Trikkyas have been eliminated. I don't know how, but my guess is their 'big fleet' was a sham, and whatever ships they had in that fleet coming at us were destroyed by our bombs."

"That's great news, Captain!" Miranda smiled.

"We're nearing the Milky Way Galaxy. I've got a big report to file when we land on Earth, and we have everything on the visual, so why don't you go spend some time with your wounded warrior in the Medic Center?"

"You don't have to tell me twice, sir," Miranda commented, saluting her captain before running down the hall to

Doc's office.

Helena came up behind Kront, although he knew she had been there the whole time. "I heard they're getting married, Captain."

"Another marriage, huh?" Kront shook his head. "My little girl is all grown up."

Chapter 27. – Thief Onboard.

"Attention! Captain on deck!" Helena announced, standing on the platform in the Hangar.

Kront stepped inside and turned on his com to the microphone setting so everyone could hear him. "At ease, everyone. As you all know, we are close to landing on Planet Earth: we are on the edge of the Milky Way Galaxy, the closest we've been in many years. Aside from regular, basic duties, you are all off-duty until we land, unless something happens." A few chuckles arose from certain members in the line-up below. Kront smiled, knowing that remark was sure to get their attention. His face and voice turned more serious. "Also, we honor those that have given their lives in the service. Please pause for a moment of silence." The Hangar was completely quiet. "Thank you," Kront said when the minute was over. "Lieutenant Holley and Mason Jung, please step forward." Helena and Mason stood side-by-side at attention. "Lieutenant, I believe you wanted to bestow the honors upon Specialist Jung?"

Helena smiled inwardly. She spoke aloud, "During the rescue of Officers Miranda Holliday and Preston Henson, Mason disabled a booby trap with such skill and precision as never before seen. Thereby, I, Lieutenant Helena Holley, do give him…" She walked over to him, stood in front of him, and whispered, "…the kiss I promised to give him five years ago." But before she could lean in to give him a simple smooch, Mason wrapped his arms around the lieutenant, swept her off her feet, and planted a big one on her ruby-red lips. Her maroon and purple hair fell out of regulation, and Mason ran his fingers through its locks. For several seconds, Kront thought the two went beyond an exchange of saliva and tongue, so he turned away, his face beet-red. The crew cheered, and Mason finally put Helena back on her feet. She interlaced her fingers with his, and they held hands, even after Kront dismissed everyone from the Hangar.

* * *

"Miranda Holliday and Preston Henson reporting for duty, sir," Miranda announced.

Kront turned around, happy to see two of his favorite people. "Welcome back! I'm glad to see both of you on your feet again." He shook their hands.

"Thank you, sir," Preston replied. "To tell you the truth, the Medic Center was very boring."

Kront laughed, "Yes, I can imagine so, but now that you're back, why don't you take to your stations and make sure things are still running smoothly?" They saluted and gladly sat in their seats next to each other. Miranda turned on her scanner and radar. Preston relieved Nielson at the com station. Kront sat at his desk and nodded. "Miranda, scan the area. I want to be sure we're not being followed. Preston, call the Helgin Camp on the com. We left instructions with them on how to build the Miranda Engine so they can send survivor flights to Earth to join us. I want to know about their progress."

"Sir?" Miranda spoke up. "The Miranda Engine?"

"Yes," Kront confirmed. "We took the satellite engine you built and enlarged it for this ship. It was your engine to begin with, so it became the Miranda Engine."

Miranda beamed. Preston laughed, "Sir, it sure is a good name." Suddenly, an alert sounded on every computer on the Bridge. Preston and Miranda whizzed through numerous reports on various monitors in front of them.

"What's going on?" Kront asked. "Why the alert?"

"Sir," Miranda spoke up, "we've received word from Planet Helgin that...no, that can't be right." She continued to open more programs and reports, reading the same alerts with the same warnings.

"Their information must be wrong," Preston continued. "It can't be the Trikkyas. I thought they were destroyed."

Kront's face turned slightly pale. "The Trikkyas? But our radar indicated they were gone. The bombs worked...didn't they?" *Now I'm leading the Trikkyas straight to Earth,* he mused. *What have I done??* John, Helena, Michael, and Drenge appeared on the Bridge.

"Sir!" Miranda interrupted Kront's thoughts. "I coded a new program when Preston and I were held captive aboard the

Protector. I realized the possibility of our information being leaked or stolen, so I created a code that could find our codes on other ships."

"Leaked?" Michael asked. "Stolen?"

"Yes," John confirmed. "Walls have ears like we have mouths."

Miranda emphatically pressed one button, and the screen scrolled with hundreds of lines of text that didn't stop. "It seems the Trikkyas got my scrambler code *and* the Miranda Engine blueprints. The Trikkyas were never completely eliminated. Many ships were destroyed, but they still have many more remaining. Since then, they've launched twenty-five new Fire Tail Class ships."

Preston looked at his captain. "They're heading for Helgin, sir. The Miranda Engine hasn't been installed on every survivor shuttle. So far, we can save only 300,000 people as of right now."

Helena stepped over to Kront and stood at his side. "Sir, what are we going to do?" Mason, Nielson, and Buck joined the group.

"What's going on?" Buck asked. Mason stepped over to Helena's side but paid more attention to the situation than his maroon-haired lover.

"I say we find the bastard traitor aboard this ship who betrayed us," Drenge shouted, slamming his fist into his other palm. The other squad leaders nodded and gave their approval.

Kront nodded to Miranda and Preston. "You two know what to do. Do it."

For several minutes, silence enveloped the Bridge except for the constant clicking and clacking of computer keys. Suddenly, Preston jumped up. "Sir, I got it! The signal ends at Daniel Blindy's computer."

Miranda continued, "After that, a signal goes out from his laptop, and a large packet of information was sent to the Trikkyas Fleet."

Kront looked up to his squad leaders and crew commanders. "Buck. Mason. Bring Daniel Blindy in for *questioning*. Helena, search his quarters and bring us his laptop." Mason and Buck left with Helena on their heels until they took separate hallways at the end of the corridor.

Mason and Buck jogged down to Blindy's working station. In his place, they found his battle buddy, Roland. "I haven't seen him around here today," the man replied in response to their questions regarding Daniel's whereabouts. "But he said something about going down to the Hangar." Mason and Buck glanced at each other before racing down to the Hangar, but just as they reached the bottom stair set, they watched in fury as the *Lindman, Jr.* took off on an unauthorized flight with an unauthorized pilot.

At that same moment, Helena walked in to Daniel's quarters. It was obvious he had left in a hurry. Drawers, clothes, files, papers—everything was scattered around the room, lying on the floor, broken or out of place. "Damn," she muttered aloud, "I'll be lucky to find anything in here." She began by looking under the bed, on the bed, in his desk, and in the bathroom. She tapped the lid of his laptop and thought, *I'll give this to Miranda. She could decode it and find out his secrets.* Leaving the computer, she walked over to Daniel's closet and opened the door.

BOOM! A huge explosion sounded. She was thrown back against the wall so hard that everything quickly went black.

The blast from Daniel's room shook the ship, even if just as a minor quiver. Miranda looked to Preston, and then to Kront. "Captain, where did you send Helena?" Kront's eyes widened. Drenge, John, and Michael took off. Miranda jumped up to follow them. "Helena!" she yelled. They ran from the Bridge, down the hall, to the left, down another corridor, and to the living quarters. The squad leaders rummaged through the billowing smoke and charred debris. A voice called out, "I found her! I've got her! Gimme some help in here!"

John and Drenge carried Helena's body from the room out into the hallway and laid her down. Doc was already rushing to the scene, two of his orderlies behind him with a stretcher and first aid kits. Drenge felt for a pulse and looked up. "Doc, it's Helena! She's got a pulse, but she doesn't look too good."

Doc knelt down the moment he got close enough to hear her breathing and used his stethoscope. "Quick, put her on the stretcher. She needs to be scanned." His orderlies moved around the squad leaders and lifted Helena onto the stretcher. Everyone moved as a group, following the lieutenant's body toward Doc's office. "Will someone tell me what happened?"

"We think the room was a trap, sir," Miranda spoke up.

"Well, she certainly found it," Doc noted, a grim expression on his face. Doc and the orderlies entered the examination room; everyone else, including Miranda, were forced to stand outside the open door.

"Where is she? I want to see her!" The soldiers in the room backed up as they heard and felt Mason pushing his way through the crowd. "Where's..." He saw Helena lying on the stretcher with the scanner going over her body.

Doc looked up at Mason and then back down to Helena. "Hold on, son. I'll have some answers to you in a little bit. Everyone else needs to leave, please. Mason, you can come on in."

"Thank you, sir," Mason replied, stepping inside the room and closing the door.

Miranda stepped back from the crowd and walked to Daniel's room to finish what Helena had started. She trudged through the wreckage lying everywhere. Black pieces of this; burnt fragments of that. She knelt down and picked up Blindy's laptop, barely held together by a few screws that happened to not fall off just yet. She gathered samples of the explosive material from around the room, as well. *Captain will want to know everything,* she said to herself. *He probably blames himself for her getting hurt. I sure hope I can give him some good news out of all of this mess.*

She entered the Bridge and approached Kront. "Sir, I found Blindy's laptop and took samples of the explosives from the blast." A very grim Kront tapped a part of his desk to his left, indicating she should leave the materials there for him to investigate. He made no other move to acknowledge her presence or words. "Sir?"

Kront leaned back in his chair, white-faced as a ghost and looking more old than usual. Miranda felt anxiety for her superior commander. Were his days of commandeering the *Lindman* coming to an end so soon? Surely he wouldn't take this upon himself like he had the deaths of all of his other crew members. "I just received word from Doc that Helena will recover, but not for four to six weeks."

Miranda smiled. "Sir, she may not be able to work, but she's not dead, and she'll kick your ass if she finds you moping about her like this."

Her words cheered Kront enough to bring color back to his face and a slight smile to his lips. "You're right, Miranda. She would kick my ass, and in the process some of that hair dye would probably land in my hair." He winked at Miranda. "Can't have a Captain with pink hair, now, can we?"

"Captain," Buck radioed in over his wrist com, interrupting Kront's recovery moment with Miranda. "Blindy took off in the *Lindman, Jr.*"

Kront laughed, "Miranda's ship? He's either dumb or…well, dumb. Kront out." The visual screen turned off. He stood up and looked down to the Academy student. "Officer Holliday, Daniel Blindy stole your shuttle. Bring him in. I want him arrested for attempted murder and theft."

"With pleasure," a tight-lipped Miranda answered. "No one steals my shuttle and hurts my friend, and gets away with it," she muttered under her breath. She jumped over to her station, opened a program on her computer, and sent remote commands to her ship from her screen. Within minutes, the *Lindman, Jr.* landed at the feet of Buck and Nielson in the Hangar.

Buck walked up the door and found Daniel lying on the floor. He called in over his com unit, "Captain, Daniel's dead. Single shot to the head."

*   *   *

"Honey, I've got some good news," Preston smiled.

"I need good news," Miranda scowled. "I'm so pissed off about Helena getting hurt yesterday, and then that traitor-bastard committing suicide so we couldn't question him. What a fucking coward!"

Preston's eyes widened. He looked up to the captain who simply sunk lower in his chair and covered his face from Miranda's view. Even he knew to stay away from Miranda when she was pissed. "Honey?"

"WHAT?!" Miranda startled herself. "Sorry, Preston. I'm just worked up about things lately. What is it you wanted to show me?"

He pulled up the blueprint of the Trikkyas version of the

Miranda Engine. "So we know the Miranda Engine design was stolen by the Trikkyas and renamed the Fire Tail ship, *but* I discovered an error in their copy."

Miranda smiled. "Show me."

Preston pointed to a specific section of the ship in the blueprint. "Remember how exposed the fuel cells were on the Trikkyas ships you took out? I designed this new ship in order to conceal the fuel cells so they would be protected, but when the Trikkyas got the design, I guess they forgot to add the armor hatch on the rear of the ship."

Kront stood up. Apparently listening in to the conversation, he walked to the lower level and joined the couple at their stations. He studied the schematic. "How can we use this to our advantage?"

"One of my ideas that I remember was a two-foot missile. It travels the same speed as our other missiles but carries only twenty-five pounds of explosives—"

Miranda interjected, "—enough to start a chain reaction!"

"Exactly." Preston stood up and crossed his arms. "And it's small enough to fit through the hatch."

Chapter 28. – Lucky Ladies.

Angelina returned to the *Protector*. When the missiles hit, the power went off and all signals were jammed. She knew exactly what was happening. She left two guards to watch over the hostages while she and the rest of the crew evacuated. *No way am I caught that easily,* she thought to herself.

"Sergeant, open the shuttle door," she commanded. He quickly followed orders, and she stepped through the doorway and back onto her ship. "Let's get this ship running again." Her Senior Officers stayed on her heels all the way up to the Bridge. "Lieutenant, I want coms online. Sergeant, go through the visual recordings. I want to know what happened on my ship after I left." She sat down in her seat and continued firing off orders. "Sergeant Paulsen, pull up the visual from the prison." He turned on the visual com screen; Angelina's jaw dropped. "What?? How the hell…WHERE ARE MY PRISONERS?!"

* * *

Miranda sat at her personal desk in her quarters with Blindy's computer in front of her. Preston was lying on her bed behind her, but he waited to fall asleep until she was done. "Honey?" he prompted. "You've been at it for six hours straight. It's 3 A.M. Let's get some shut-eye before some other catastrophe happens, okay?"

Miranda sighed. "But I'm so close to being done with recovering the files, and I haven't even started to search them to see what Blindy even has on this thing." Her fingers tapped the keyboard incessantly, clicking and clacking commands and codes until they suddenly stopped. "All right, I can barely stay awake. I'll finish this later." She shut the lid on the laptop and lied down on the bed beside Preston, her back to his chest. He began to massage her shoulders. "Ohh, that feels so good." She let her eyes close, knowing she would fall asleep in seconds if she'd just let go.

"Miranda?"

"Hmm?"

"Do you think we'll stop this Trikkyas ships before they

reach Helgin?" Preston stopped massaging her back and wrapped his right arm around her. "It's not just my family I'm worried about. These people have already survived their planet exploding once. I don't think they could emotionally handle it happening again."

Miranda turned around and buried her head in Preston's warmth. "Honey, with you and me, those Trikkyas don't have a chance."

Preston smiled, kissed her forehead, and laid his head down on the pillow. Within seconds, the couple that seemed to know it all slept like they hadn't for days.

*   *   *

Helena's hand moved. Her feet stirred. Finally, she opened her eyes. A very tired Mason was staring at her, watching her every move. "You know, you watching me like this would be creepy if I didn't like you so much."

Her remark made him chuckle. "How are you feeling, beautiful?"

"I've been better, dumbass."

He smiled again. "Well, you've been unconscious for a week."

Her eyelids flew open. "Ohh," she mumbled as the pain hit her head in the form of a headache. "A week? Are you sure?"

"Well, yeah, I haven't left the room except to shower." He winked. "Even then, I've only done it once."

"No wonder I was unconscious," she joked. "Your odor kept me under."

Tears built up in Mason's eyes. He gently rubbed her hands and kissed her fingers. "I was really worried about you. Kront's been blaming himself this whole time, but don't tell him I told you. Miranda reminded him that you'd kick his ass when you were better if he moped and blamed himself."

"Hell, yes, I will," Helena stated, a little too loudly for her unused voice. She coughed, and Mason helped her drink a few sips of water from a plastic cup. "How's everyone else?"

"Seems that Preston and Miranda couple found a way to stop the Trikkyas from invading Helgin. They're working on it as we speak."

* * *

Sergeant Gregory Hiskyk worked as fast as he could to pull the visual recording from the prison cell. He decoded it and sent it to the large visual com screen at the Bridge. He radioed in to his supervisor who put him on the speaker. "Commander Francis, I have the recording of what happened in the prison cell. It's all right here." He pressed the play button from his location in the Conference Room aboard the *Protector*; it showed Angelina everything: Helena and the S.S.A.U. team, Buck stunning the two guards, Mason disabling the trap, and the couple being rescued from the Hepro-toxin administered to the hostages in their food. The video concluded, and Angelina leaned back in her chair.

"Well, since those two are back with their daddy," Angelina mocked, "at least we still have the upgrades they left us." No one said anything. "Gentlemen, am I right?" No one was brave enough to answer. Her black-painted nails dug into the upholstery of her chair; her voice rose in leaps and bounds of frustration. "Will someone answer me?!"

"Ma'am," Sergeant Hiskyk spoke up, "the missiles were jammers, and they...wiped...everything...out..."

An alert sounded on the radar. "Incoming com from...Earth..." a female lieutenant timidly announced."It's the Chairman of the Joint Chiefs of Staff."

Angelina's face turned white. Her knuckles turned white from clenching the arms of her chair so tightly and for so long.

"They're demanding your surrender."

* * *

"And we have liftoff!" Preston shouted from his station. Miranda reached over and squeezed her man's hand. Over the next several minutes, the radars continued to scan the area.

The Intel Officer searched through Blindy's laptop, hoping to find information in the files she finished recovering from the burnt hard drive. One particular folder popped up on her screen. She opened it, thinking it was no different than the others, but to her surprise, the laptop began running itself. She tried to stop it, but she found even she was having a hard time controlling its functions. "Captain, do you have a minute?" she asked Kront.

"What's up?" He walked over to her station on the lower level.

"A random folder popped up on Blindy's computer, and when I opened the folder, the laptop went nuts." She moved her chair back slightly so the captain could have a better look. "I don't understand what's going on."

"We'll, what are the codes linked to?"

Miranda entered some search commands, but Preston beat her to the answer. "Sir, I think I just found our answer." He brought up images of the three Trikkyas ships on his local screen. "Those Fire Tail shuttles are being controlled by that program on Blindy's computer, and look, sir." He transferred the images from his monitor to the large visual com screen. "The ships are holding civilians and human prisoners, not Trikkyas troops."

Kront slammed his fist on the desk. Preston quickly plugged some numbers into his computer. "I think we can stop the missiles, *and* override the program, if we disarm the weapons one at a time."

"Miranda?" Kront asked.

"Already on it, sir," she responded. The ID numbers of each missile appeared on her screen, along with a countdown of the minutes until detonation. "First missile, three minutes to detonation, ID number 45-JED-729."

Preston entered the numbers into a coded program on his computer. Disarming the missile, he waited until the green dot on the radar turned red and then disappeared. "Okay, Miranda, next one." One by one, the missiles were disarmed, turning from green to red and then disappearing from the radar.

"Ten seconds to detonation for the last two missiles," Miranda declared. "Damn it, we didn't make it. Those poor people…"

"Just give me the numbers. Let me try."

"Son," Kront spoke up, "it's over."

The three crew members at the Bridge looked up at the radar. One of the Trikkyas ships filled with civilians and humans *blipped* slower and slower, fading from the screen as the missile hit its target and killed everyone onboard.

Kront walked over to Preston and clapped his hand onto the young man's shoulder. "Henson, don't take this on yourself. We're at war, and war has casualties."

Preston shook his head. "Sir, how many people were on that shuttle?"

"Preston, please," Miranda begged.

"I need to know," he retorted, the agony in his eyes staring her down. He turned to his Captain. "Maybe it's against protocol. Maybe it'll cause more harm, but right now I need to know for how many deaths am I responsible?"

Kront returned to his desk and pulled up a digital roster. "Eighty-two."

Preston lowered his head. "Eighty-two."

Chapter 29. – The Book.

"Officer Henson, I have a special mission for you."

Preston, wide-eyed, looked up to his commanding officer. "Sir?"

Kront nodded. "I need you to work with Lieutenant Holley and write up a Peace Treaty to offer the Trikkyas."

"But, sir, Doc still has her under strict orders not to—"

"I know her orders, Preston," Kront reassured the young man. "Staying in bed and helping you with a peace treaty isn't against doctor's orders."

Preston smiled. "I'd be honored, Captain."

Kront smiled. "Good. Grab a laptop and report to Lieutenant Holley in her recovery room in the Medic Center." Preston saluted Kront, turned to kiss Miranda on the cheek, and then set off to accomplish the enormous task. The commander turned to the Academy student. "As for you, Miranda, your mission is Classified: Top-Secret, and I didn't want to break it to you in front of Preston. You can tell him on your own time when you're ready, *if* you choose to tell him at all."

Miranda nodded, "Understood. Where am I going, and what will I do when I get there?"

"Come look at my monitor." She walked up the few stairs to the higher level at the Bridge and sat down in a chair to his left. On his screen was a picture of an old document. "This document tells a story about a forgotten book belonging to the Trikkyas people, their secret book of the Holy Temple. No Trikkyas has seen this book in over 300 years, but the only way to secure a treaty is to offer them the book as a token of good faith."

"I'm looking for one really old book out of the entire galaxy?"

"Basically, yes."

Miranda shook her head. "Sir, even I don't have that kind of capability or know-how. What am I supposed to do?"

"Well, I happen to know where it is." Miranda's eyebrows rose in surprise. "I've had it hidden in a secret place for a very long time."

Kront opened a folder of pictures from his younger days. She smiled and laughed when he tried to flip past the ones showing his daring adventures involving women and…well, things involving more questionable antics. He finally stopped at a group of photos titled 'Random.' She thought the title funny for a bunch of photos that seemed to be from the same trip. The first photo showed a group of soldiers running towards a fortress with dead Handlon guards at the entrance. The next photo displayed piles of gold, silver, titanium, platinum, and thousands and thousands of Credits. A few more photos showed soldiers filling their pockets and bags, but then the photos took the viewer on a path away from the riches and glories.

A solitary photo of a hidden door in the background was followed by a photo showing a huge library, obviously hidden behind the door, filled with an innumerable amount of books. Several subsequent photos displayed the titles of various books in the library; most of them Miranda could only half-translate. Her skills in the Trikkyas language were not up to par compared to the linguists at the Academy. The last photo was of the front cover of a thick, heavy book. The title was buried beneath a layer of dust, but Miranda picked out enough letters to figure it out.

"Trikkyase I," she stated. Gwibst hrkols niyths, the subtitle read. "'Trikkyas Book of Holy Beliefs and Standards'," she translated.

Kront closed out of the folder and turned off the computer monitor. "I was on the squad that plundered the Library of Handlon all those years ago."

"The Handlons had it?"

Kront shook his head in the affirmative. "Yes, they did. The Handlons stole it in the Great War of the Trikkyas Planets in the year 2419. The Handlons attacked the Trikkyas Holy Temple and killed the Prior and his followers, unarmed people of peace. The Handlons stole the book, and the Trikkyas have been searching for it ever since." He stood up and stretched. "After the plunder, I decided to hide the book. I've never read it, but now I see I could use it to stop the war we have with the Trikkyas."

"So, where is the book?"

"The only place I knew no one would ever look." He leaned down to Miranda and whispered, "In their own library. It's in a secret compartment behind a shelf of books on Handlon History."

"How am I supposed to get it? Sing and dance my way in there? Take this book that's been under their nose this whole time, and bring it back so *we* can have peace with the Trikkyas people?"

Kront shrugged his shoulders. "Sure, why not? If you want to do it that way."

She shook her head. "I'll do it my own way, but I've got to admit, you're pretty sneaky, Captain Tallin. We already have a peace treaty with the Handlons, and they've always had the upper hand against the Trikkyas people. Sealing the deal between the Trikkyas and our race of people? Sneaky, sneaky."

He raised his hands in his defense. "I'm just doing my job as a Freedom Fighter, but this time I'm using the words of a pen instead of the blade of a sword."

Miranda jumped out of the *Lindman, Jr.* She landed in an area of low elevation between a valley and a hill approximately two miles from the Handlon State Library. The planet of Handlon 8 had a very small population, despite the presence of the Handlon State Library. Even Miranda was surprised at the lack of organized territory and civilization in the immediately surrounding areas. She scaled the wall of the library, landed onto the roof with a "bump," and searched the area for guards. She jogged over to the sky window, staying in the cover of the shadows that the Helgin 8's moon cast.

Suddenly, her wrist radar alerted her. *Blip. Blip.* Two green dots marked two guards pacing the north wing of the library. She slowly pried open the window, aware of the possibility of creaking hinges; the window opened, and she slipped a long rope inside. Anchoring her side of the rope to a metal pipe extended from the cement roof, she slid down the rope and landed on the floor. *Thud.* For three seconds, she paused in a kneeled position and listened for footsteps. She heard the guards talking and walking around in the room to the left.

"Tasfret, did you hear that the Blazing Handlons of Handlon 3 won the game last night?"

"No," Tasfret replied. "You know I don't watch those games, Hetlyjd. I hate Grittiam ball. It's just a bunch of grown-up

Handlons beating each other up over a ball."

The Handlon named Hetlyjd laughed. "It's certainly no different than those dumb Earth games that you like. Soccer, football, wrestling. Humans are so ancient."

Miranda waited until the two Handlons were four rooms away before she exited the room and snuck down the hallway to her right. Using her wrist radar, she followed the map of the building to the main room of the library. She walked past several shelves of books; the temptation to stop and read a book or two nearly replaced her will to accomplish the mission.

"Section 8, Shelf G-92," she whispered, reading Kront's notes aloud. "Look behind the back board." She took the first row of books down from the shelf and put them on the floor, careful to keep them in the same order they were on the shelf. "Don't want to leave behind any evidence," she muttered while smiling. "Now, about that shelf...how to get it out without making noise is the hard part." She pulled a knife out of her utility belt and pried the board away at a corner. Unfortunately, it squeaked loudly.

Miranda froze. No rush of guards into the room. Her scanner showed no signs of change in the guards' patterns. Turning back to the library shelf, she found the hidden compartment, exactly as Captain had told her. Inside, she found a small bag with the treasured book. She put the bag over her shoulder and closed the compartment up with the board she pried away from it. She returned the books to their proper places on the shelf. Quickly, Miranda shimmied up the rope, climbed back onto the roof, and closed the window behind her. She made her way back to the *Lindman, Jr.* She remotely flipped on the scrambler button and jumped into the pilot seat. She silently maneuvered the shuttle upwards into space, and when she reached high orbit she blasted the engine to full power and headed for the *Lindman.*

The *Lindman, Jr.* landed in the Hangar next to the *Jamie.* Preston stood at the top of the stairs and waited for Miranda to exit the shuttle. She jumped out, handed Buck the keys, and walked up the long flight to join Preston at the top. Although his arms were crossed, she leaned in and gave him a big kiss. "Hi, honey. I'm home."

Preston smiled. "It's a good thing I already knew you had the highest level of clearance before we got into a relationship." He winked. "Glad you're back." He put his arm around her, and together they walked up to the Bridge.

"Captain, mission was a success, sir," she stated, saluting her superior commander.

Kront smiled at her. "Great! How'd it go?"

Miranda dropped the bag from her shoulder. "Exactly as planned."

Kront turned to Preston. "How is the Peace Treaty coming?"

Preston smiled, "Sir. We finished it this morning, and I have news from the Doc. Helena will be leaving the Medic Center Today, she have recovered in record time, the Doc. Says it have something to do with Love and Friendship."

Chapter 30. – The Trikkyas Meeting.

"Sir, we have a response to our com," Preston announced. "It's a visual."

Kront smiled, "Put it on the big screen."

"Yes, sir."

The commanding officer of the Trikkyas ship Dragon Flames appeared on the screen. "Captain Tallin, I am General Flasif. I've received your com, and we accept your surrender."

Kront stifled his laugh, covering it as a cough. Preston and Miranda had to do the same at their stations. "General Flasif, our com stated that we seek a truce with the Trikkyas people, not to surrender to them."

Flasif shook his head. "Captain, you cannot force a truce simply because we are three days' time from Helgin. How do we know this isn't a con to give you more time to rescue your loved ones from the planet?"

Kront stood up straight and took a demanding pose. "General, I'm in possession of an item that I will offer as a token of good faith in showing that my people wish to have a peace treaty with your people."

"What could you possibly have that could dissuade us from destroying Helgin?"

"Trikkyas I: Gwibst hrkols niyths." Kront held the book up for the general to see.

Flasif's eyes opened wide. "How did you…where did…" Composing himself and gathering his words, as well, Flasif started again. "I don't understand Captain. What is the meaning of this? You hold one of our most beloved treasures for ransom – a missing hallmark of our history, I might add – in exchange for a treaty of peace?"

"General, it's quite simple. I give you the book, and you sign a peace treaty that is recognized, accepted, and adhered by the entire Trikkyas people."

Flasif nodded. "I will contact the King and return with an answer. Flasif out."

Over the next two hours, Miranda kept a close watch on the

Trikkyas ships still headed to Helgin. Although the two ships of humans and hostages landed safely on Helgin, they were followed by four more Trikkyas ships full of actual soldiers prepared to invade Helgin and take control of the people.

"Sir, the shuttles are slowing down. They're at half-speed, and still decreasing."

"Thank you, Officer Holliday," Kront replied.

Suddenly, a small dot in the corner of the Delta Sector caught her attention. "Sir, the *Protector* is heading for Earth." She turned to face him. "Should we intercede?"

Kront shook his head in the negative. "While you were out, Miranda, I sent a com to Planet Earth concerning my future intentions in landing the *Lindman*, staying for a while, and reporting Angelina."

"And?" she prodded.

"They've already caught the little prison escapee." Kront smiled. "Seems she was already going to trial for treason when she escaped with her crew, stole a ship, and impersonated a commander when we had the unfortunate pleasure of meeting her. Add to her list of crimes the murder of Sigu Flort, the kidnapping two senior officers aboard an intergalactic ship under the Presidential Service, and the attempted murder of those two officers, and you've got a prison sentence for life...in the *least*."

* * *

Helena sat in the pilot seat on the *Jamie*, the only unarmed shuttle aboard the *Lindman*. Kront sat in the copilot's seat as she steered the shuttle down through the atmosphere of Trikky Talos. The day of the peace treaty signing had arrived. "Sir, I've received the landing coordinates. E.T.A. in three minutes."

"Thank you, Helena," Kront remarked. He turned around and faced the others sitting in the back. "Remember that we are here on a mission of peace. Keep your opinions to yourself and be polite."

Preston sat in the chair at the com station and called back to the *Lindman*, "*Lindman*, this is the *Jamie*. Over."

Nielson's face instantly appeared on the visual com screen. "Preston, is everything all right? Is Jamina okay? How's the baby?"

"Nielson, they're both fine. This is just a regular call in," he reassured the expectant father. "We're approaching the landing zone with clear skies. Captain is confident we'll have a successful mission."

"Good luck, and God speed." The man on the other side smiled through his concern for his wife and unborn child. He knew that bringing a pregnant woman – his wife – to a truce meeting would show the Trikkyas by leaps and bounds the good faith and honest effort of their people in wanting to stop the war. He sighed and nodded, "Nielson out."

The Jamie landed on the indicated platform. Twenty armed guards surrounded the immediate area. Kront snickered, "I guess they don't trust us quite yet, but stay calm. Open the doors." Helena flipped the switch to open the rear doors, and Kront stepped out with Adriahna, both individuals helping a very pregnant Jamina exit the ship. Miranda and Preston followed, and Helena turned the keys over to the senior ranking Trikkyas when she stepped onto the platform.

A Junior Admiral stepped forward and greeted Kront. "Captain Tallin and crew, welcome to Trikky Talos. I am Junior Admiral Brantis."

"Admiral," Kront acknowledged.

"According to protocol that you have already received and should have read through, we must inspect the ship and all accompanying persons for any weapons."

"Understood, Admiral." Kront gestured to Jamina, "May Ms. Nielson sit down while the protocol is completed?"

"Absolutely!" Brantis snapped his fingers, and a chair was immediately set forth. Kront and Adriahna helped Jamina to sit, and then stood back up, prepared for the pat-down. Of course, as Kront already knew, his party and ship were clean.

"All clear, sir," the chief guard stated.

"Very well," Brantis responded. "Let's make our way to the Grand Hall."

Kront's crew was loaded into a very large land speeder that took them directly to the entrance to a vast and open hall filled with important dignitaries from several Trikkyas planets and floating fortresses. The building reminded Miranda of the Greek amphitheaters from Ancient Earth History courses at the Academy.

"Amazing," she whispered. "It's breathtaking." Preston squeezed her hand in agreement and smiled.

The *Lindman* crew members were led down the steps to the front row of seats at the bottom of the building and directly in front of a large stage-like area. In front of them, a table and two chairs sat empty, waiting for a truce to call an end to the bloody war. They had barely sat down when an important announcement was made by one of the king's speakers.

"Rise for His Majesty, King Seriten Avar!"

Kront and his crew bowed when King Avar entered the room. Kront was flanked by four Trikkyas troops and directed up a set of stairs to the left in order to meet the king on the stage. He bowed again when he stood closer to the king. "Your Majesty, it's an honor to meet you. I am Captain Kront Tallin. I come to offer you a token of good faith in hopes that we may sign a treaty of peace and end the war between our peoples."

The King nodded. "I hear you have something of great worth to us, a piece of our history. Is this true?"

Kront nodded, "Yes, sir. If I may?" He reached into his pockets and looked at the guards who nodded, asserting that they knew he had no weapons and could no harm the king. He pulled the Trikkyase I book from inside of his coat jacket and handed it over.

The king accepted the book from Kront. "You bring this in good faith, as well as a woman with child. You bring honor to your people, and peace to this meeting. We accept your token and shall sign a treaty of peace with your people." They sat down and signed the documents. So many years of fighting were politically finished in a few seconds' time, and yet the treaty meant so much more. It included an oath made by the Trikkyas people to provide food, shelter, and shuttles to the survivors of the Troklon tragedy, and an oath to seek out peace before rushing into war with any race or species, interplanetary, intergalactic, or otherwise.

Kront saluted King Avar. "Your Majesty, again, it has been an honor, but we must return home. Our time here is done."

King Avar shook hands with Kront and snapped his fingers, signaling applause from the audience. Several troops surrounded the *Lindman* crew members – now viewed as heroes – as they walked up the stairs from the bottom of the open area and back to the speeder that took them to the *Jaime*. They boarded the shuttle, waved goodbye to the Junior Admiral and the troops that stood with him, and buckled their harnesses.

Kront sighed as he settled in to the copilot's seat. "Good job, troops. Let's go home."

Chapter 31. – Dreams of Earth.

Nielson set the *Lindman* on auto-pilot for Earth, left his station, and walked up the few steps to the higher level of the Bridge. Kront leaned back in his chair and offered his friend a seat to his left. Nielson accepted and smiled. "Sir, what are your plans for when we arrive to Earth?"

Kront's years in the service finally seemed to settle into the wrinkles of his face. "I'm thinking about retirement."

"But, sir!" Nielson gasped. "Truly? I can't imagine the Federation without the *Lindman*, without you."

"Face it, Nielson; I'm not getting any younger. Forty-five years puts mileage on the mind...and the heart," he solemnly added. "I think I need to settle down and find a hobby." He turned the conversation on Tyler. "What about Jamina and you?"

"What can a com officer do on Earth?"

"There's always the Earth Defense Guard," Kront suggested. "I hear it's pretty elite."

"Sir, you're kidding, right? Me join the EDG? I'm going to be a father," he reminded his commander. "I need something safe, something steady. I need a regular paycheck. I could care less about the actual job. I care more about my Jamina and our little one."

Kront put his hand on Nielson's shoulder. "I know the Admiral that runs the Old American base in Kentucky. I'm sure I can put in a good word for you."

"Thank you, sir."

*   *   *

Preston lied down on the bed next to Miranda. "So, where are your family members from?"

"Alaska."

He raised his eyebrows and sat up. "Alaska? That's cold stuff up there."

Miranda laughed, "I'm kidding." Preston lied back down. "Actually, I have no idea where they're from. I was born on Planet

Dringls, but right before it blew up my parents were transferred to the *Grimond Wolf...*"

"...and the rest is history," he finished for her as he hugged his love. "You'll love Earth. We'll travel around and find somewhere to live together."

"Where's your family from?"

"Nevada. About 100 miles from a city called Las Vegas."

Excitement and curiosity filled her eyes. "Las Vegas? That's one of those cities originally built on gambling and prostitution, right?"

Preston doubled-over in chuckles. "Is that the only reason you're excited?" She shook her head in the negative, but he saw a shy smile prick at the corners of her mouth, so he continued. "About 850 years ago, some gangsters decided to build a few casinos out west. Not long after that, there came the Hoover Dam. The workers who built the dam needed to live close to the worksite so they didn't have to travel thousands of miles every day. Being so far from home, these lonely men wanted 'company,' so when they weren't working on the dam, they went to Vegas and spent their paychecks on gambling and prostitutes."

"Is it still the same now?"

"Not quite," he explained. "Gambling has limitations: no person can gamble more than 30% of what he or she carries in cash."

Miranda sat up. "Why not?"

"The government stepped in and offered Vegas a deal when the economy was so down on its own luck that even Vegas was going to crash and burn. The then-president came up with the 30% deal as a way to offer people the chance to continue gambling without losing their beloved city as a whole to the economic woes of the time. In exchange, the government would increase job efforts in the area to bring the city back to its former days of glory."

"What about the prostitutes?"

"In the year 2286, it became illegal to perform sexual favors for strangers for any reason. About 400 years ago, an all-woman farm needed their farm houses painted, but couldn't pay with money, so they recruited four male painters with the promise of payment in the form of sexual favors. Needless to say, they got reported, lost the farm, and were sent to prison. The men, too."

"Well, Officer Henson," Miranda seductively stated, "you won't have to worry about paying me when it comes to certain...*favors*." She tiptoed her fingers over the buttons of his shirt up to his chin. Her other hand slid up and down his arm, caressing the strength of his muscles.

Preston arched an eyebrow. "Oh, yeah?" *I like where this is going*, he thought to himself.

She quickly stood up and skipped away, calling over her shoulder, "Once we're married!"

*　　*　　*

"Mason, do you ever think about your family?" Helena asked.

He lowered his head. "Sometimes, but they're not exactly the kind of people who would miss anyone." He raised his head and looked at her. "You know what I mean."

"I do. I remember you telling the story when you joined the force."

Mason laughed, "Yeah. Prison dad. Druggie mom." He stopped laughing but still smiled.

"Do you want to look them up when we get to Earth?"

"I don't think so. Dad will probably still be in jail. Killing four cops in a bar fight isn't a ticket to freedom."

Helena quietly nodded. "What about your sister?"

Mason's shoulder slumped forward; he sunk into his seat. "Frankly, I haven't thought about her in years. She joined the Monastery of Oregon right before I joined the Presidential Service. I don't know if she'd want to even see me after all this time."

Helena shakily stood up from the recovery bed. Mason helped her to the chair next to him. She leaned over and gave him a hug. "Don't you think she'd like to know her only brother – her only other sibling – is getting married?"

Mason smiled. "I supposed your right."

The lieutenant tossed her hand into the air. "Pssht. I'm always right."

He grinned at her response. "What about your parents?"

"My parents have chosen to stay on Helgin, for now." Her

eyes betrayed her confidence in her support of their decision. "I think they're just looking to take some personal time before returning to Jaime's birthplace."

"It's still fresh on our minds."

Helena gulped. "It'll always be fresh on *my* mind…"

*　　*　　*

Knock, knock, knock. Miranda stirred in bed. She heard someone knocking at the door again. Still half-asleep, but using her half-conscious part to focus, she answered, "I'm coming. Just a moment." She tumbled onto the floor and pulled on a pair of shorts that she knew didn't match her raggedy t-shirt. She threw her hair into a messy ponytail and opened the door, regretting the bright hallway light that directly shone into her eyes.

"Miranda?" a small, timid voice asked.

Miranda peeked through her fingertips to see who stood before her. "Melissa? Melissa Heart, right? Hi!" She took her hands down and stepped into the hallway to greet her former team member. "I'd invite you in, but my room's a mess. Let's go get a Slonga Water in the rec room." Quietly, Melissa accompanied Miranda and sat across from her in a small booth. Miranda took notice of the broken-hearted woman's motions, emotions, facial expressions, body language, and general lack of regular behavior. "Are you okay?"

Melissa shrugged. Miranda walked a few steps away to grab the Slonga Waters from the cool box, and came back and set one in front of her friend. She sat down, opened her own drink, and relished the feeling of a cold liquid draining down the back of her throat.

"I feel sick."

Miranda nearly spit the Slonga back out. "Do you need me to take you to see Doc?"

"No!" Melissa jumped at her. She nervously looked around. "Sorry, no, it's nothing like that. I just haven't…I don't think I can talk to anyone about this but you."

"Why me?"

"Because you knew Sigu better than I did."

"What does Sigu have to do with this?"

Melissa looked up at Miranda with tears in her eyes. "Because I loved him."

Miranda closed her eyes. She was beginning to cry, too. *Sigu gave his life the day that Preston and I were kidnapped,* Miranda remembered. *A random killing that wouldn't have happened if we would have just gone with Angelina in the beginning.* "I'm so sorry, Melissa. I had no idea."

Tears fell without command down Heart's face. "I never got to tell him how I felt."

"And it's all my fault. You probably hate me, don't you?"

Melissa shook her head. "No."

"No?"

"No," Heart echoed. She even smiled a little bit. "I just wanted to know how to move on. Helena and you lost Jaime, but I can't ask Helena because she's still recovering in the Medic Center. I don't want to cause her to get hurt all over again." Melissa's eyes showed apology. "I know that you were really close to Jaime, and her death still hurts you, too, but I was hoping you could use that to help me. I need to get over Sigu and move on."

Miranda half-smiled. "You probably won't feel better for a long time. A lost love is hard to get over, but trying to get over it is half the battle. I loved Jaime like a twin sister, like a kindred spirit. I don't forget the fact that she died doing right. I just choose to remember the good impact it had for the rest of us instead of the end result of her choice on her own self." The two stayed quiet for a few moments. Melissa was first to break the silence.

"When we go back to Earth, I'm staying with my brother."

"That's good," Miranda encouraged.

"I heard you've never been to Earth. I'd love to give Preston and you a show around. I'm very familiar with most of the countries and cultures."

Miranda smiled, "I might just have to accept that offer."

Chapter 32. – Home Sweet Home.

Kront stood at the Bridge by himself. Most everyone else was gathering at the bottom level of the Hangar while the leaders and other designated persons were talking at the platform at the top level. Helena and Mason slowly made their way down the hallway toward the Bridge; Helena caught sight of Kront before they exited to the Hangar. She put her hand on Mason's hand which helped steady her, and he looked to her.

"What's wrong?"

"Give us a moment?" she pleaded with her eyes. He nodded. They walked over a few steps to the Bridge. Kront heard them coming and smiled.

"Helena, Mason," he nodded. "Getting ready for a life on Earth?"

"Soon, Captain." She looked up to Mason and smiled. He left the room and closed the door behind him. She turned back to Kront who sat down in front of her and held her hands in his. "Thank you, Kront. Thank you for a wonderful adventure."

His eyes filled with tears. "You know, the first time I saw you at the Academy with that goofy-colored hair, Lieutenant," he started, "I thought I was nuts to take you on board. Sure, I saw your records, your accomplishments, your scores. But that stripe of purple and green in your black hair threw me for a loop."

She laughed. "I thought you were an old fart."

He wiped the tears from his eyes. "Helena, I need to tell you something."

"What is it?"

"I feel responsible for Jaime's death."

Helena's happiness sunk to a new low at the mention of her late sister. "Kront, it's not your fault. We all know she made her choice, and—"

"But that's not the whole story, Helena."

She stopped talking for a moment. "Captain, you can tell me anything, and I'll forgive you. It still hurts to talk about her and remember her, but ultimately she made the call that ended her life."

"I will never know if my actions could have prevented it."

She shook her head. "I can't hold that against you." She looked at him. "But if you'd feel better telling me anyway, then let it out."

He sighed and let go of her hands, interlacing his fingers with his own as he stared at the floor. "I tried to convince the Handlons to release King Avar long before Angelina showed up and told us that she was ever involved. I was afraid my actions were too late, and then by the time they listened, the Trikkyas were so upset that they took it out on Jaime." He shook his head. "I feel like I caused her death more than she did."

Lieutenant Holley wrapped her arms around her superior commander. They hugged for several moments before parting. Standing up, he helped her walk out of the room to the platform in the Hangar. It would be the last time they would ever spend as commander and second-in-command on the Bridge of the *Lindman*.

"Today, we depart from each other to take our own personal journeys into life. Some of you will settle down and live a normal life." He looked to Nielson, proudly holding Jamina at his side. "Some of you may seek adventure and travel the universe." He winked at Miranda and Preston. They laughed. "But always remember that we are a family from the *Lindman*. Our family has lost many family members. As I read off the names, please remember them in your hearts and minds, in your hearths and homes: James Montas. Moniqé Nastas. Heidi Kalt. Regan Drogly. Mort Klav. Robin Sammy. Linda Milas. Steven Blisy. Tom Raven. Adam Pander. Sergeant Sigu Flort…Com Specialist Jamie Holley…" Most of the tears fell when the last two names were read aloud. Everyone was called to attention, and they saluted a flag at half-staff for the rest of Kront's speech. He stepped back and allowed Helena to speak for a few minutes until the pain caught up, and Mason helped her away from the podium and into a nearby chair. Then, it was Miranda's turn.

She walked up to the microphone and took a deep breath. "We are here. We have accomplished our missions, succeeded in space, made peace with the Handlons and Trikkyas, and landed on Earth. We must have pride in what we have done, and have hope in what we can still do. As most of you know, Officer Henson and I are engaged, but our plans to stay grounded have changed."

Whispers started throughout the ranks below, but Miranda hushed them with her hands. "When we heard that the infamous Captain Kront and his glorious ship, the *Lindman*, were retiring, we thought of no better thing to do…than to buy up the ship and begin renovations!"

The crew members shouted and cheered. Kront cried tears of joy, knowing his years of hard labor on that ship were not gone to waste upon his choice of move to retirement. He stood up and hugged Miranda. "You make me proud, Miranda." He kissed the top of her forehead. Preston ran up the stairs and joined them at the platform. Preston shook Kront's hand and hugged the man who felt more like a father than commander.

Miranda turned back to the microphone. "In five years, the *Lindman* will begin hiring crew members for an exploration of the Blazik Galaxy. All interested parties should begin to prepare their applications now. Captain?"

Kront stepped up the platform, fresh tears on his cheeks. "This will be my last order as your Captain, so I hope you all will follow it well." He stood at attention and saluted his crew members. "Make a good life, and make it count. Dismissed!"

EPILOGUE.

Captain Kront Tallin attended every court hearing for Angelina Francis until she was convicted. Six months after the first hearing, she was found guilty on one count of treason, one count of escaping from prison, one count of robbery in stealing an intergalactic shuttle, one count of impersonating a military commanding officer from Planet Earth, one count of murder for the murder of Sigu Flort, and two counts of kidnapping and two counts of attempted murder for the kidnapping and attempted murder of two senior officers aboard an intergalactic ship under the Presidential Service. Various members of Angelina's crew were sentenced to prison, anywhere from several years to a few months of community service. Angelina was sentenced to life in a maximum-facility prison camp in former Afghanistan.

Captain Tallin had to testify against her, which was no easy feat when he had to remember their friendship in recalling the entire truth of how he knew her. But as he recalled her actions before, during, and after being aboard his ship, he had no emotion for her but pity. His evidence from the secret visual com recordings blew Angelina and her defense attorney away. She had no idea that Kront had recorded everything. Even the judge was surprised at Kront's wit against the woman, but Kront had never denied how happy he had been in listening to his gut that day.

Once the judge had declared Angelina's sentence, the woman tried to jump the barrier and attack the judge. Three officers tried to control Ms. Francis. She looked to the audience and saw that Miranda and Helena had joined Kront to hear her sentencing. She swore revenge on Kront, his crew, and his ship, but the officers finally escorted her out to the transport that would take her to a life in the hot and unhappy sands of prison time.

Miranda and Preston traveled around the globe before and after Angelina's final sentencing, settling themselves in a custom-built home in the outskirts of Las Vegas. The happy couple bought a small slot machine manufacturing plant that had been shut down several years before due to workers' strikes. Using their intellect and general conniving natures, the business turned out to be a hit. It wasn't long before nearly every casino in Vegas had a Henson-Holliday Slot machine. But they still had the marriage to discuss.

Only one year after landing on Earth, the entire *Lindman* crew attended the Henson-Holliday wedding. Kront gave Miranda away to Preston, and Buck was the best man. Instead of announcing a pregnancy a few months later, Miranda reported that renovations to the *Lindman* had been completed much faster than anticipated, and she would fly in another year and a half.

Mason and Helena moved to Hollywood, California, and started a small private investigation company. With Mason in charge of the finances and Helena behind the investigations, the success of the company allowed them to focus more on their own relationship. Just shy of being on Earth for two years, Mason got hitched to his slightly curvier bride. She tried to hide it, but everyone knew they were expecting. What no one was expecting was twins. Mason even fainted on to the floor when the doctor announced it. At the reception, Helena made sure to throw her bouquet in Adriahna's direction, and she did catch it, but confessed that Buck and she had a shotgun wedding in Vegas just a few weeks back. For a few moments, everyone was stunned, but then the congratulations started up again. It seemed a happy ending was in order for the entire *Lindman* crew...well, almost everyone...

Kront spent the beginning of his retirement attending Angelina's court hearings and the weddings and baby showers for several members of his crew. When the excitement calmed down and everyone headed in their own directions, he started to collect various weapons as the hobby of choice. Still young at heart, the rarest weapons tugged at his bank account more than caution could tug at his heart.

He knew how to be careful. After all, he was Captain Kront Tallin of the *Lindman*. Even if he *was* a washed-up, old captain, the memories and moments were not lost upon him. Universal enemies sought common territory and mischief in the black market, a place that he found the weapons he wanted the most. And then he heard that the weapon of his dreams had come to light: a Bloghuv Blaster. An extinct race of people, the Bloghuv's were killed on their planet when their sun engorged another star. No one had seen it coming. They cared more about their weapons of war than the changes in atmosphere or distance of the sun relative to their planet. The temperatures of the Bloghuv's planet rose so quickly that no one had a chance to escape. Kront contacted the man presumed to have the Blaster, but the man demanded more money. Double the money. Kront walked away, sure he would never find another, but still looking in hopes that another would turn up.

Like a second miracle, the original man offered the gun to Kront at the first price. Kront was stunned and curious, but the man apologized and claimed no other buyer could offer the price, so he felt bad and searched Kront out. Kront accepted, but as he left with his new weapon, eight men surrounded him and opened fire quicker than he could pull the trigger on his new toy.

When the news hit the fan, Miranda immediately thought of Angelina's last words, threatening to take revenge on Kront, his crew, and the ship, but everyone knew that Angelina had no contacts out in the deserts of Afghanistan, or so they hoped. Preston's wife cried for days. Helena went into false labor and ended up in the hospital for an unexpected two-week stay until her health improved as a result of Kront's death. Nielson and Jamina named their first son after the captain: Stephen Kront Nielson.

Finally, the days were counting down until the *Lindman* and a new crew would take to the skies and explore outer space once more. Miranda and Preston took Buck and Adriahna on board in the preparation process. Miranda, as Captain, hired Adriahna as Crew Recruiter. Preston hired Buck as Mechanical Chief Engineer and Advisor.

With a crew of 70 members, Miranda knew that her additions of more living quarters to the ship were not only costly but quite necessary. In addition, she purchased forty new fighters and twenty new shuttles. She wanted everything to be ready for the ten-year exploration of the Blazik Galaxy. She had done all the research herself and learned about the horrific tragedies incurred by the Space Navy only 300 years earlier. It had sent thirty-five ships to the galaxy for pure study and observation. After six months inside the galaxy, only three battered ships with starving, psychologically-beaten crew members returned to tell the horrific stories of cruel and unusual species. The Space Navy had been armed to the teeth, so Miranda knew her civilian freighter of Freedom Fighters had always been prepared to fight for the freedom of others. This time, they may have had to prepare to fight for their own freedom…

Continues in the *Lindman* Story – Undiscovered Worlds

ABOUT THE AUTHOR

Originally from Denmark, B. B. Hartwich visited Washington State in 2004 and met his future wife, Angela. Two years later, he made the physical move to the United States, and the couple was happily married, making him an immediate stepfather to two wonderful girls; they are now joined by two more children, one girl and one boy.

B. B. Hartwich worked as a Security Officer in downtown Portland for four years. During that time, he wrote his first book, but it took another four years to find Kimberly Dunn of Dunn Editing (http://www.dunn-editing.com/), an editor whom he believed was just the right one. Together they have refined the manuscript into a finished product. And Kaysie Donat a local artist that with B. B.'s ideas made a wonderful cover for his first book.

B. B. is a family man, spending most of his free time with his kids and wife, and works swing shifts for a rental car company driving the shuttle bus. Aside from writing, he enjoys the outdoors, prospecting, metal detecting, coin collecting, and computer gaming.